DEATH MINUS ZERO

Born in Hull in 1942, and educated at the university there, John Baker has worked as a social worker, shipbroker, truck driver and milkman, and most recently in the computer industry. He has twice received a Yorkshire Arts Association Writers' Bursary. His first Sam Turner novel, *Poet in the Gutter*, and the latest in the series, *King of the Streets*, are both available in paperback. John Baker is married with five children and lives in York.

John Baker

DEATH
MINUS ZERO

CASSELL PLC

VISTA

During the writing of any piece of extended fiction, many people make contributions to the narrative in the form of information, advice and comment. While I would like to express my thanks to Anne Baker, Sue Brown, Tim Crawley, Jenny Jones, Maria Lovatt and Simon Stevens for their help in the production of this novel, it is also necessary to say that any offended sensibilities are the responsibility of the writer alone.

First published in Great Britain 1996
by Victor Gollancz

This Vista edition published 1998
Vista is an imprint of the Cassell Group
Wellington House, 125 Strand, London WC2R 0BB

A catalogue record for this book is
available from the British Library.

ISBN 0 575 60202 3

Printed and bound in Great Britain by
Cox & Wyman Ltd, Reading, Berks

98 99   10 9 8 7 6 5 4 3 2 1

Playin' leapfrog and hearin' about Snow White

Bob Dylan

chapter 1

When the politicos hit the transport Norman got out of there.

Some moments passed after the explosion when he didn't do anything. Maybe it took a minute for the men in masks to come in and get the Eye-talian out, whatever they called him. Isaac, something like that. Two of them led the guy to a motorbike, gave him a crash helmet and he was on the pillion and away.

Then there was just Norman and the black guy. Both of them sitting there like old age fucking pensioners on a bench. Norman couldn't think later which of them moved first, but suddenly they were both on their feet and heading for the gap where the cab of the transport used to be.

Jesus, what a mess. The cab, the guys who were driving, the whole front section of the transport had gone. You can say what you like about the politicos but they don't do things by halves. Norman knew about guns, handguns, rifles, things you might call weapons. But these guys were using artillery. What did they use to do that? Mortar bomb, some kind of rocket launcher?

Norman didn't know the answer, only knew he was glad the guy who pulled the trigger actually hit the target. If he'd hit the transport a yard and a half further back Norman would've disappeared.

The lead escort car had been hit as well, with something smaller, though, as it hadn't actually disintegrated like the cab of the transport. There was an acrid smell in the air and something that made your eyes smart, though there were no actual fires. One of the filth from the rear escort car was crawling about on the road, and behind him was another one, limping but trying to help his mate. They didn't look at all interested in Norman or the brother.

Most of the masked politicos had gone already. Norman caught a glimpse of the last of them closing the back doors of a van. They had a gun in there big enough to kill Jesus. Blow Him to kingdom come.

There was the road and there were fields, open country. A tall chain-link fence alongside the road. The brother was already heading towards it. If you're gonna go, go, Norman said to himself. Any way you like, but move.

The alternative is to stay banged up for the rest of your life. The governor had told him that's what it had come to. 'We're never going to let you out, Norman. Even when you're old and grey. The only way out for you is in a coffin.' Norman ran faster than he'd ever run before. That 'old and grey' bit really put the shits up him. If this was his chance, well, take it man. Let's show this brother what running is all about.

He hit the fence at a hundred miles an hour, taking off and up from about six feet back. The black guy was only a yard ahead of him now. Norman clambered up behind him and they both got to the top at the same time, slowing down a little to get past the barbs. The brother got his trousers caught there and had to leave a piece of them behind. Norman didn't get anything caught. He was flying.

Crash-landed and cracked one of his toes. An instant later the brother was beside him, both of them on all fours. Like the beginning of a race at the Olympics, sprinters waiting for the gun. The filth who was still on his feet was coming up behind them now, but a long way off. Neither Norman nor the black waited for the gun. They were off out of those starting blocks like a simultaneous ejaculation at an adolescents' gang wank.

Heading for the horizon. Norman could see the brother on his right, sticking close. Norman veered slightly to the left and the brother stayed with him. He veered further left and still the brother was with him. Jesus, he thought, the daft bastard's following me.

One thing Norman knew for certain. The brother was not

gonna get far. Even the dimmest cop in the country would spot him a mile off. The guy was six foot seven, maybe taller, slim, nothing to him but he was really high off the ground. He had that flat top haircut, tribal scars on his face. Wherever he ran the cops would pick him up before nightfall. And he was following Norman. Jesus, this guy's gotta be unloaded.

Norman spurted ahead and veered to the right, try to shake him that way, but still the guy followed him, like he couldn't think for himself. Norman just stopped running, let the brother go wherever he would go, then took off himself in another direction. The filth was still behind them, but he followed the brother, leaving Norman alone on the map. Every time he looked around the brother and the filth were further away, over to his right. Eventually he looked around and there was no one behind him at all. No one in front of him. He couldn't hear anything either, couldn't smell anything except fresh air.

Norman just kept going. He kept going till nightfall, only stopping to lie still when one of the helicopters came overhead. When it got dark he stopped for a while in a ditch, get some of his breath back. Then he carried on. He had to be well clear by morning, out of the county. The dogs would be out. The manhunt would be on.

If he knew something about the stars Norman would have been able to work out where he was. But they were just pretty. He had the feeling he'd been travelling south, which was not ideal, because it meant he'd be travelling back towards the prison and have to pass the moor again to go north. He knew enough though to find a fixed point in the sky and keep going in the same general direction he'd travelled already. Parts of the moor turned to bog from time to time, and he had to make detours, still keeping his eyes on that one point in the heavens.

At least it was warm. Make a break in the winter and trudge through snow, you'd never make it. Now though, in June glorious June, with the whole summer coming up round every corner, shit, it couldn't have been better if he'd planned it.

Another two hours brought him to a road, and shortly after that a little outpost called Poundsgate. Should be able to find some wheels here. Norman was wary, though. Lot of screws lived in these villages on the edge of the moor. He left the village behind and followed signs towards Widecombe. But less than a mile down the road he heard the sound of a car approaching. Norman headed for the ditch, but stopped before he got there. The sound was obviously not a police car. More like one of those old bangers, what they call them? Vintage cars. Jesus, at this time? Must be three o'clock in the morning.

Norman laid himself down in the middle of the road. Stretched out full length, his head on his arm so he could see the car approach. Norman playing dead or injured, thinking whoever it is in the car, he probably smokes. Norman hoping the guy has plenty of cigarettes and maybe half a bottle of good Scotch in the glove compartment. With a bit of luck he'd have a daughter too, or a new wife, then it'd be party time.

The car's beam came over the brow of the hill, then the lights themselves hit the straight and Norman felt himself illuminated, bathed in light. It was like a play they'd done one Christmas at school about a million years ago. Only then it was shepherds. Norman had been the one who was supposed to shine the light on the shepherds as soon as the angel began singing, but he shone it on Annie Bristol instead, the girl who was playing the Virgin Mary. That would have been all right most times, except that this time Annie Bristol wasn't on the stage. She was in the girls' changing room in her knickers and vest, and when the light hit her she set up a scream which drowned out the angel and evacuated the audience because they thought the place was on fire.

But this was now, and it was a game of chicken. Norman was stretched out on the road and the car was heading towards him. Maybe the guy behind the wheel was blind and couldn't see him, didn't seem to be slowing down. Norman was on the point of rolling over to the side of the road when he heard the car change down. One, two little pumps on the brake, and then it changed down again and came to a stop about fifteen feet away, the engine idling.

First thing the guy did was to kill the beam, then he switched off the engine. Norman didn't move a muscle, just listened to the silence. As soon as the engine died the quiet rushed into all the spaces of the night. As the car cooled down there was the odd creak or crack as metal parts contracted, but none of these sounds was anything like the car door being opened.

Norman counted seconds like a gym teacher had once taught him, putting an *and* between each number . . . one *and* two *and* three *and* . . . until he had counted a full sixty seconds. Then he started again. The guy sat behind the wheel trying to make a decision for a full two and a half minutes before he opened the door and got out of the car. Norman watched his shoes walking along the road towards him, brown brogues with some kind of patterning, little holes punched in the leather and those big floppy tongues. The only other thing Norman could make out was the bottom of the guy's trousers. Grey cotton, probably a suit. Norman guessed the guy was old. There was something uncertain about his step, which might have meant that he was old, or it could be he was young and frightened.

He stopped about a yard away, shifting on his feet and spoke with a northern accent, could even have been Scottish, said, 'Are you all right?'

Norman closed his eyes but didn't move or reply. He needed the guy to come just one step closer, then he'd have him. The guy said, 'What's the matter? Can you hear me?' He leant forward but still didn't move his feet. Norman waited. He'd waited seven years behind the tall walls, what was a few seconds more?

When the guy straightened and came over to him, actually touched him on the shoulder, Norman took hold of both his ankles and yanked him over on his back. The guy squealed as he went over, and then squealed again as his head cracked on the road. He squirmed a little, but not with enough conviction to stop Norman sitting astride him, pinning his arms to the ground, and giving him a couple of good cracks on the nose. 'Help,' he said.

Help? Jesus. Norman looked around, like the guy was expecting the US Cavalry to come down the road. 'We're on a moor,' he said. 'It's the middle of the night. Where you gonna get help?'

Norman looked down at him. Yeah, he was old. Sixty, maybe sixty-five. His eyes staring up at Norman, real surprised looking little eyes, as if he'd been attacked by the devil. 'I want your clothes,' Norman told him. 'I want your car. That's all. I'm not gonna hurt you.'

The guy didn't say anything.

'You listening to me?' Norman asked, slapping him across the face.

This time the guy nodded. Whimpered a little.

'We gonna exchange clothes. OK?'

'Yes,' the guy said.

'You drive a hard bargain,' Norman told him. He pulled the old guy up by his shoulders, careful not to make too much of a mess of the suit. The guy's nose was bleeding a little. A trickle running down by the side of his mouth and heading for the neck of his shirt. Norman wiped it clean with his hand. 'Don't wanna mess that nice shirt up, now do we?' he said. He managed to get the guy to his feet, but as soon as he let go of him the guy started tottering around and ended up back on his butt again in the middle of the road.

'What's wrong with you, man?' said Norman. 'You gonna ruin the fucking suit before I even get it on.'

He stood the guy up again and pulled him over to the car, propped him against the bonnet. 'Take your clothes off,' he told him. 'Jacket, pants, the whole lot. Just leave them on the car.' Norman pulled his own clothes off and threw them on the ground. He had a little shank he'd made out of a spoon, sanded it down real good so it'd cut paper. He put this on the bonnet of the car. He stood in his underpants and vest and waited for the guy to get a move on. But the guy'd only managed to get one arm out of his jacket. 'Jesus,' Norman told him, 'we ain't actually got all night.'

He took the guy's jacket off and unbuttoned his shirt, let

his trousers fall down around his ankles. Then he put the guy's clothes on. Everything several sizes too big, but felt a whole lot better than prison clobber. He had to roll up the waistband of the trousers, and they were still too long. He left the guy sitting on the road in his undies while he put on the shirt, knotted the tie, and fitted the jacket. The sleeves were three inches too long, so he turned them up. He picked up the shank and tucked it away in the top pocket of the jacket. Finally he sat down next to the old guy and put on the socks and the brown brogues. When he stood again, he said, 'Trouble with guys like you, you don't have no taste. I had a choice of anything else I'd put all this stuff in the ditch.'

The shirt, the jacket, everything smelled of the old guy. The kind of smell you wouldn't find anywhere, 'cause you'd never go anywhere where people smelled like that. You knew anyone who smelled like that you'd tell them to get lost.

He helped the guy into the discarded prison clothes with great difficulty. The guy didn't say anything but he was shaking all the time, couldn't seem to keep anything still. His hands and legs were shaking, his head nodding away like a puppet. 'The fuck's wrong with you?' Norman asked him.

He got the guy back on his feet again and dragged him over to the ditch. 'Lay down there,' he said. 'And don't even think about moving.' The guy was flat out on his belly, his face in the dirt. Norman went looking for a stone, something heavy. He found a big one, could hardly lift it, and brought it back. He dropped it on the guy's head. Something cracked, Norman didn't know if it was the stone or the guy's head. He lifted the stone again, high as he could, and threw it at the guy's head one more time. The stone hit the head and bounced away along the bottom of the ditch, rolled out of sight. The guy's face was half buried in the boggy ground now. His left leg was doing a kind of dance on its own. The other leg was completely still.

'What do you think about that?' Norman asked him.

But the guy wasn't saying. Never breathed a word.

'They find you,' Norman told him, 'they'll think you're

me. At least for a while. Till they get an ID. By the time they find out who you really are I'll be long gone.'

He walked over to the car and got in the driver's seat. Leaned over and opened the glove compartment to see if there was a bottle. There was no bottle. A pair of gloves though and a big bag of sweets. Those boiled ones, all different colours, but they all taste the same.

Norman shook his head. He felt in the jacket pockets for a pack of cigarettes, but came up with only a small bar of chocolate. He threw it out the window. He got out of the car again and walked back to the ditch, said to the guy down there, 'You eat this kind of shit, man, you just end up with bad teeth.'

But the guy didn't say fuck. Never moved a muscle.

chapter 2

'You should get a dog,' Geordie said.

'I shouldn't get a dog,' Sam Turner said. 'I've got enough on my plate with your dog. I spend half my life taking your dog for walks so he can do his pee-pees. I feed your dog at least as many times as you feed him. I wake up in the morning and find your dog sleeping in my flat, while you're upstairs in your flat without a dog. So tell me, for why do I need a dog? I ain't got a dog, that's true, but it seems equally true to me that if I got a dog of my very own I'd have two dogs instead of the one I haven't got at the moment but that lives with me.'

'It would be company for you,' Geordie said. 'And if you got a big dog instead of a small dog like Barney, I don't know all the names of dogs, but maybe an Alsatian, or one of those others, what're they called? Really fierce fuckers?'

'Canine psychopaths?'

'No. Like a bulldog, but that's not it.'

'A pit bull?'

'Yeah, pit bull terrier, one of those. Then you could train it like a guard dog or a police dog, and then you can get them to smell things, like if you're looking for a guy who's hiding out and you don't know where he is. What you do is, you give the dog something belongs to the guy, like an old jacket, or something he's worn, and then the dog starts sniffing along the street and leads you straight to the guy.' Geordie hobbled across Sam's sitting room with only one trainer on, retrieved his missing shoe from under the sofa and sat on the floor to put it on. 'I've seen it in the movies. S'real cool.'

'Why'd you think I need a bloodhound?'

'Who said anything about that?' Geordie asked. 'I'm talking about normal dogs here, like what you really like. I'm up in my room at night minding my own business playing some music or reading a book or something and when the music stops I can hear this droning coming from down here, so I open the door to find out what it is. You know what it is?'

'Could be a model aeroplane,' said Sam. 'Or a model submarine, anything that drones could produce a sound like that.' Sam fingered his chin, the bristles there, and found himself thinking about his face. He was forty-nine years old now and looked all of those years plus a few more. He had started out as a young man with boyish good looks, fine features that had hung around until he was well into his thirties. But the last decade had visited his face with a vengeance.

'It's you,' said Geordie, finishing lacing up his shoe and springing to his feet to check it. 'It's you sitting down here talking to Barney. God alone knows what you're talking about, because, like I say, by the time it gets to my room it's just a drone. But it sure goes on a long time, like you've really got a lot to say to him. And Barney, being like I've brought him up to be polite and have good manners and that, he doesn't interrupt, he just sits there and listens to whatever kind of drivel people have to say to him.'

'That's how he is,' said Sam. 'The dark silent type. He doesn't say much himself, but he files it all away in his doggie brain, and he thinks about it. One day he'll come out with a real gem.'

'I'm not talking about Barney, here,' said Geordie. 'I know Barney's all right. What I'm talking about is someone who hardly ever goes out of the house any more, and who spends almost all his spare time talking to somebody else's dog. I'm talking about somebody who's supposed to be a private detective, living an exciting life of adventure and mayhem and anarchy and stuff like that, but who actually doesn't do nothing but talk to dogs that can't actually understand what he's talking about.'

'Tell me if I'm wrong, Geordie,' Sam said. 'But I get the feeling you're upset with me. Could this actually be the case?'

'Why? Because I think you should get a dog? You're paranormal.'

'Noid,' said Sam.

'Noidnormal?'

'Paranoid,' said Sam. 'And I'm not. I just don't want another fuckin' dog in the house.' Sometimes people said he looked like Gene Hackman. Well, to be honest a couple of women had said that, but then one of them had gone on to say he looked like Gene Hackman after Gene Hackman had fallen off a cliff and been involved in major surgery. The other woman, after Sam had got through explaining to her who Gene Hackman was, said the resemblance was astonishing, she'd just not noticed it until Sam pointed it out. She also said that Gene Hackman, if indeed it was Gene Hackman she was thinking about, had more hair than Sam.

If his face was shot, his main torso had managed to stay fairly trim. He kept himself fit, worked out in the gym a couple of times a week, but two days ago the doctor had told him that he should stop smoking. Sam's blood pressure was too high. Nothing to worry about, yet, but he should do whatever he could to get it down. That's what he had been talking to Barney about the last couple of evenings. His blood pressure. Stopping smoking. Well, who else was there to tell?

'I know something's wrong with you,' Geordie said. 'You're not so much fun. You don't even play your tapes any

16

more. Look at you, you didn't even get shaved the last couple a days.'

Geordie had the ability to drag up out of himself the most despairing look imaginable, and he did this now, at the end of his little speech. He showed Sam two empty palms and put on that look which was designed to get a compassionate response, and never failed.

Sam began to melt. 'OK,' he said. 'I've been a bit depressed.' He told Geordie what the doctor said about his blood pressure and stopping smoking.

'Well, at least you know about it,' Geordie said. 'Like you've caught it in time. You just stop smoking and you'll be all right.'

'Uh-uh,' Sam said.

'You don't think it's that simple?'

'Maybe.'

'You mean there's something else?'

'Hell, I don't know,' Sam said. 'You gotta start worrying when your body fails. You start coming unglued, things dropping off. Christ, I need to understand it.'

Geordie didn't reply immediately. He knelt down on the carpet and scooped Barney up into his lap. He held the dog's jaws together, so Barney had to struggle to get free. Sam was not sure of Geordie's age, but there seemed to be some kind of consensus that he was now eighteen years old. After a period in various children's homes in the North East, Geordie had been homeless, hanging around various doorways in London, Manchester, Liverpool, Leeds. When he arrived in York Sam had befriended him, and managed to get him installed in a flat of his own. Geordie also had a job. He was a trainee Assistant Private Investigator in the Sam Turner – Investigations detective agency. He looked at Sam from across the room, released Barney's jaw and let the dog back on to the carpet. 'When did you last have a screw?' he asked Sam.

Sam laughed, got out of his chair and filled the kettle with water. 'Thank you, Mr Freud,' he said as he plugged the kettle into the mains. 'But I don't think that's gonna solve my problems. In fact it'd probably give me more.'

'No, it'd cure you,' Geordie said. 'I've seen you before, when you're in love, or even when you're not in love, but somebody you fancy fancies you as well, and you turn into a different person. It's true, Sam.'

'You know,' said Sam, 'people like you put back the cause of female emancipation a hundred years. Like, what you're saying here is that if I get a dog or a woman I'll be cured. Correct me if I'm wrong, Geordie. But that is what you're saying?'

'You should start going to the Singles Club again.'

'Geordie,' Sam said, 'give me a break. I'm trying to rethink myself right now. A woman wouldn't fit into the picture. Christ, I'm still reassessing my image since I realized all the women I attract are menopausal. I don't want more of that.'

'Menopausal? What's that?'

'It's one of my problems,' Sam said. 'Nothing for you to worry about.'

'Like an old woman? Is that what it means? Come on, Sam. I'm trying to learn new words.'

'Yeah,' said Sam. 'Not old. Oldish. Someone who's finished with child-bearing.'

'What's wrong with that? A guy your age doesn't want a young woman. You could get really unlucky and end up marrying one of those high-pitched voices.'

Sam placed two mugs on the counter and poured a jot of milk into each. 'Listen,' he said, 'if a woman happens, that's OK. I wouldn't say no. But I'm not gonna push anything at the moment. Thanks for your concern. It's good to know you care. But don't push it any more, not tonight, anyway. If I want any shit out of you I'll squeeze your head. Savvy?'

Geordie came over to him and reached for the tea pot. 'Friends at last,' he said.

chapter 3

It wasn't a vintage car, it was just an old banger of a Renault 4, must be ten years if it's a day. Shit, when it was new it wasn't much. Now it was a liability with only one speed, like slow. Not even a radio. And it smelled like the old guy, the old guy's clothes. Have to get rid of it quick, find something with a bit more class.

Norman headed for Exeter, get a new car there before going on up to Bristol, then change again before heading north. Keep changing. Make sure if they were following him they couldn't follow him far.

Shit, that carnival going on around the transport, the politicos playing at target practice, the authorities wouldn't know who was alive and who was dead. Might be days before they sorted out all the bits of bodies. By that time he could be miles away. If Norman had his way he'd be hundreds of miles away.

When they finally found out he was missing they'd expect he'd gone back to London, start hitting his old haunts. But Norman had no intention of going anywhere near the Smoke. Once he ended up there they'd pick him up within hours. Norman wasn't gonna be stupid this time. He was going somewhere nobody knew him. Somewhere he didn't even know himself.

On the outskirts of Exeter he pulled into a side-street and took stock. The old guy's wallet was stuffed with credit cards and a hundred and forty pounds in tenners. There was a driving licence in there as well, in the name of George Sketch, photographs, a library membership card for Carlisle Library, in fact a whole new identity kit. It wouldn't last for long, once they found George's body and identified it the credit cards would be useless, but for the time being it was a ticket to ride. Should he find himself anywhere near Carlisle, which he hoped wouldn't ever happen, shit, he could get something to read.

In the boot was a small bag – must be George Sketch was going on holiday or something – full of unbelievable clothes. That smell again. Jesus, didn't the guy wash? Norman didn't want any of these clothes. The size was wrong, but even if the size had been right they would still have been shit. He found a wire coat hanger, which would certainly come in useful, and a wrench, and put them to one side.

Norman took the gloves and the car keys, took George Sketch's little bag after he'd emptied the contents into the boot, locked the car and walked away from it. Didn't even look back, didn't ever want to see it again.

Dawn found him in the middle of a housing estate, still on the way into Exeter. All the curtains drawn, everybody sleeping away in their cosy little beds, dreaming about all the sex and violence they ever wanted. Nice little black BMW, probably souped up, parked outside its garage, with real leather upholstery inside, teak dashboard, radio and stereo tape deck there too, with a little cabinet full of tapes. Looked promising.

Norman unwound the coat hanger he'd taken from the Renault and pushed it down the side of the driver's window, felt around for about a minute until he located the lock mechanism. A sharp pull on the hanger, then, while he held the door catch, and he was inside.

Oh, nice smell, all that leather to breathe in. He used the wrench to smash the plastic around the steering column and hot-wired the beast. Before starting it he pushed it out into the road. Didn't want the sound of the engine to wake the owner, have him legging it down the road after his favourite car, reporting it to the police before Norman got off the estate.

The engine sounded like the growl of a lion. Norman put it in gear and headed back the way he'd come, out to the M5 which would take him all the way to Bristol. Exeter wasn't gonna be worth a visit, too close to the scene. The place would be crawling with cops.

The tapes were a mixed bag, but he found one of Tina

Turner, picture of her on the front, all legs. And inside, Jesus, picture of her wearing hardly nothing at all. He put that picture on the dashboard so he could see it good while he was driving, and he slipped the tape into the system and switched it up real loud. He felt good for several minutes after that, before he remembered he hadn't eaten in a long time. Then he felt crap, aware of a big hole in his stomach.

He had the money and the credit cards, could easily stop at the first service station, get a fucking big big breakfast, and have something to eat and drink after it. Get a carrier bag and fill it with sandwiches, enough to last him for a week.

But he wouldn't do it. They'd be sure to have police in all them places. Christ, they see him walk into a cafeteria in a suit fifteen sizes too big for him, Mr Plod would have him in the back of a van in two minutes flat.

Norman checked the petrol gauge and then sang along with Tina for a few minutes 'Simply the Best' . . . Could just imagine putting your hand up that little bead dress of hers. Wouldn't have to go very far before you lost it. Norman did a smile and settled back in the leather bucket seat. A full tank, and just feel the power every time you touch the accelerator. Who needs food?

Well, yeah, you can tell yourself you don't need food, but your stomach doesn't listen. Just keeps on rumbling away there. Your mouth goes dry. You feel like shit. Especially now while you're sailing past a service station at ninety miles an hour. Slow down, man, you wanna get picked up for speeding? Sailing past a service station so close you can smell the bacon and eggs. Double bacon and eggs. Sausages. Coffee in one of those glass jugs. Toast and fried bread, two slices of that. Tomatoes. Little side order of mushrooms. Beer on the side. A pack of cigarettes. Little waitresses looking like Tina, butts sticking out in those tiny black skirts.

Christ, it's turning into a torture chamber.

One cigarette would solve the hunger. But he couldn't afford to take the chance of buying any. Maybe pick up a hitch-hiker? Ask him if he smokes before you let him get in

21

the car. The guy doesn't smoke he can wait for another ride. What do you think this is, man, a fucking bus service?

Only nobody was hitching.

By the time he got to Bristol the morning traffic was building up. Lots of cops around. Best to change the car quickly and get out of here. Don't get caught on the street. He followed road signs to a multi-storey car park and drove straight up to the top level. A couple of wiggers were trying to break into a Vauxhall Astra, and when Norman drove past they left it alone and made out they were taking a morning stroll. Shit, fifteen years old, maybe less. But the younger one was about Norman's size. Black jeans, sweatshirt, something you could walk in the street with.

Norman drove around the top level again and slowed down to drive alongside the wiggers. He hit the window switch and leaned his elbow on the door. 'Mornin', gents,' he said. One of the kids was ready to run, the elder one, but the younger one stayed cool.

'Mornin',' he said, glancing over at Norman. 'You lost something?'

'Might have found something you want,' Norman told him.

The kid looked straight ahead, but he was interested. 'What's that?' he said.

'These wheels,' Norman said. 'Real fast, and nobody round here's looking for them.' He pulled into a parking space, killed the engine and left the car in gear.

The kid stopped, walked alongside the car and glanced at Norman again. His eyes went past Norman and took in the broken steering column. 'Jeez,' he said, 'did you wire that?'

Norman put his smile on. Didn't say anything. Just let the kid appreciate his work. 'How'd you get into it?' the other kid said. 'The lock's still sound.'

'Course the lock's still sound. You punch the lock out, you might as well put a sign in the windscreen: *This is a fucking hot car.* Anyway, it spoils the look of the thing. You wanna drive a car round, or you wanna drive a wreck?'

'How'd you do that?' the younger wigger said. 'How'd you get the door open?'

Norman looked into his eyes, his fresh face. Never had a shave in his life. Well, he thought, kid's've got to learn somewhere. They won't learn nothing useful in school, nothing they can actually use in real life. Might be years before they go to prison and start learning real skills. 'I could show you that one,' he said. 'Maybe one or two other things. But we'd have to make a deal.'

'What's that?' the younger kid asked.

'I don't wanna show on the street,' Norman said. 'But I need something to eat. Also I need some real clothes, get out of this shit I'm wearing. You get me some food and give me your clothes, I give you a few lessons on how to open a car properly, and you get to keep this one with the radio and the stereo. Everything 'cept the Tina Turner tape.'

'You're not having my clothes,' the kid said, backing off a little.

'Shit, I'll give you the money,' Norman said, taking the old guy's wallet out and fanning the tenners. 'You can go down to the shop and get new ones.'

The elder kid said, 'You give us the money, we can buy you sandwiches and clothes.'

Norman felt like kicking the shit out of him. 'Hey,' he said, 'you think I'm from the moon, or what? I give you money and you've spent it before I've put my wallet away.' He flipped the wallet closed and put it back in his pocket. 'Fuck you,' he said. 'I'll find someone wants to do business. Someone can understand a good deal when it's staring them in the face.' He started the car and put it into reverse.

'Hang on,' the younger wigger said. 'I didn't say I wouldn't do it. How much money you gonna give me for the clothes?'

'A hundred,' Norman said. 'For the jeans, the sweatshirt, the shoes if they fit. I don't want the cap or the jacket.'

'Two hundred.'

'I'll go a hundred and twenty,' Norman told him. 'That's all I've got. And a credit card. You can have one credit card.'

The kid scratched his chin. 'OK,' he said. 'Let's do it.'

Norman switched the engine off again. Got the wallet out

and held up two tenners. 'Get in,' he said to the younger kid, and waited until the kid walked around the car and got in the back seat. To the other one Norman said, 'You get the food. I want pies with meat, meat sandwiches, a six pack of beers. As much as you can get for twenty. You don't come back I'll eat your friend.'

The kid smiled as though he thought Norman had made a joke, took the two tenners and went for the sandwiches.

Norman told the younger kid to get his clothes off. He undressed himself, stripping back down to his prison underwear, passing old George Sketch's clothes back to the kid. When they'd finished the wigger was dressed in the old guy's pants, shirt and jacket, even the brogues. Norman was sporting a sweatshirt which had Orlando Magic emblazoned on the front, black jeans, and a pair of Nike shoes. Feeling good, cruising around the car with a swagger he'd misplaced somewhere seven years ago, and was only now beginning to find again. The shorn wigger stayed in the car, saying if anybody saw him in this shit he'd kill himself.

When the other wigger returned with the food Norman ate a meat pie and swigged off a can of cold Bud. The younger kid asked for his money, and Norman smiled and gave it to him 'Now I'm gonna show you how to open a car properly,' he said.

He led them over to a Scorpio auto on the other side of the car park. Blue job with black leather inside. Norman checked through the window to make sure there was some sound equipment inside. Using his bent coat hanger he had the thing open in about ninety seconds.

'How do you do that?' the younger wigger asked.

Norman locked the car again and fitted his wire hook down inside the window frame. He fiddled for a moment, said, 'Now you try.'

The younger wigger took hold of the coat hanger and jiggled it about.

'Just about there,' Norman said. 'You feel the little lever inside? Don't pull so hard. That's right, you can feel it moving.'

'Yeah. I got it,' the kid said.

'OK,' Norman told him. 'Push the handle in and pull it up slowly.'

The door of the Scorpio opened. 'Easier than a can of sardines,' Norman said. He told the elder kid to get his bag from the BMW. When he brought it Norman shoved it in the back of the Scorpio. 'And the Tina Turner tape,' he said.

'I've got something else to teach you,' he said to the younger wigger.

'What's that?' The kid was eager to learn everything this character could show him.

'Put your back here,' Norman said, pointing to the door of a VW camper. 'And hold the door handle with both hands.'

The kid did as he was told.

Norman came over and stood in front of him. 'You got hold of it with both hands?' Norman asked.

The kid nodded and Norman butted him hard in the face. The little wigger dropped like a stone. His friend ran off down the car park, putting about seventy yards between himself and Norman. 'You're a fast learner,' Norman told him. The little wigger was sitting on the concrete shaking his head from side to side.

'That's the best lesson you've had today,' Norman told him, retrieving his hundred and twenty pounds from the kid's pocket. 'Don't forget it.'

Norman left him there, got behind the wheel of the Scorpio and wired it to go. He waved to the elder wigger as he drove on past, slammed Tina into the tape deck, and stuck a chicken sandwich into his mouth.

Bristol was humming. Cars and pedestrians everywhere. The shops buzzing so you could almost hear all the cash flowing into their tills. Plenty of cops as well, some of them in pairs, looking for escaped convicts. They look at a Scorpio and they think businessman or executive or something, never dreaming that what they're after is behind the wheel. Norman just kept going, remembering everything anyone had ever told him about the Highway Code. Stopped at all the red lights, even slowed down a couple of times when there were no lights showing, let a woman with a dog go across the road. Shit, he could've been a driving instructor, didn't hit the horn even one time. Twenty minutes later he was back on the M5 heading towards Birmingham.

Those kids learned pretty good, he reckoned. If he'd been born on the other side of the tracks Norman thought he could have been a school teacher. He'd have been a much better teacher than any of the teachers who taught him. The kids would respect him for a start, not run rings around him like they did most teachers these days. First thing, first time he walked into the classroom he'd tell them, *OK motherfuckers, you might be thinking you got a ticket to ride, but while I'm standing up here and you lot are sitting at your little desks, only one thing's gonna happen. I'm gonna spout and you lot are gonna shut the fuck up and listen.*

He reached for the inset of the Tina tape and stuck her picture up on the dashboard. Maybe he'd get himself one like her in Birmingham. He shook his head. Maybe not. In Birmingham he'd change cars again and head on out for Manchester. Get one there instead.

He had to take stock, try to think the thing through. Maybe make some kind of plan. The first day after the riot in the prison Norman and two other so-called ringleaders had been taken to a transport. The Eye-talian Norman had never seen in his life before. Either they'd had him banged up in solitary, or he'd not been there long. The black brother he'd seen before, in fact he'd followed him for a while during the riot. Just after it started. The screws'd got out immediately, kitted out the mufti-squad, started bolstering up no-man's-land between the buffer and the perimeter fence, bringing filth in from the neighbouring towns. The way it looked that first day it wouldn't be long before they brought the army in.

Guys were already up on the roof, throwing slates at anything that moved, making banners out of sheets and somebody's blood. Probably one of the nonces they kept wrapped up in cotton wool. Serve the bastard right. But it just went to show, Norman thought, the worst kind of shit can come in handy in an emergency. Use the fuckers as blood donors. Everybody running around like it was a carnival.

Least that's what it looked like. The library and two kitchens were on fire, smoke everywhere so you could hardly breathe.

He followed three black guys who'd made a crowbar out of some piping and looked like they might have a plan. They made for the admin office which was swarming with cons, must've been about six fires going in there. Filing cabinets were overturned, records being heaped on the flames. Guys were smashing desks, ripping calendars and charts off the walls. Anything wasn't smashed already they would smash it. The black guys didn't stop there, but went through another door into a little pantry the screws used to make tea and coffee. Everything in the pantry had already been smashed.

There they started levering the bars off the window. That's where he had seen the brother. The one in the transport. Looked like he could've just bit through the bars, but he didn't, he levered them out of the stone and mortar like they were daffodil stems. Every time one of the bars came out the other two brothers cheered and said something in that language they use. Norman couldn't understand a word of it. He just felt happy for them.

When the bars were all out the brothers went through the window and Norman followed, keeping some distance in case they turned on him. They seemed to know the lie of the land and as long as they knew that, he was quite happy to follow. In a little alley now, high walls on both sides. The brothers were running along it and turning a corner at the end, heading towards the sounds of shouting and something exploding. When he got to the corner the blacks had disappeared.

Still from inside the alley Norman could see the buffer fence, a long way off, but there it was. Cons were running towards it from all directions, slates and bits of drain pipe coming down from the revellers on the roof, sirens screaming like it was a war. Some of the cons were climbing over the buffer fence and being chased by screws on the other side, having their heads opened with batons. Norman could see this wasn't gonna be a normal prison day. Maybe not even a normal prison week. He didn't intend missing any of the fun.

His shank was originally made as protection, like a defensive weapon against some mad bastard who kept touching his ass; but now it would be an offensive weapon, help him get over that buffer, maybe even over the perimeter and out into the world. Shit, just do it, Norman told himself. If one of them tries to stop you, stab the bastard.

Once outside of the alley he saw the three brothers again, halfway across the open area now, heading towards a place on the buffer that didn't seem to have any screws at all. Norman took off after them. They'd been good luck up till now. Might as well stay with them till it runs out, then dump them.

A slate from the roof whistled past his head so close it almost took a layer of skin off, but Norman didn't stop. Didn't stop until he was over the buffer and one of the screws smacked him across the head with a baton. Then he stopped good. Woke up in hospital and missed the rest of the fucking riot.

Norman left the M6 at Junction 21 and drove through Salford into the centre of Manchester. He was behind the wheel of a white Escort diesel, which was the best Birmingham had had to offer at short notice. He double parked behind the Royal Exchange Theatre, took the bag and left the car with the keys in the ignition. Somebody'd use it.

The weather was hot and dry. Manchester, shit, it should be raining. But the air was dry, too dry. So you had to take it in short gasps through your mouth. Women had sleeveless dresses on, and the men were all carrying their jackets over their shoulders. Norman leaned against a shop window and had a good look at some of the women. Legs, hair, occasionally caught a sniff of perfume when one or the other passed real close. They'd pretend he wasn't there. But they knew OK.

Completely new territory, but it felt good. Norman had been born in Southampton and moved to London as a teenager. Before today he had never been further north than Watford and had half expected to meet peasants and wild animals. He smiled to himself at the thought. Manchester looked just like parts of London, hardly any difference at all, even some of the shops had the same names. Good job as well. He'd come up against peasants and wolves, shit, he'd probably be making his way back south again.

He went in a burger bar and got a double cheeseburger and two cups of coffee. Winked at the waitress who sneered at him in return, asked him if he had a problem with his eye. Norman asked her if she got many tips with an attitude like that. She came back with something else, 'nother mouthful of garbage, but Norman picked up his tray and found a table by the window. Shit, the first woman he'd talked to in years and she gives him a mouthful. Fucking accent like *Coronation Street*. Maybe works in the Rovers Return at night, but Norman wouldn't give her a job cleaning dishes. Face like a dog. Shit, no body. Greasy apron. Great fat legs. Like a peasant. Even if you put her on the street she'd be trouble. Have to smack her every day.

Norman understood women. Knew how to handle them. He hadn't had to learn it either. It just came natural.

Norman went to the gents and counted his money. He put six tenners in the pocket of the sweatshirt, another two and a fiver and the loose change in his trouser pocket, and the rest of the tenners he put in his sock.

When he'd finished eating, drunk his second cup of coffee, he walked down the street to a taxi rank. 'I want a girl,' he told the driver when he'd got himself settled in the passenger seat.

The driver sniffed, glanced at his St Christopher dangling from the rearview mirror, and said, 'Anything particular?' He was a little guy, face furrowed like a ploughed field, wearing a sweater and sweating, long thick nails on the ends of his fingers. Like claws, Norman thought. Maybe he was one of the wild animals.

'Black,' Norman told him. 'Something like Tina Turner.' He laughed. 'She don't have to sing, though. I mean, she *can* sing, that's OK; but she don't *have* to.'

The driver didn't say if he thought that was funny. His face said he'd heard all the jokes before, and even if he hadn't heard that one before he still wasn't gonna find anything funny. His face was so cracked already, it wasn't gonna crack any more.

'Where we going?' Norman asked him.

'You wanna black girl,' the driver said. 'Place called the Star, they got Indians, Chinese, and real black blacks. Even got whites if you change your mind.'

'Star?'

'Yeah. It's not a house. Jus' a pub. You buy a drink and the girls'll find you.' He glanced at his St Christopher again, then started chewing something, though there was nothing in his mouth. Then another thought somehow got into his head. 'Won't be busy tonight,' he said. 'Too bleedin' hot.'

The cab stopped outside the Star and Norman got out and gave the driver a tenner. The driver handed him a fiver and two pound coins, and Norman took the fiver and left the two pound coins in the guy's hand. 'Buy yourself a new face,' he said.

The guy looked at him deadpan before pulling away from the kerb. Norman watched him go, then stood and wondered at the vision of Tina Turner coming down the road towards him, wobbling along on heels like stilts, wearing a pair of bright red shorts and a black sequinned shirt that was tied round her middle. She started smiling as she got closer, then swept round into the entrance of the Star and said, 'I have to buy my own drink, or we going in together?'

The *smell* of her. Jesus, this was a woman. He'd forgotten that, that they smelled so different. 'Shit, babe,' Norman told her. 'You're not going anywhere without me tonight.'

There were around half a dozen people in the bar, men and women. The room was no bigger than an average living room, but the ceiling was higher and supported a large brass fan. A couple of girls like Tina, though not so lush, were talking to their Johns at a table behind the door. They both said something to her as she passed, but Norman still hadn't got the Manchester dialect and assumed they were using too many words to say Hello. The bar was six or eight feet long with a middle-aged woman behind it. She gave Tina a grin and asked what Norman was drinking. Tina was drinking Scotch and Norman had the same with a beer chaser and turned his attention to the next most interesting thing in the room.

At the far end of the bar was a brother must've been over seven foot tall. His neck was the size of a bucket. Rings everywhere, ears, nose, hands. The front of the guy's shirt was open and there was a ring through his left nipple. Norman couldn't see the guy's toes, but he would've bet there were rings there as well. The brother didn't move apart from a slight twitching of his nostrils. There was a mirror behind the bar so he could see everything that was happening without moving.

Tina went over to him and put something in his pocket. Norman assumed it was money. The guy still didn't move. Norman hoped he never would.

When Tina came back, Norman asked her, 'That your daddy?'

'Sometimes,' she said. 'Shall we sit down?'

She led him to a table behind the black giant and asked him his name, said she was called Sue. Norman told her he was gonna call her Tina and she said that was cool and what was he looking for.

'I've bin away,' he told her, 'so I want everything at once.'

'A girl can only do her best,' Tina said.

Norman drank half the whisky, put the glass down and swigged a quarter of the pint of beer. 'How about a good fuck now?' he said. 'When we've finished this.' He motioned to the drinks on the table. 'Then we come back here and have a few more beers, maybe get a bit sloshed. Then we go back to your place and take it more slowly. Finish up about two or three in the morning. I got to be on the road by then.'

Tina looked at her watch. 'Sounds cool,' she said, reaching into her bag and putting a small calculator on the table. 'Can't add up,' she explained. She punched a couple of numbers on the keypad. 'You gonna want a blow job?' she asked. 'Anything kind of specialized?'

'Maybe a blow job,' he said. 'I don't know yet.'

Tina punched more numbers on the keypad, said, 'We're talking between eighty and a hundred quid here.'

Norman pulled the six tenners out of the pocket of his

sweatshirt and counted them on to the table. 'That's all I've got,' he said. 'You ask Daddy if we got a deal?'

Tina reached for the notes but Norman covered them with his hand. As she moved forward he found himself taking in a good lungful of her scent. She went over to King Kong at the bar and talked some. The guy didn't move. Norman watched very closely and he didn't see anything move, not even an eye.

Tina came back to the table, sat down and showed Norman her teeth. 'It's a quiet night,' she said. 'And I like you.' She picked up the six tenners and went back to the brother at the bar. When she came back the tenners were gone. 'I'm all yours,' she said. 'But you leave at midnight.'

Norman shrugged, he'd been away a long time. 'Jus' call me Cinderella,' he said. Then he had another thought. 'Don't suppose you've got a dress made out of beads?' he asked.

They left the Star and went round the corner to a house that was falling down. Two brothers in the hallway downstairs, playing cards. Loud music coming from one of the rooms behind them. Norman followed Tina upstairs to a tiny room with a bed and a table and chair. Nothing else. 'How you wanna do this?' she asked.

'Quick,' he told her. 'But check this out first.' Norman loosened his belt and motioned Tina to put her hand down the front of his trousers. 'Surprise for you.'

'It got teeth?' she asked, reaching down there.

Norman drew in his breath when she made contact. 'Lower,' he said through his teeth. 'I got four balls.'

'Jesus,' she said, her hand deep in his trousers. 'You ain't bullshitting.' She felt some more, her eyes wide with something only a little short of wonder. She unzipped him and let his pants fall to the floor, then she got down on her knees to get a better look. 'I've come across singles,' she told him. 'They's a lot more common than you'd think. Twos, of course. Though most of the guys with two, to hear them talk you'd think they had more. And I came across a three once. Guy who had two normal ones and a little one, could actually have been a piece of gristle or something. I mean it might not have been a real ball. But let's give him the benefit of the doubt. He had three. But this little cluster, here,' she said, weighing them in the palm of her hand, 'it sure takes the biscuit.' Her eyes opened wider. 'Honey, if you never say or do anything else, you certainly made a little history for me.'

She gave him a condom and began undressing. Norman put the condom on and told her just to take her shorts off.

Seven minutes later they were back in the bar.

Norman left his bag in Tina's room. You carry a bag around people think you've got something worth taking.

When they walked into the bar the big black guy still didn't move. Norman knew the man was never gonna be impressed. He ordered drinks and they sat down at the same table, talked about the state of the world, how everything used to be good and was now turning sour. 'The fucking thing is,' Norman told her, 'jus' when Margaret was beginning to get everything together the bastards got rid of her.'

Tina nodded through her glass. 'She was good for us,' she said. 'Wanted the cops to leave us alone and chase real criminals. Terrorists and that. People making money, she was into that.' She took another swig and looked at her empty glass. 'I think she'll be back.'

'Hope so,' Norman told her, picking up Tina's glass and his own in one hand. He went to the bar and looked at the giant while he waited for the drinks. Fucking *neck*! The guy didn't move. Norman thought if the guy would look at him he could give him a wink. But the guy didn't look. Screw you, he thought. Bit too big to take on, though, unless you wanted eating. Even though he did have all that money. Maybe after a few more drinks he wouldn't look so big.

'What's with him, anyway?' he asked Tina when he got back to the table.

'Nothing,' she said. 'He only gets involved if there's trouble. Long as he's there there's no trouble.'

'He your pimp?'

'One of them,' she said. 'It's all family down here. Sisters do the work, brothers collect the cash.'

'Nothing wrong with that,' Norman told her. 'You know anywhere it's different?'

'Heaven?' said Tina, and swigged more whisky. She put her glass down and licked her lips.

'Heaven, shit,' said Norman. 'It'll be jus' the same up there, 'cept with wings.'

The third time he went to the gents Norman had some difficulty getting through the door, like it had got narrower since the last time he went. He had a long piss and shook the drops off, then stood in front of the mirror smiling at his reflection. 'How long since you had a good skinful?' he asked himself. 'And a woman?' Hell, he was *free*. Getting shitfaced. Sitting in there having a normal conversation, talking 'bout politics and religion, gonna fuck himself stupid in an hour.

On his way back to the bar the door had got narrower still. Had to go through sideways.

'You gotta wife?' Tina asked him. 'Family?'

Norman leaned forward and had another sniff of her. 'You looking for a husband?'

She laughed. 'Christ, no,' she said. 'I'm just interested.'

'Why should I get married?' Norman said. 'Everybody I know got married, they're all trying like hell to get unmarried.'

'I was married twice,' Tina told him. 'The first guy was a hundred and eighty years older than me. We lived together two years and at the end I was a hundred and eighty years older than him.'

'You work that out on your calculator?'

'The second guy was gonna put me in pictures, but somebody stoled his camera.'

'What happened to him?' Norman said.

'He's still there,' she said. 'The brothers chased him off. Comes in here occasionally, complains about the price, but he always pays.'

'For his own old lady?'

'Johns like to pay,' she said. 'They don't pay they don't think they've been screwed.'

'Yeah, I know,' Norman said. 'Used to run a couple of girls one time. You ever need a new pimp, you can look me up.'

Tina looked around, see if anyone was listening. 'The brothers run everything here,' she said. 'There's no opportunities.'

Norman eyed the big one at the bar, see if he'd got any smaller. Maybe a little. Now he was only medium huge. 'I can hear what you're saying,' he said.

'What about girlfriends?' she asked. 'You must have somebody.'

'I told you. I've bin away.' He picked up a packet of cigarettes off the table and shook one out. Lit it up. 'I had a girl before,' he said. 'Snow White.'

Tina laughed again. 'Snow White. Shit. You putting me on?'

Norman laughed along with her. 'No, it's true,' he said. 'She was called Selina White, really. But when I first met her, she signed her name S. White, so I called her Snow White after that. Everybody did.'

'She work for you or the seven dwarfs?'

'She worked for me a while,' he said. 'But when I went away she split with my stash. Cleaned me out.'

'Sometimes happens,' Tina told him. 'Not very often. A girl goes astray here the brothers find her before you can say jack shit.'

'I'll find her,' said Norman.

'You know where she is?'

'Yeah. She married a guy and went straight. Living in York.'

'She know you're coming after her?'

'Not yet,' Norman said, finishing the last of his drink. 'But she will when I get there.'

Back in Tina's room Norman checked his bag. Somebody had been in it, but nothing was missing. He got undressed and took sixty quid's worth of flesh and sweat off her, then slept for an hour.

'It's ten to twelve,' she said, waking him. 'You're not out by twelve they'll come up for you.'

'Did I get my blow job?'

'You got everything you're getting,' said Tina.

He dressed and left her. 'I come by again I'll look you up,' he said. At the bottom of the stairs the two card-playing brothers had gone. The big one who'd been in the bar was standing by the door. Norman waited for him to move out of the way.

The guy eyed Norman's bag. 'You got a long piece of wire in there,' he said, 'with a hook on the end.'

'The guy's got X-ray eyes,' said Norman.

'What's it for?'

'Hot weather,' Norman told him. 'My ass sometimes gets sticky. I can put the wire over my shoulder and scratch my ass with the hook. It saves me turning round.'

The guy thought about it a moment, then moved aside.

Norman took a few steps along the street, then turned round and went back to the brother. 'From time to time,' he said, 'I come across cars and dope and shooters, things like that.'

'Ain't you the lucky one?' the brother said.

Norman shrugged. 'I got a market already,' he said. 'I jus' thought I could combine it with Tina up there. She's my kind of girl, and if I was coming through with merchandise I could put her on my expense account.'

The brother looked down on Norman from a great height. 'Shooters?' he said.

Norman nodded.

'We'd look,' the guy said.

'You got any more questions?' Norman asked him.

The guy said nothing. He'd gone away again.

Norman found a little Fiat van, something he could stretch out in. Drove it out of town and parked in a lay-by. He got in the back and slept until noon the next day, dreaming of Tina and all the things he'd forgot to do to her.

When he woke up he ate a sandwich out of his bag. Opened a can of beer. There was no tape deck, only a radio, so he listened to the news. The authorities said the rioting inmates had caused more than ten million pounds worth of damage. One prisoner and one prison officer had been killed. The prison officer was a married man with two small children and had been well loved by colleagues and prisoners alike. Norman couldn't think who that was. No one he knew had loved any screws. Wait a minute, still more to come. Three prisoners were still missing after the politicos had hit the transport carrying some of the ringleaders of the riot. Isaac Bova, white, five foot eight, forty-five years old, serving twenty years for terrorist activities, and two other men. There was some evidence to suggest that one of these men was involved in the murder of the well-loved prison officer. All three men were believed to be making for the London area, though travelling separately, and none of them should be approached by the public. Christ, Norman, they're trying to pin the murder of the screw on you. Shit, he thought, I never even had the chance.

And what was this shit, anyway? Isaac Bova and *two other men*? How come they give out the name of some twat called Isaac Bova, and Norman Bunce doesn't even get a mention? Like fucking Isaac is important and Norman doesn't even exist. How many people did Isaac kill, for Chrissake? Who is this guy, the world record holder?

But Norman smiled. They didn't know where he was. Thought he was on his way to the Smoke. Maybe he should go to York, like he'd told Tina. It was true that Snow White had moved up there, and he might look her up for old times' sake. Maybe get something out of her.

Norman switched the radio off, then he found the M62 and drove to Leeds. Last leg of a long journey.

He parked the Fiat outside the railway station. Went to the ticket office and got a single ticket to Scarborough. 'That's seaside, right?' he asked the guy behind the glass.

'Seaside? Sure,' the man said.

Norman held up his bag so the guy could see it through the glass. 'Got my bucket and spade in here,' Norman said. 'Little swimming costume. Might do a bit of fishing as well.'

He walked off down the platform. Sat in an orange plastic bucket and lit up a cigarette, watched the ladies while he waited for the train to arrive.

chapter 4

'Could I speak to Gus, please?'

It was a sweet voice, a low voice, a voice that had waited and thought about it before picking up the telephone and dialling the number. It was a voice that had counted the number of rings, and had hoped that it would be Gus who answered. And then when Sam Turner had picked up the receiver and said whatever he said into it, the voice had gone automatically into secondary mode, trying to sound like a general enquiry and failing badly.

'Gus's not here,' Sam said. 'Can I take a message?'

'Oh. No, it's not important. I'll try later. When is the best time to catch him?' Sam ignored the words. They didn't mean what they said. Each syllable was tinged with disappointment. Something else as well, a barely concealed Teutonic accent.

'Try after four,' he said. 'Between four and five. He should be here then.'

'Thank you. Bye.'

Sam put the phone down. On the office floor, where it lived for the moment, there being no furniture in the room. Jesus, he thought, the stupid prick's having an affair. He brought the makings out of his pocket and rolled a tight cigarette. Lit it up and looked round the room. Then he remembered his blood pressure and stubbed the cigarette out on the wooden floor.

Gus was Sam's oldest friend. Long before the private detective business got under way they had played snooker together, shared the same musical tastes, and driven thousands of miles backwards and forwards to rock concerts all over the country. Even made the occasional foray into Europe. The last Dylan concert in Oslo. They had a date lined up for the coming autumn when the Cocker was playing Amsterdam.

But Sam had known Marie, Gus's partner, for longer than he had known Gus, and the thought of her being cuckolded again was enough to remind Sam what the world really smelled like. Someone had told him a long time ago (or maybe he read it in a book – he couldn't remember) that under the toothpaste and the powder, civilization stank of stale cooking and piss.

Sam drove the Volvo over to the Stonebow and went down the cellar steps to the snooker hall. 'Must be the coolest place in town,' he said to Gus and Geordie when he got to their table. Barney, Geordie's dog, came over to Sam and rubbed up against his leg. Sam bent over to pat the dog on the head.

There were two other tables occupied, four women playing doubles on one of them, and two old age pensioners on the other. 'Is this a game?' Sam asked.

'No, we was jus' practising,' said Geordie. 'Gus's bin showing me how to put backspin on the ball.' Geordie was dressed in white Reeboks with black jeans about four inches too long for him. Today he was sporting his purple New Deal sweatshirt and a baseball cap with 'Indianapolis 500' written on the front. Only when he played snooker he wore it back to front, so the legend was at the back, and at the front a little leather tag to adjust the size. Gus called it Geordie's IQ reducer. 'When he wears it normal,' Gus would say, 'it reduces the IQ to about half. But when he wears it back to front, like that, then the IQ goes through the floor.'

'Backspin? Maybe you should learn how to pot them first,' Sam said.

'I can, Sam,' said Geordie. 'I potted two the other day, including one was a black one.'

'Yeah, and the other was the white one, which is not supposed to be potted.'

Geordie laughed. 'It was a fluke,' he said. 'Watch this.' He put the blue on its spot in the centre of the table and the white midway between the blue and one of the centre pockets. 'I'm gonna pot the blue and bring the white back into this pocket,' he said.

He chalked his cue and got right down on the table, feathering the white carefully, then drawing his stick back and striking the white hard and low. The blue missed the centre bag, ricochetted off the heel of the pocket and broke up the reds. The white stayed in the middle of the table.

Geordie stood up. 'See,' he said. 'That was bloody close.'

Sam and Gus both laughed. 'OK,' Sam said. 'It only takes practice. You're better than you used to be.'

'He'd have to be, wouldn't he,' said Gus. 'Time was when he'd miss the white.' Gus was thirty-two years old, slightly built, an inch taller than Sam. He wore the same slacks and shirt he'd worn for the last five summers, and sandals over black socks. They began collecting the balls, putting the colours on their spots. Geordie racked the reds and rolled the white down to Sam at the baulk end of the table.

'So,' Sam said. 'We cracked another case.'

'*We?*' said Gus. 'Don't remember seeing you there. Me and Geordie cracked another case while you were painting and decorating the office.'

'Jesus, Sam,' said Geordie, 'we was shitting ourselves in that restaurant. If it'd been the Mafia instead of those kids they'd've burned the place down with us in it. Turned us into pastrami, whatever it is they eat.'

'Mafia don't work like that,' Sam told him. 'If they'd been involved there wouldn't just be a few cases of arson, they'd have blown the place off the face of the earth.'

'Yeah, that's what I mean,' said Geordie. 'Then where would we be?'

'I give in,' said Gus. 'Where would we be?'

'Fuckin' vanished,' said Geordie. 'Sam'd be playing this game with nobody. Every time he missed a pot it would still be his turn.'

'You know there's a reward?' Sam asked them.

'How much?' said Gus. 'Will we be able to retire?'

'Dunno exactly. Couple of thou. Buy you some records and a new suit.'

Geordie got down to play the ball and then stood up again. 'Jesus,' he said. 'I'm gonna get one of those CD players.'

'Yeah,' said Sam. 'And you could take some driving lessons.'

Geordie was down on the ball again, but couldn't concentrate enough to hit it. 'Me and Gus get a thousand each,' he said. 'Is that enough to buy a car?'

'Maybe,' said Sam. 'But you should take the lessons first.'

Geordie nodded, not convinced. He feathered the white again, then stood up to ask another question. 'If I get a car,' he said, 'and I get a licence to drive it, can I go abroad and drive it?'

'Sure,' said Sam. 'You just remember to drive on the other side of the road.'

'Yeah,' said Geordie. 'I heard that.' He got down on the table again, then looked round at Sam. 'You'll be telling me people in Australia are upside down next.' He looked back at the ball, then stood up again.

'Jesus Christ,' said Gus. 'Are you gonna hit the ball?'

'OK,' Geordie told him, getting down on the table again. 'I was only asking a question. How'm I supposed to learn things if I can't ask questions?' He struck the white and potted a red. The white ball finished straight on the pink. 'Look at that,' he said. 'Steven fuckin' Hendry, look out!'

'So, what's next?' Gus asked Sam. 'Much lined up for tomorrow?'

'Only the slush pile,' Sam said. 'Forester, the solicitor, we've got a few jobs outstanding for him. Be a chance to clear up.'

'We should close down for the summer,' said Gus. 'Get a villa in France. Something like that. We could all go together.'

Sam shook his head. 'We've just finished the office,' he said. 'Something'll turn up. This weather people go crazy.'

'We run out of jobs?' Geordie asked.

'Not quite,' Sam told him. 'Only they're not very exciting.'

'Jesus, I don't care about that,' Geordie said. 'Long as there's something to do. If there's nothing to do then I get restless.'

'Yeah,' Sam told him. 'You never miss your water till your well runs dry.'

*

'There was a call for you,' Sam told Gus. They were sitting together in the car outside Sam's flat. Geordie had already got out of the car with Barney and disappeared into his own flat. 'At the office.'

'Any message? Who was it?'

'No message,' Sam said. 'Woman's voice. I said you'd be there after four.'

'Probably Marie.'

Sam looked across at him. 'I'd know if it was Marie,' he said. 'I've known her a long time.'

'Yeah,' Gus said absently. 'I wasn't thinking.'

'I got the impression it was somebody Marie wouldn't be too happy to hear about.'

Gus turned towards him. 'What are you, then, an oracle? For all you know it coulda been my grandmother, my auntie Doris, my niece from Edinburgh. Sam, just because a female voice asks for me on the telephone and it isn't the female voice that I live with, you immediately have to think I'm having an affair. I don't know what's wrong with you, 'less it's that you've got a dirty mind. I mean, think about it a minute. Is it at all conceivable that you could be wrong about this?'

'No, Gus, it's completely inconceivable that I'm wrong about this. I heard the woman's voice on the phone. When she said your name her tongue was hanging out. Don't ask me why her tongue was hanging out. Because if thinking about you makes her tongue hang out she must be blind as well as stupid. But that's about her, and I never even met the woman. What I want to talk about is you. And you I have met, more than once before, and this isn't the first time I've met you in the same kind of situation. That is, with your prick hanging out for some floozie that for reasons which will always escape me, thinks it's the best thing she's seen since celery with mayonnaise. And you know for why? I know you know for why, because Marie is a friend of mine, and friends of mine I take care of. You wanna go round screwing some little baggage you just happened to run into, that's fine, it's actually none of my business, and under some circumstances I'd even be happy for you. But under the present circumstances all I see coming out of it is a friend of mine, namely Marie, getting hurt. And she'll be the only one in the whole situation who didn't do anything to deserve it.'

Gus opened the passenger door and got out of the Volvo. 'I don't have to take this shit,' he said. He slammed the door and walked off down the street.

Sam got out of the car and followed him. 'You can't run away, either,' he said. 'Every time you look round I'll be sitting on your shoulder. I'll haunt you, Gus. I'm telling you, you gotta sort this one out.'

But Gus kept on walking. Didn't look back. Didn't say another word. Sam looked after him in disgust. Socks and sandals. No wonder the guy had no self-respect.

What did these women see in a guy like Gus? Sam couldn't understand it. Socks and sandals? It wasn't like he was a dork, more like a blank. He was like a blank canvas, the kind some women like to paint their dreams on.

chapter 5

When he got to Scarborough Norman followed the signs down to the front, stopped at a shop and bought himself a sleeping bag and a pair of shorts, some shades to cut out the glare. At a grocery store he spent the rest of his money on sandwiches and beer, some cigarettes and matches, filled up his bag. Then he walked along the cliff, south, away from the town.

He took his sweater off and tied it around his waist, get a little sunshine on his body. After another half hour, when there were few people about, he took his trousers off and put them and the sweater into his bag. Got his new shorts on and felt the sun on his legs. Maybe the first time in twenty years. Last time that happened Norman had been a school-boy. But Jesus, who wants to remember that?

Norman intended to sleep under the stars, find a little

nook in the cliff somewhere and curl up. But after he'd been walking for a couple of hours he came across a small shack halfway down the cliff. He climbed down to it and kicked in a couple of planks to get inside. The place had been built as a small café but abandoned for some reason. Maybe because of the recession, or probably because it had been built in such an isolated spot that it never got any customers anyway.

There were some items of crockery, an old coffee-making machine so corroded it would never be used to make coffee again, a tea urn with a stiff lid. There was one broken chair and a table that still had three legs. At one end was a long counter covered in dust, made of solid deal. Behind the counter were sliding doors, and when he opened one of these Norman found a place a little longer than himself, about four foot wide, that would make an ideal bedroom. He got his new sleeping bag and unrolled it into the space. Perfect. He could get in there and pull the sliding door closed from the inside. Sleep like a baby. During the day he could sit in the sun and drink beer, eat a sandwich, have a paddle every now and then. Spend a few days like that until the heat died down. By then he'd have a beard. When he arrived in York even Snow White wouldn't recognize him.

The evening of the second day Norman walked to the village and emptied the local telephone box to see if he could still do it. It was easier than slipping on a banana skin.

The morning of the third day he was half asleep under the counter when he heard sounds. Somebody coming into the shack. Quiet voices, whispering. First he thought it was the law tracked him down and what he was hearing was some kind of armed assault force coming in to get him. He kept completely still, barely breathing.

'It's a café,' one of the voices said, not whispering any more. A high-pitched voice, could have been a woman, but it wasn't. Must be kids. That was a boy's voice. Young boy, so young his voice hadn't broken. Norman kept still. With a bit of luck they'd go away.

'This's for making coffee,' said another voice. 'Sound. We

44

could make a den here. Look at all this stuff.' Another unbroken voice, like the first one.

Oh, Jesus, don't make a den here. Go and play on the beach. Make sand castles, whatever it is you're supposed to do. The trouble with kids today, they've no respect for private property.

There were only the two voices. No more. One of them jumped up on the counter and did a little dance. Jesus, like being inside a drum. Then he jumped off on to the bare boards of the floor, and the other one jumped up on the counter and did the same.

Norman wanted to get out of there and sort the little bastards out. Scare the living shits out of them.

'There's a cupboard here,' the first voice said.

'Where? Let's see.'

'Under the counter.'

The door at the far end of the counter opened about eighteen inches. Norman watched the light stream in.

'Anything in there?'

'Can't see. It's too dark.'

Then a head and a hand appeared through the cupboard door. Norman stopped breathing.

'There's something,' the voice said. 'Feels like a blanket.'

'Anything else? Any money?'

'No. There's something wrapped in it. Feels like a . . . like a . . . foot.'

Norman said, 'Jesus. This's all I need.'

The kids panicked and were out of the shack before Norman could get rid of the sleeping bag and crawl out from under the counter. When he got outside the shack the two boys were about twenty yards up the cliff, unsure if they should carry on going up or come down and see what the foot had been attached to.

'Come back,' Norman shouted. 'I'm not gonna hurt you.' Jesus, he'd have to play it by ear, but kids like these he could get to do whatever he wanted. They were about twelve, maybe thirteen years old. A small blond one and a dark one, slightly taller than his mate. They came down the cliff slowly, the dark one first. Norman watched them and waited. Both wearing shorts and a T-shirt.

'Christ, we thought you was a ghost,' said the dark one.

'Or a dead man,' said the blond. 'I thought you was a dead body.'

Norman laughed and went back inside the shack. The two boys followed him. He reached under the counter for his bag and opened a can of beer. He took a swig and passed it to the taller of the two, obviously the leader. Then he shook a cigarette out of his pack and handed the pack to the boys. They each took a cigarette and Norman lit them all up with one match.

He reached into his bedroom again and came out with a plastic bag and emptied it on to the counter. A million ten-pence and fifty-pence pieces spread themselves over the surface, some of them rolling off on to the floor.

'Jesus,' said the little blond kid. 'It's a fortune.'

Both pairs of eyes shone at the sight of the money. 'Where'd you get all that?' the dark one asked.

'I could tell you,' Norman said. 'But I don't know if you can keep a secret.'

'Oh, we *can*,' they both said in unison. And only a fool would have believed that they didn't mean it. Shit, whatever it was, they weren't gonna tell anyone. Not ever.

Norman passed the can of beer around again. 'Broke a telephone box open,' he said. 'Last night.'

'Sound,' said the little one.

'Yeah,' said his friend. 'How'd you do it?'

'Can opener,' Norman said, taking the beer from the blond one and sipping a little.

'What you sleeping under there for?' the dark one asked.

'I'm on the run,' Norman told him. 'Police're looking for me.'

The two boys exchanged glances. This was turning into the best summer they'd ever had. The blond one shook some ash from his cigarette and looked at Norman with his mouth wide open. Like he couldn't believe what he was seeing, something unheard of, like a sea monster.

Norman shrugged. 'I suppose you'll turn me in?' he said.

The little blond one shook his head. 'No,' he said. 'We wouldn't do that.'

'Why're they after you?' the dark one asked.

'I escaped from prison,' Norman told him. 'Been on the run for three weeks. Trying to set up a record.'

'Record?'

'Yeah. The record for staying out of the joint I was in is four weeks. I wanna try to stay out five weeks. Then I'll break the record.'

'No one'll find you here,' the dark one said. 'You could stay here for ever.'

Norman laughed. 'No,' he said. 'After five weeks I'll turn myself in. I'll be a hero when I get back. No one ever stayed out that long.'

'We won't spragg you,' said the little blond one.

His friend agreed. 'No,' he said. 'We'd never do that.'

Norman smiled at them. 'Good,' he said. 'Maybe you could help me?'

Two voices said, 'Yeah.'

'You could take some of the money,' he said. 'Get me something to eat, a newspaper, some fags. I can't go out during the day. Get something for yourselves as well.'

Norman needed only a couple more days. He knew, when they returned with a chicken tikka sandwich and a blackberry pie, that he could string them along that long. Shit, something like this happening, they'd probably keep it a secret the rest of their lives.

The following day they brought him fish and chips from the van at the caravan site, a new six pack of beers, and forty cigarettes.

A couple of nights later Norman broke into a house on the outskirts of the village, got himself some clothes more suitable for the town, and a hundred and seventy pounds in cash. Could have taken a car as well, just standing there outside the house, but he would have to dump it in York, and that might lead the police to think he was there.

Norman didn't want anyone to know he was in York. Not yet. Not while he was on holiday.

Not until he found Snow White. After that he didn't care what happened. By that time he'd probably be finished with the town as well as the girl.

chapter 6

They brought the desk up the stairs and placed it next to the window. 'You wanna look out the window or have your back to it?' the chief humper asked.

'Have my back to it,' Sam Turner said, following them into the room with a swivel chair. 'Need to get this between the desk and the window.'

'It was my office I'd have it so I could see out,' the humper said. 'See the grand ladies going into Betty's, all those little students with next to no clothes on. Can't blame 'em though, in this weather.' He went to the window and looked down on the square. 'They could go naked for me,' he said. 'I wouldn't make no complaints.'

'I've got to work,' said Sam. 'Pay the landlord for all this space. If they take their clothes off I don't mind standing up to get a look. I think that's a better way of handling it, don't you? Rather than arranging the whole office on the off-chance that I might see somebody's bare ass?'

The humper and his mate went back down the stairs muttering something about work and bringing the drawers up and why in God's name was it so hot?

The room still looked bare, but what the hell. Sam smoothed his hand over the surface of the desk. Old, weathered oak. Here and there someone had gouged a piece out of the surface, but it would do fine for Sam's use. He picked the telephone off the floor and placed it on the desk. It didn't ring.

Sam took a large glass ashtray off the window sill and placed it next to the telephone.

He rolled a cigarette and put it to his lips, let it dangle

there, unlit. He sat in the swivel chair with his feet up, looked around the room. There was a radiator under the window behind him. On the far wall was the door and a filing cabinet. The filing cabinet was locked, and in the middle drawer was a small pistol and ammunition, and an empty bottle of whisky. The pistol was for emergencies. The empty whisky bottle was a symbol of the full bottle of whisky that all private detectives keep in their filing cabinets. All private detectives except this one, who couldn't handle it.

The right hand wall had a sink and a small draining board, place for a kettle and some cups. Then there was a door to Celia's room. To the right of that was a bookcase with nothing in it, but Sam had some books at home he would bring tomorrow.

Over to his left were two more desks, one each for Geordie and Gus, and a shelving unit which housed a radio and tape deck together with a stack of tapes to keep them occupied when they weren't solving cases or reading books. There was also a spare chair over there.

There was another chair in front of Sam's desk, for clients. But no one had ever sat in it yet.

Behind him the window had been stencilled so that the name of the business showed itself to the square outside. Sam got up from the swivel chair and walked round the desk. He sat in the client's chair and looked down at the front of his shirt. He had to move the chair slightly to get the effect he wanted. Then he smiled. The shadow of the stencil had thrown itself on to his chest, and proclaimed:

Sam Turner

Investigations

Sam was wearing a green chino short-sleeved shirt with a button-down collar and a pair of loose cut gabardine trousers with metal buttons on the pockets. He was too hot. He got out of that chair and went over to the entrance door. This led to a small anteroom, so when they had customers queuing up to get in they would have somewhere to wait. There was nothing to sit on in there yet, but judging by the noise coming up the stairwell a couple of chairs would arrive soon.

The pubs looked more inviting in this weather. But it was a trick played by the subconscious and the booze. They got together and ganged up on you. Would take you for a sucker if you insisted. Like you might find someone in the pub, behind the bar, at the bottom of a bottle. He laughed to himself. That was the trick the booze played. There *would* be somebody at the bottom of a bottle, only you might have to go through more bottles than you could drink before you found who it was. Then when you found who it was you'd remember all the other times you'd drunk yourself insensible.

He'd stay off it, though. One day at a time.

Sam walked back into his office and put *New Morning* on the tape deck, 'cause that's what it felt like. Then he went over to Celia's door. He opened it and poked his head through. 'How're you doing?' he asked.

'Oh, Sam,' Celia said. 'I'm doing fine. Thought I heard you through there.' Celia had compromised with her desk, placing it at right angles to the window so she could look out or not, depending how she felt. Celia Allison was Sam's secretary, sixty-eight years old and going strong. When he talked to guys who told him their secretary was a treasure, Sam would tell them, 'Hell, mine's a gold mine.'

She was dressed in a navy button-through top with short sleeves and a matching spotted skirt with pleats. Shoes were navy too, with pointed toes and little heels. She wore a three-colour gold Russian bangle on her left wrist. Tiny wrinkles on her wrist and ropy veins running down the back of her hands.

Her room was not large, slightly smaller than Sam's. She had a new computer desk with a modern system on it. Multisync monitor on a tilt and swivel stand. Laser printer. Scanner. Little mouse on a mouse mat which Sam had not mastered yet. Every time he moved it the pointer disappeared off the screen. Worked OK for Celia though.

There was also a combined fax and telephone on the desk, and one of those little trays with three tiers so you could have In, Out and Pending all going at the same time. Celia had also brought a small carpet from home. 'To make the place a little cosier.'

On the wall behind her desk she had a filing cabinet and several shelves containing discs and the programs she used on her computer, accounts, desktop publishing, word processing, and other things Sam couldn't understand. He knew how to use the database though. Had found his way around that little cookie. And if anyone could ever explain to him how a spreadsheet could improve or simplify his life, he'd crack that one too.

'There's some mail for you,' she said.

'Anything interesting?' He took the sheaf of papers from her and looked through them.

'Not much,' she said. 'Couple of cheques. Oh, and you've been invited to join the Rotarians.' She laughed.

'God,' said Sam. 'Few months ago I couldn't fall out of a tree and hit the ground. Now I've solved a couple of cases, had my name in the paper, everybody wants me to come to dinner.'

'You're a celebrity, Sam.'

'Hell, Celia, it'll be the Masons next.'

'What shall I tell them?' Celia asked.

'To get stuffed,' he said. He walked over to the window and looked out at the square. All the bench space was taken up by tourists. People were queuing to get into Betty's for a cold drink. A couple of buskers were playing an old Charlie Parker number and a horde of Scandinavian teenagers were crowded around taking photographs or dancing, some of them doing both at the same time.

The humpers got to the top of the stairs and banged their way through the anteroom with the remaining drawers and chairs. Sam went through to be with them and Celia followed.

'I like the desk,' she told him. 'Where did you find it?'

'I've got another just like it,' the chief humper said. 'Could deliver it tomorrow. Matching chair as well.'

'No thanks,' she said. 'We've got plenty of desks. Yesterday we didn't have any and we managed all right.'

When they left, Celia went back into her office. Sam

followed and found her trying to open the window, but it had been jammed for centuries. 'I can't open any of 'em,' he told her. 'Leave it. I'll get somebody to fix them tomorrow.'

She left the window and turned to face him. 'You got anything else to do here?' he asked.

She shook her head. 'No. All done and dusted.'

'We could go over to Betty's,' he said. 'Have a lemonade or ice cream, something to keep the heat at bay.'

'That would be lovely, Sam.'

'I dunno why people want to go to Italy,' he said. 'Weather like this.'

Sam walked past the queue of people waiting for a table at Betty's, Celia following him. He caught the eye of the maître d' and was shown to a small table by the entrance to the kitchen. The maître d' held Celia's chair until she was settled, winked at Sam, and left them to it.

'I don't know how you do it, Sam,' Celia said. 'Some of those people have been waiting for ages.'

'Just a little arrangement,' Sam said. 'Saves me a lot of time.'

Celia shook her head. 'Goodness,' she said. 'There's corruption everywhere.'

'Yeah,' said Sam. 'Even at Betty's. The last bastion of the British Empire.'

A waitress who looked like the coolest person in the whole place took their order, ice cream and coffee for Sam and ice cream and Earl Grey tea for Celia. A couple of minutes later she came back and served it.

'How are things going with Wanda?' Celia asked.

'So-so,' said Sam. 'She's been going out with this guy from the Solo Club. Big mistake. Turned out to be married.'

'Oh, no,' said Celia. 'Poor Wanda. Why don't *you* marry her and get it over with?'

Sam choked on a piece of ice cream.

'Celia,' he said. 'I've been married twice. I'm not gonna do it three times. Not unless I start drinking again. That usually does the trick.'

'I can't think why not, Sam. You really like each other. It would be good for both of you.'

'Celia,' he said, 'give me a break. It could also be bad for both of us.'

She shook her head. 'It would be lovely,' she said. 'For those two girls as well. Little children like them, they need a father.'

'Christ, Celia. I don't wanna be a father.' Sam scraped the last of his ice cream out of the tall glass and put it down in front of him, pushed it away. 'Wanda's a good friend. I'm a good friend to her and she's a good friend to me. We look after each other. I look around at other people's marriages and I don't see much of that going on. I don't want a wife if it means losing a friend; and that seems to be the equation.'

'It's not that you're frightened, then?'

'Frightened? Hell, if it comes to marriage I'm terrified. Wanda would have a nervous breakdown if I asked her to marry me. Christ, terrified. Wouldn't you be?'

Celia laughed. 'Yes,' she said. 'But at my age it's not really on the cards, is it?'

'Oh, I don't know,' Sam said. 'Everybody should try it at least once.'

Celia took a sip of her tea. 'Anyway,' she said, 'we're not talking about me.'

Sam sighed. 'Let it go, Celia,' he said. 'Last time I got married I bought myself more troubles'n God gave the Jews.'

'Someone keeps ringing for Gus,' Celia said. 'A woman.'

Sam didn't meet her eyes. 'Yeah?' he said.

'Yes,' said Celia. 'A woman. Not Marie.' She looked hard at Sam. 'Do I have to spell it out for you, Sam?'

'What, like a femme fatale?'

'Maybe. I've only spoken to her on the phone. She sounds like somebody who's very keen about Gus.'

'Someone lusting over his body?'

'Sam,' Celia said, 'I do believe you're trying to shock me.'

'I should know better,' he said.

'Also, you know more about this than you are saying.' She was silent for a moment. 'Does Gus have trouble keeping his zip up?'

Sam laughed so loudly people at nearby tables put their cups down. The waitress hovered on the borderline between kitchen and restaurant. Sam covered his face with his hands and regained control. 'Yes, you're right,' he said, still wreathed in smiles. 'He's having an affair.'

'Does Marie know?'

'No. Not yet.'

Celia pursed her lips. 'He's a silly boy,' she said. 'If he loses Marie he'll have lost more than he could ever replace.'

'I tried to tell him that.'

'Try again, Sam. I don't want to stand around while he hangs himself.'

'Yeah,' Sam said. 'I'm just waiting to catch him in a more amenable frame of mind. Women make him stupid.'

'Don't make sexist remarks,' she said. 'Gus, all of you chaps, you don't need *women* to make you stupid.' She pursed her lips tightly together and glared at Sam. Then had another thought. 'Oh, my goodness,' she said, 'I almost forgot. My niece, Jennie, is coming today. She'll be staying with me for a while, and I've managed to rent her a little room down the hall. Somewhere she can work.'

'Didn't know you had a niece, Celia. Does that mean you'll be spending time with her?'

'A little,' Celia confessed. 'But not as much as I'd like. She's going to be working. You should take the time to meet her as well, Sam. She's a psychologist. She'll be working with some of the people over at the women's prison.'

'Askham Grange.'

'Yes. She's involved in some kind of research project. You'll probably get on quite well together.'

'Is this another attempt to get me fixed up, Celia?'

'Good gracious, no,' said the old lady. 'Jennie is my own flesh and blood. My little brother's girl. I wouldn't throw her to the wolves.'

chapter 7

Norman was surprised at York. It wasn't that it was big, but
it was a hell of a lot bigger than he'd expected. He couldn't
remember exactly what it was he had expected now – not
that he'd get off the train on a little wooden platform, see a
town with fields around it. Maybe an old station guard with
a white beard, doddery old fucker. And Norman would go
up to him and ask him where Snow White lived, and the guy
would say, 'Oh, yeah, Snow White. She lives in the house on
the hill.'

Yeah, that was what he'd expected. Something like that.

What he hadn't expected was a station with several
platforms, modern trains, and when you got outside the
station, modern cars and shops and thousands of people
walking around the town, many of them talking in foreign
accents. Not just north of England foreign accents, but real
proper German and Japanese and American foreign accents.
That was what he hadn't expected, and together with that he
hadn't expected all these new-looking glass-fronted hotels to
put them in.

Norman was surprised at York, and after walking around
it for an hour or two he didn't mind being surprised. It was
a place you could get lost in, and that was a real nice feeling.

Only problem was, how would he find Snow White?
Norman wasn't even sure if he wanted to bother finding
Snow White. The prospect of hurting her made him think it
would be worthwhile. But he had the feeling that a whole
new world was about to open up for him, and he didn't want
aspects of the past to clutter it up.

One thing Norman discovered on his first day in York was
that he was the only tourist without a camera. He realized
this when he followed a party of what he assumed were

Scandinavians and Americans up an artificial mound to a huge castle keep called Clifford's Tower. When they got to the top of the mound the cameras started clicking and everybody except Norman was looking at the world through a viewfinder. For a minute Norman didn't know what to do. He tried to remember his classes in social skills in Dartmoor, and although he knew that a situation similar to this had been discussed, he couldn't remember exactly what it was. While he was still racking his brains he became aware that the guide was talking about William the Conqueror.

William the Conqueror had been here. The guy had actually built a fort on this hill. There'd been riots here as well, against some Jews, battles, and at one point someone had blown the roof off. Norman couldn't remember a time before when he'd stood somewhere that William the Conqueror or any of those historic types had actually stood. For a time there he had a really strange feeling about it, made him forget all about being the only one without a camera.

On the way down he sidled up to the guide and asked him, 'When was that again? William the Conqueror and all that?'

'Ten sixty-six,' the guide told him.

'Jesus,' Norman said, but was distracted by the sight of a Japanese woman placing a Nikon with a huge lens on the grass at the bottom of the mound. She just left it there. Put it down on the grass and walked away after one of her children.

So it was Norman the tourist, with a camera he'd probably never learn to use slung over his shoulder, who walked away from Clifford's Tower, past the fire station, and into the heart of the city.

Jesus, York was the place to be. No wonder William the Conqueror came here. Not surprising at all, though, 'cause like the tour guide said, old William, he was a Norman.

Night time.

During the afternoon Norman had checked into a boarding house run by a Mrs Lee. Middle-aged woman who wore thick glasses and had no husband. A kid somewhere at a boarding school. Been doing this job for ten years, five years in Brighton and five years in York. Lots of other things she'd told him about herself, couldn't seem to keep her mouth shut for more than a minute at a time. Norman got her life story between her opening the door and her showing him the room. But she never asked anything about him. Just gave him the *Yellow Pages* when he asked for them, together with *What's On*, *The Good Beer Guide* and several maps of the city.

Night time.

Norman had found the address of the gun club in the *Yellow Pages* and borrowed a car to get out here on the ring road. Done a complete recce. Round about now it looked as though the place was closing down for the day. Most of the cars had gone from the car park. Only two left. One of them a truck, the other a silver Merc. There had been several trucks earlier, farmer-type trucks, and the farmer types had come out of the gun club and got into them and driven away.

Another one came out while Norman watched. Great fat guy with a white handlebar moustache and side-whiskers, checked jacket. Got in the truck and left. Now there was only the silver Merc. Norman waited twenty minutes, smoked a cigarette while he sat there. The guy who came out and locked the door was about Norman's size. Looked like an ex-cop. That's the kind of thing they do when they take early retirement. They buy a pub or become security advisers or start a gun club. What would he be, maybe fifty, fifty-five years old? Silver hair to match his Merc. Probably got a silver watch in his pocket, a little silver-haired wife at home.

When the Merc pulled out of the car park Norman took off after him. Followed the ring road for a mile or two, and then instead of turning back into York, the guy turned the other way and headed for the outskirts. Eventually he entered a new housing estate and pulled into the driveway of a detached house. The garage door opened all by itself, like it had just been waiting there for the guy to come home, and the silver Merc disappeared into it. After a moment or two the guy came to the garage door and closed it. He closed it so that he was inside. Must be a door in the garage that led into the house.

Norman noticed there was a large bell box above the front

door, probably with infra-red sensors inside, maybe pressure mats. The guy obviously had something to protect. Find out tomorrow. For now there was still time to get back to York before the pubs closed. A few beers and early to bed seemed like a good idea. Maybe watch the TV for a while in Mrs Lee's lounge.

Next day Norman decided to have another look at York. Played the tourist still, the camera slung over his shoulder, the shades keeping out the glare of the sun. There was always the possibility that he would bump into Snow White on the street. Say, 'Hi, babe. Remember me?' Then watch her face.

He could imagine her doing the double-take. Sucking in a little breath and her eyes glazing over as she decided if she should run or try to brazen it out. He'd play with her. He'd be a big cat with a baby mouse. Except this particular baby mouse had previous experience of Norman. She would know all the way along the line that he wasn't fooling. She'd know she was going to die, but that wasn't the most important thing. She'd also know that she was gonna see a lot of pain. So much pain that by the time her death came round she'd be begging for it. He kept seeing the meeting, like constantly rewinding a video tape. He turned a corner and there she was. 'Hi, babe. Remember me?' Then watch her face. Then rewind the tape.

But that didn't happen. Only in his head. He didn't know how he'd find her. York was a neat little town draped alongside a neat little river and half an hour after his walk round the city centre Norman the tourist sat on a bench in a historic square, a bag of fish and chips on his knee, his new camera between his feet, listening to a couple of buskers singing 'Why Do They Fall in L-ove?' While he was listening he looked up at a large stone building on one side of the square. Large wooden doors, and at the top of the building in gold letters, carved out of the stone, it said: YORKSHIRE INSURANCE COMPANY – ESTABLISHED MDCCCXXIIII. Norman knew about Roman numerals, and tried for a moment or two to work out what the total number was. But he didn't know these Roman numerals. He knew the X and the I, and thought maybe the C was a hundred, but the rest he couldn't work out. His eyes caught a sign on one of the windows in the building, and suddenly he smiled. The sign said, SAM TURNER – INVESTIGATIONS, but Norman smiled because he knew now how he would find Snow White. He'd get a private detective to do it.

Easy as that. One minute you have a problem, the next minute you've solved it. Just like with the camera.

Norman didn't intend to go see the private detective right away, first he'd have to think up a good story, why he wanted to trace Snow White. He'd think about it today, come back again tomorrow, then go see the man. But he'd have a good look at the building, make sure he'd remember where it was. While he was looking at the building Squish-squash came out of the door.

Norman's first impulse was to run. If it hadn't been for the fish and chips, the camera between his feet, he might have done just that. But he didn't. She hadn't seen him, and even if she did see him she probably wouldn't remember him. She'd never seen him with a beard.

She stood outside the door for a moment, as if she didn't know what to do next. Then she walked across the square, passing within six feet of Norman. She looked in the window of a shoe shop, and Norman watched her back. Yeah, it was definitely her. He remembered her long legs, her butt, her black hair cut off short at the bottom of her ears. Squish-squash, Jennie Cosgrave, psychologist. Norman had spent six weeks on one of her research projects in Dartmoor. Filling in questionnaires, answering bloody stupid questions like, How far would you go? (a) Steal a raincoat, or (b) Kill someone on a 'contract'? There were lots of other questions as well, Norman couldn't remember them all, parking a bike illegally or robbing a bank at gunpoint, questions like that. You had to tick the ones you'd do, then they put all the answers in a computer and sent you back to your cell. Never did tell you what they found out. Maybe they found nothing, or maybe they found out what colour to paint the bogs.

She turned now and walked back across the square, wearing a short yellow silk dress with a V-neck, buttons all the way down the front, canvas shoes. Norman crumpled his bag of fish and chips, picked up his camera, and followed her. At the corner of the square he threw the bag of fish and chips at a rubbish bin about five feet away. Went in first time.

Norman smiled at her walk. All the cons called her Squishsquash because of that walk. Little steps, one after the other. She'd take two steps to every one of Norman's. On the first step the top of her tights, the bit you couldn't see round her thighs, would go squish, and on the next step it would go squash. That's how she got her name. Walking around Dartmoor, squishsquash, squishsquash, squishsquash. Nearly caused a riot.

She walked past McDonald's and turned right, past the theatre. She stopped there for a moment to look at the photographs of some dancers in a glass case. Then down a long street with cars backed up bumper to bumper. Ended up taking another right and going into a big house in Lord Mayor's Walk. Got you, Norman thought. While the private detective was tracking Snow White, Norman could have a bit of fun with Squishsquash. Give her some questionnaires to answer. Every time she put a tick in the wrong place she'd have to forfeit something. He could teach her social skills she hadn't even dreamed of.

chapter 8

The guy who came into Sam Turner's office the following day was about five eight. He was slim but solidly built, and wore a yellow jacket with white jeans. Under the jacket a white T-shirt. He sported a short beard, clipped close to his skin, and he carried an expensive Nikon camera over his shoulder. Didn't look as though he had a problem in the world.

Sam was playing the *Budokan* album when the guy walked in. He stood and turned the tape deck off, offered a chair.

'You could have left the music on,' the guy said. He looked around the office, flared his nostrils. 'Stinks of paint in here,' he said. 'Are you open?'

Sam smiled and went behind his desk, sat down and looked over at the man. 'What can I do for you?' he asked.

The guy shook a cigarette out of his packet and lit it with an expensive and kitsch lighter. Didn't offer a cigarette to Sam. Sam pushed the ashtray over towards him. I can manage this, Sam thought. Let him smoke. I'll be righteous.

'I'm looking for a missing person,' the guy said. 'A woman. Are you the detective or the painter?'

Sam reached into his drawer for a pad and pen. 'You want your house painting?' he said. 'Business is slack at the moment. I could do either.'

'Shit,' Norman said. 'I wanna detective.'

'Can I get some personal details down?' Sam said. 'What's your name?'

'Norman Brown,' the guy said. 'Call me Norman.'

'Address?'

'Yeah,' Norman said. 'I'm actually working for someone else on this. I wanna be anonymous.'

Sam put his pen down and looked across the table. 'I might need to contact you,' he said. 'Who's paying the bill?'

'I'll leave some money with you,' Norman said. 'I'm doing a lot of travelling at the moment. I'll look in every other day or so. See how you're getting on. Keep you topped up with cash.'

'D'you wanna start at the beginning?' Sam said. 'Tell me who we're looking for?'

Norman smiled. 'She's called Snow White,' he said.

Sam looked at his pad. He'd written *Norman Brown*, and then an *S* for *Snow White*, but hadn't gone any further. He put his pen down again. 'She's been missing a long time,' he said 'From all accounts she was some kind of nymphomaniac. Into little chaps, preferably in gangs. Not that I've got anything against that sort of thing. Always think it's OK, whatever it is turns you on. What people do behind closed doors, so long as it doesn't hurt somebody else, that's fine. A girl gets off on a gang of dwarfs, and they decide to live together and run a family business, that's up to them. It's not even against the law, so far as I know. Except maybe if they're keeping her there against her will. But from what you've told me so far, well, what I'm trying to say to you is that I don't think I'm the right guy for the job. In fact, I don't think you'll find her. In my opinion, Mr Brown, you'd have better luck flying.'

'No,' Norman said with a smile. 'That's not her real name. It's like a nickname.'

'Good,' said Sam. He wrote on his pad, *Snow White alias*, and then looked over at Norman again. 'What's her real name?'

'She used to be called Selina White,' Norman said. 'But then she got married, so maybe she's changed it now.'

'How old is she?' asked Sam.

'Yeah,' Norman said. 'She was twenty-three seven years ago, so she'll be . . .' He closed his eyes to work the sum out. Sam watched him count it out on his fingers. 'Christ,' Norman said, 'she'll be thirty.'

'Do you know her date of birth?'

Norman shook his head. 'No, but her birthday was the twenty-fourth of June,' he said. 'I remember that 'cause it was the day after mine.'

Sam wrote on his pad. Without looking up at Norman he said, 'My secretary's got a computer. If we feed all this info in, we might get her date of birth.' He looked up and smiled. 'What do you think? Is it worth a try?'

'Go for it,' Norman said. 'Might even tell us where she's living, computers these days.'

'You don't know where she was born?' Sam asked.

'She came from Leicester,' Norman said. 'Had some family there, but she didn't keep in touch. Little sister.'

'And a wicked stepmother?' Sam tried.

'Dunno,' said Norman, missing the joke. 'Could've had.'

'What about a photograph?'

Norman shook his head. 'There was some photographs, but I don't have them now.'

'Just a general description, then,' said Sam. 'What she looked like.'

'Yeah.' Norman leaned forward, put his elbows on the desk. 'You see that *Star Wars* film?' he said. 'She was like the girl in that. The princess.'

'Princess Leia?' said Sam.

'Yeah. That's her. Could have been a film star.' Norman nipped the lighted end of his cigarette into the ashtray and put the butt into his top pocket. Sam inhaled deeply, got as much as he could of the remaining secondary blast.

'You sure she's in York?' Sam said.

'Yeah. She's here,' Norman said.

'Only, from the description you're giving me,' Sam said, 'I think I'd remember her. You know, she should sort of stand out.'

'Shit, you'd remember her,' Norman said. 'Snow White, she's a good-looking girl. You see her one time you'd know what I mean.'

'I bet,' said Sam. 'But I don't have a lot to go on.'

Norman stood, pushing his chair back. 'You don't want the job,' he said. 'I'll find somebody else.'

'I didn't say that,' Sam told him. 'We could give it a go.'

'OK. How much you want?'

'Couple a hundred,' Sam said. 'I'll keep detailed accounts. Anything we don't spend you get back.'

Norman fished in his back pocket and brought out a wad of notes. 'I'll give you a hundred now,' he said. 'Drop the rest off tomorrow.' He wet the tip of his right index finger to count the money.

'You can give me a cheque if you like,' Sam told him.

Norman was concentrating hard on the counting. He stopped when Sam spoke, then carried on again without replying. When he'd finished, pushed the cash over the desk, he said, 'No need to get complicated.'

On his way out Norman stopped at the door to Sam's office and turned back, looked around the room. 'This must be a really old building,' he said.

'It's not modern,' Sam agreed.

Norman laughed. 'You can say that again.'

'It's not modern,' Sam said, deadpan.

Norman shook his finger at him. 'Says when it was built outside,' he said. 'I reckon it was built by the Romans.'

After Norman left Sam put the *Budokan* tape back on and sat down in his chair. The guy was an ex con. That business with the cigarette, nipping the end off and then stowing the tab away in his top pocket. Only place Sam had ever seen that was in prison. And the guy was mean as well, trying hard to cover it up, but underneath the mask he was someone you wouldn't want to trust. Look out, Snow White, Sam thought. If this guy finds you, you could end up with the poisoned apple treatment.

Still, he thought, it's a job. First of all find the girl, see what she thinks. If she wants Norman Brown to find her that's OK. If she didn't wanna be found Sam'd give the guy his money back.

chapter 9

George, the founder of the men's group, a twenty-eight-year-old of Italian descent who had recently taken to calling himself Giorgio because it 'sounded softer', introduced the theme for the evening: betrayal.

'We all know about the outer betrayals,' he said, 'how we manipulate and fight each other for the possession of a female, or the possession of anything really. All material goods. But I hoped we could talk around the inner betrayals a little, the ways in which we betray ourselves.

'Our instincts, for example, especially sexual instincts, driving us to procreate. We just follow them blindly, though we know it's not in our best interests. Our bodies betray us as well, leading us into emotional situations we aren't equipped to deal with. We are betrayed on all sides, by apathy, ambition, pride, greed. And as long as we are unconscious of these processes we are at their mercy.'

Bock, the guy who looked like a Christmas tree because of all the rings in his ears, nose and on his fingers, had four children all under four and whatever theme was introduced he always thought it was about them. He said, 'I *only* rely on my instincts. They're all we've got left. I look at my youngest, Rosy, and I don't know what to think, she's so helpless, man. I'm giving her a bath, or I'm changing her nappy, whatever it is it's all the same. She's reaching out to me and I'm reaching out to her, and there in the middle, between her reaching and my reaching, right there in the middle is love. And I see that love, and Rosy, she sees that love, and I don't think either of us is being betrayed.'

Sam was getting to like these guys. It had been a long process. It was hard work because they were as full of shit as Rosy's nappy.

But who wasn't?

That's the way he thought about it now. He knew he'd betrayed himself in countless ways. He thought wryly that he might even have been betrayed once or twice, as well as betraying others who had relied on him. To Sam, the whole thing was an ecological whole now. Whatever went round would always come round one of these days. And everything went round. There were no exceptions. Some things only limped round, others went past doing a ton, but nothing ever stopped or got spun off, everything was contained within the totality.

These guys in the group seemed to think they could stop everything. Like if they met together and talked about it the world might suddenly one day fall into a different shape. And they were right, of course. They believed in magic. They believed in the reality of magic.

At least they got out of the house, they didn't sit at home being programmed by the box. They were searching for something, bringing all the baggage of their preconceptions with them. But still searching. For the wild man, for the feminine side of their nature, hell, they had all kinds of names for it, this something they had lost along the way, or that had been stolen from them.

You go on a search, you look long enough, hard enough,

sooner or later you'll find something. It doesn't matter if you're blind, you've been blinded by everything you ever read, or by everything you ever learned. Get down and start searching, sooner or later you'll stumble across it.

They were all detectives, even Bock with his Rosy. They didn't have a clue. Just a hunch that some day they'd find one.

This meeting had some of the same qualities as the AA meeting. Sometimes in either meeting, Sam could find himself wondering which one it was. In both meetings the participants were reaching out for another kind of reality, something which alone they were not capable of achieving, but which together they might occasionally grasp. Both groups had grown in numbers over the past few years, in direct proportion with a recession that was itself approaching drinking age. The main difference between the two groups was that this one closed down for the summer. This was the last meeting they would have until the autumn. Whereas the AA meetings went on for ever. The day they stopped the world would start to wind down.

Sam didn't say anything about inner betrayals. He kept those for the AA meetings. He listened to the discussion with one ear. Bock talking about his daughter brought back memories for Sam of his own daughter. Of Donna, his first wife, and their small daughter mowed down by a hit-and-run driver. Bock's image of Rosy reaching out in the bath became Sam's own image. The picture filled his mind for a time.

Bronte had been two when she died. Slim and dark like her mother, but still with all that puppy fat little kids have. For an hour after the accident they hadn't found her body. They'd found Donna by the side of the road, still alive, unconscious; but without witnesses no one had thought to look for Bronte. A man coming home from work had found her in his front garden, nearly every bone in her body broken. The impact had sent her through the air, almost fifty feet. The driver must have been doing ninety, the coroner said. And then he'd said, 'Accidental death.' Sam had to shake his head to make it go away. The picture. It hung on for a moment, then it collapsed like the pieces of a kaleidoscope, turning slowly into something else.

chapter 10

Norman opened up a Nissan Stanza 1.65SGL hatchback in the Castle Museum car park in York. Chosen because it had a sunroof and he'd been sweating all day. Central locking with electric windows and power steering. He'd never opened one before but had heard how to do it in the slammer. Learned it good as well, took him about eight minutes. Next time he'd do it in four. The time after that probably two.

He drove out to the ring road and followed the route to the house of the guy who ran the gun club. Pulled into the driveway and parked in front of the garage. The street was quiet. Norman kept his gloves on, took his holdall from the passenger seat and got out. He walked round the garage to the back door and leaned on the bell.

The woman who answered the door was around fifty, a little younger than her husband. She wore glasses with thick lenses and pale blue frames, and her hair had those blue bits at the front, dyed, all heaped up and bouncy like she'd just been to the hairdresser's. She had long teeth. 'Yes?' she said, looking at Norman with his holdall like he'd just crawled out of a hole in the ground.

'Fuck this,' he said, pushing her back into the house and closing the door behind him.

She staggered back into a kitchen area, nearly fell over but not quite, and steadied herself against a cooker. 'What on earth do you think you're doing?' she said, still with that tone that made Norman want to slap her. Made him want to spit.

'Doing?' he said, putting his smile on to show he wasn't intimidated. He put his bag down on the carpet tiles and took the washing line out. 'I'm tying you up. That's what I'm doing.'

She started to scream then. It was going to be long and loud like they do in those horror movies, so Norman had no option but to smack her in the mouth. He hadn't thought about hurting her, cutting her lip like that, sending her glasses across the room. That wasn't part of the plan. But a man has to do what a man has to do. She stopped the scream immediately, started whimpering, saying her husband would be home soon. Saying Norman could have the money, take anything he wanted, only please don't hurt her. She was pushing herself back into the corner, like she was trying to get through the wall.

'Where's the money?' Norman asked.

She took him upstairs to a large blue bedroom, blue curtains and carpet, blue cover on the bed, with a little pink patch in the centre of it. A pink diamond. Norman told her to keep away from the window. She took a cashbox out of the bottom drawer of a chest. Inside the cashbox was a wad of notes, about four inches thick.

'How much is there?' Norman said.

She shook her head. 'I don't know.'

'What about guns?' he said. 'I need a gun.'

'He doesn't keep guns here,' she said. 'Sometimes there's one in the office. I don't know.' Her speech was hesitant and she didn't seem to be in control of her body. She was twitching all over and every now and then she took in really deep gulps of air.

The office was next door to the bedroom. It had a desk and a filing cabinet. On one wall was a bench with gun parts, a couple of dismantled pistols. The stock of a rifle and a few cartridges. 'That's all there is,' the woman said.

Norman pushed her back into the bedroom and made her lie down on the bed. He hog-tied her, legs roped together and pulled up her back so that her feet were tied to her hands. She was whimpering all the time, saying the rope was cutting into her skin, could he not tie it so tight? Norman pulled the rope tighter, then took it around her neck so if she struggled too much she'd strangle herself.

He found her underwear drawer and shoved a pair of smalls into her mouth, stop her from trying that scream again. Then he went back into the office for the parcel tape and wrapped it a couple of times round her head and mouth. She looked ridiculous, just her eyes staring at him. He put his hand down the front of her dress to see if there was anything doing, but there was only skin there. 'The story of my life,' Norman told her. 'Thirty years too late.'

Then she wet herself. Just let it go. No control. Norman shook his head. People were unbelievable.

He opened the door of a wardrobe and shoved her in there, on top of all her shoes. He pulled out four matching suitcases from the top shelf. Closed the door and went downstairs with the suitcases. Wait for the hubby.

The Chief was confronting a load of women anti-abortion demonstrators, but Norman switched it off when he heard the silver Merc arrive. It was too complicated to be a good programme. Abortion, anti-abortion, who cared about stuff like that? People like those women, they don't live in the real world. The real world's different to that, about life and death, about filling the space in between with as much as you can cram into it. Nothing to do with abortion. And that Chief, Jesus, he was a complete fantasy. Who ever heard of a cop with a conscience? Or a cop who gives a toss about anybody else who's not a cop?

Norman didn't like television. They always did things like that on television. Told lies. Made out like there were cops who were human beings, when in reality everybody knew they were pure shite. Norman had his way he'd ban television altogether, just have videos. Bring some reality back into the world.

Key in the front door, the guy would be a bit narked because somebody'd blocked his way into the garage. Norman didn't move from the leather armchair in front of the box. He reached for his glass and had a little sip of the old malt he'd found in the sideboard. Kept it in his mouth until it got warm, started tingling on the back of his tongue, then let it trickle down his throat.

The front door opened and closed. The sound of it being locked. Then the voice, 'Helen, I'm home.'

And there he was, framed in the doorway, large leather briefcase in his hand. Looking a little tired after a hard day at work. A smile on his face that slowly drained away when he saw Norman instead of the little wife.

'You don't look too happy to see me,' Norman told him, placing the empty glass on the small round table in front of him.

The guy was confused. He blinked a couple of times. Came into the room then, blinked again and said, 'Do I know you? Where's Helen?' Looked around the room, like he thought she was there, only he hadn't located her yet. He looked at the four suitcases Norman had left by the wall.

'She's not here,' Norman said. 'Been kidnapped.'

'What?' The man's head wasn't working. Either that or he was deaf.

Norman raised his voice just a little. 'I know it's a nuisance,' he said. 'But she's been kidnapped.'

The man put his briefcase down. 'I don't understand,' he said. 'Who are you? Are you from the police?' He looked over at the stack of suitcases again.

Norman reached for the bottle of malt and unscrewed the top. 'Sit down,' he said. 'I'll explain it to you.' He poured from the bottle, kept pouring until the liquid reached the top of the glass and spilled over on the table. The guy stood and watched him. 'I said sit down,' Norman said, this time getting an edge to his voice which shook the guy. 'On the fucking chair.'

The man went to the chair and sat down. 'What's going on?' he said. 'You're not the police. Where's my wife? Why are these suitcases here?'

Norman carefully lifted the glass and took a sip off the top. 'Cheers,' he said. 'Now you ask the questions one at a time, and I'll do my best to answer you.'

The man wasn't comfortable in the chair. He didn't sit back and relax, just sat on the edge there, like he might get up any minute and do something. But he couldn't think of anything to do. His head was nodding up and down and from side to side, like he'd lost control of it. Nodding away there, twenty to the dozen.

Then he formed a question. 'Who are you?'

'Isaac,' Norman told him. 'The name's Isaac. Israeli Secret Service.'

The head began nodding even faster. If the guy kept it up his head would come off altogether. Go bouncing over the carpet and out the front door, down the street like the meatball song. 'Where's ... Helen?' he said, with a big gap between the two words. 'Where's ... Helen?' He licked his lips, wiped the back of his hand across his mouth.

'I don't know the answer,' Norman said.

The man looked at him, looked away, then looked back again. 'You said she'd been kidnapped,' he said.

Norman nodded.

'But you don't know where she is?'

Norman nodded again. 'You're starting to get it,' he said.

The man licked his lips. 'And you said Israeli Secret Service?'

'You're the memory man,' Norman told him.

The man wiped his brow. He looked down at his hands, trying to put the information together. Norman took another sip of the malt while he waited. The man looked over at the suitcases, like they might be a clue.

'I don't get it,' he said. 'What do you want?'

Norman smiled. 'You're slow,' he said, 'but you're getting there.' He put the glass back on the table. 'Guns and ammo and money,' he said. 'We get guns and ammo and money, and you get the little wife back, if you want her. What I saw she's not the best woman in the world.'

The man stood up, made as if he was coming over to Norman, but thought better of it. 'If you've hurt her ...' he said. 'Jesus, if anything happens to her ...'

'Sit down,' Norman told him. 'She's OK. You've got two hours to get back to the club, load up the guns and the money. Don't forget the ammo. One hour after I leave here with the goods she'll be released.'

The man sat back on the chair. 'And if I don't?' he said.

Norman smiled at him. 'My boss,' he said. 'He can be a real cruel bastard.'

The head just nodded away faster than ever, this time with its eyes closed. Eventually he opened his eyes and licked his lips. 'OK,' he said. 'OK. OK.'

'You take the suitcases,' Norman said. 'I want the guns packed in suitcases.'

The man went over to the stack of suitcases and began tucking them under his arms. Norman walked to the front door with him.

'If you want to see your wife again, don't do anything stupid,' he said. 'I leave in two hours whether you're back or not. And if I leave without the goods the little lady gets the chop.'

The guy knew what he meant.

'We want handguns mostly,' Norman said. 'Handguns and silencers. Plenty of ammo. A few shotguns and a couple a rifles. Don't forget the money.' He pushed the guy out into the street and closed the door. Then he had another thought, opened the door and walked down the path to where the man was getting into the Merc. 'Another thing,' he said. 'You got any shoulder holsters? Y'know, you can put a pistol under your arm, so nobody knows you're carrying.'

'You want some of them?'

'Jus' one.' Norman said. 'I jus' want one of them.'

The Chief was still at it, fighting the anti-abortionists. Norman switched channels and watched a guy who was a DIY disaster area, but after about five minutes he turned the sound down and had a think.

Guys in prison talked a load of bollocks most of the time. *When I get out, when I get out.* It was always the same thing. When I get out I'm gonna get drunk every night of the week. When I get out of here I'm gonna have the longest fuck of my life. When I get out I'm gonna be really clever. When I get out.

Norman had never got into that. He'd really thought he never would get out. And look at this. All those cons still giving it *When I get out*, while here was old Norman with his feet up drinking best malted Scotch, nearly five grand in his pocket, and a woman upstairs in the wardrobe he didn't even bother fucking because there was better meat about.

He's got a private detective working for him, searching out Snow White, another guy getting some guns together. There's Squishsquash waiting in the wings for Norman to arrange her tick tests. He'd already had Tina Turner. Jesus, sitting in a cell for seven years he'd forgotten what life outside was like. But now he was starting to remember. It was all coming back. So long as you didn't get picked up you could do anything you thought of. Anything that turned you on.

You had to be straight with people, make sure they understood what was going on. But if you wanted something you only had to ask, most people'd get it for you right off. And when you did come across somebody who wouldn't play – well, you just blew the fuckers away.

You needed some kind of talent to be able to read people, but once you had that you were almost untouchable. This guy, for instance, the guy was out getting the guns for him. He wouldn't try anything. He'd just do exactly as he was told. Somebody else might drive straight round to the cop shop, or come back into the house with a gun in each hand. But not him. Right now he'd have loaded his silver Merc with everything he could find in the gun club and be bringing it all back home. Pleasure to do business with him, a guy like that, you knew exactly where you stood.

It was the same as before. The silver Merc pulling up outside, the door slamming, and then his key turning in the lock. He didn't say anything this time, didn't shout his wife's name. And when he came to the entrance of the room he didn't stand framed in the doorway. He walked straight in, stood a few feet away from Norman and said, 'It's done. All the suitcases are packed. This is all the money we have.' He handed over an envelope, felt like around another grand.

'You haven't got any money here?' Norman asked, pushing himself out of the chair.

The guy shook his head. 'No,' he said. 'You've got everything now.'

Norman shook his head. 'That's not right,' he said, 'telling porkie pies like that. Thing like that could get you into real trouble.'

The guy hung his head, knowing he'd been found out. Looked like a schoolboy in front of his headmaster.

Norman waited a few seconds, just make sure the guy didn't have another stash somewhere else in the house.

'We found the cash upstairs,' Norman told him. 'The money box you was hiding from the tax man. Very naughty.'

'OK, you've got everything,' the man said. 'Can I have my wife back?'

'I jus' wanna check the car,' Norman said. 'Now we know you don't always tell the truth.' Norman walked past the man, taking the keys to the Merc from his hand, and left the house. He went to the Merc and opened the boot. He took a handgun and silencer from the first suitcase and loaded it as he walked back up the path to the front door.

The man was still standing in the same position when Norman came into the room. He was watching the television, the pictures with no sound. He didn't turn around, just stood there watching the pictures.

Norman said, 'Apart from that one little porkie you've done real good. So we're not gonna penalize you. Your wife's upstairs.'

The man didn't take it in immediately. He stood staring at the pictures for about fifteen seconds. Then he shook his head and went to the stairs. Norman followed him.

The man took the stairs two at a time. Halfway up he shouted, 'Helen, are you there?' He walked into the bedroom and came out again as Norman got to the top of the stairs. 'Where is she?' he said, going into the office. Then he stood at the entrance to the office, and his head began nodding again. 'You bastard,' he said to Norman. 'She isn't here.' His knees began to sag and Norman thought he might cry.

'She's in the wardrobe,' Norman said.

The man pushed past Norman, back into his bedroom and walked to the wardrobe, opened the door. 'Oh, my God,' he said, going to his knees. 'Helen, are you all right?' He began dragging his bound wife out of the wardrobe. Pulling on the ropes, bringing her out of there head first, a few shoes coming out at the same time.

The smell of piss again. Almost too much to bear, yet the guy didn't seem to notice.

Norman put the gun to the back of the man's head and touched the trigger, shot him once. The man slumped forward over his wife, and they lay together there in a tangle of shoes, half in and half out of the wardrobe.

Norman reached over and pulled the man off his wife, so he could give her the same treatment as her husband. But there was no need. She was dead already, must have suffocated. Norman shrugged. That's why there had been no sounds of her struggling or kicking. And he thought she was being a good girl.

Norman put the gun in the man's right hand, wrapped his index finger around the trigger, so it would look as though he'd killed his wife and then shot himself. The filth would think it was an open and shut case, for a while anyway. It was difficult working with gloves on, but he managed it OK. Shit, if they found Norman's dabs anywhere in the house they'd close the town down and bring the military in.

He looked through the wardrobe at the guy's clothes. There was a lightweight suit in there, pale blue with a label said it was made in Finland. Norman threw it on the bed and looked through the man's shirt drawer. He took a couple of good ones, one with short sleeves, and another with pockets the same blue as the suit. Then he found a packet of unopened socks and carried them all down to the silver Merc, only stopping briefly in the living room to pick up what remained of the good malt.

He drove back to York and parked behind the railway station. He put his new clothes into one of the suitcases and then carried all four of the suitcases around to the Station Hotel. They were heavy too, he had to stop every few yards to put them down, give his arms a rest. At the entrance to the hotel a couple of porters came to help him and Norman went over to the reception desk and asked for a room.

For a moment or two it looked as though they weren't going to give him a room because he didn't have a reservation. But then they changed their minds and the porter and a young lad showed him up to a room on the second floor.

The room had its own shower and a colour TV, and Norman turned the TV on and stretched out on the bed. After a minute or two he opened the bottle of malt and took a swig from the neck of the bottle. He kept the liquid in his mouth to warm it up, only letting it trickle down his throat when it began prickling on the back of his tongue.

chapter 11

Sam was out of bed and wandering around the flat at six o'clock in the morning. Geordie had stayed out the previous evening, and Sam had spent it with Barney, Geordie's dog, played a couple of tapes and ended up with a book Celia had lent him. *Remains of the Day* by Kazuo Ishiguro. The book had disturbed him. He had not identified with the characters who were situated in a different time and connected to an order Sam knew nothing of. But there were echoes of Sam's own experience in the book. Nothing concrete, nothing he could definitely say, *Yes, I remember a time like that*. Only echoes. Echoes that went on through the night, so that he slept fitfully and found himself with wide staring eyes at first light. Wide staring eyes and a mouth felt like it was a camp site.

Barney couldn't tell the time. He slept in his basket until someone else got up then whatever time it was he thought it was breakfast time. He was usually right.

By seven the two of them were in the office. Barney curled up in his office basket and Sam, looking out at the square, wondering why he hadn't waited for Geordie at home, had breakfast with him, started the day slowly. The only thing on the cards was Mr Norman Brown coming in with a hundred quid. And it was going to be another scorcher. Not a cloud in the sky.

Every time there was a foot on the stair or the street door opened, Barney would lift his head and look at the office door. 'Geordie's stayed out rutting,' Sam told him. 'Took a little break. It's just you and me.'

The dog looked as though he understood – but it didn't make him feel any better. He wasn't used to being without his friend.

Sam had always been alone. Apart from the time with Donna, and a brief time with Brenda, his second wife. Brief? Yeah, about forty-eight hours as he remembered it. Forty-eight hours before they both realized they'd made a terrible mistake.

There'd been other women along the way. Some of them seemed to count for a time, but when he looked back there was always something missing. He couldn't remember her name, or maybe it was what she looked like. Others he couldn't remember a single thing they'd said to each other. There was one called Samantha, couple a years back. *Call me Sam.* It'd seemed to be really hot for a month or two, all he could think about was being with Sam. But when he tried to bring her back now that's how it was. He couldn't remember one conversation they'd had. He could remember waking up in the morning, looking at her lying next to him, sleeping, and thinking: *Where did you come from?*

Hell, she could walk past the window now and he probably wouldn't know who she was. That's how it went, people drifted into and out of each other's lives. Every once in a while one of them would be right, or nearly right, right enough for you to tell yourself they were right. Once, maybe twice in a lifetime one of them would be *it*.

Wanda was nearly right, and Sam, he was nearly right for her. They were both right for each other, most of the time. Sex was good with Wanda. And they could talk, it didn't seem to matter what the other one said. They could certainly talk, most of the time.

'Tell you what, Barney,' he said to the dog. 'If this guy

comes in before twelve we'll take a little holiday. Drive to the seaside for the afternoon.'

Barney lifted his head, cocked one ear, then put his head down again. He looked at Sam with one eye, his mouth open and his tongue out. Sam did the same back to him.

When Betty's opened Sam went down there for coffee. Sat at a table by the window and rolled a cigarette. Watched the door to his office so he wouldn't miss Norman Brown when he came with the money. The only person went in was a woman, thirty-four, thirty-five years old. Long legs and a distinctive walk, taking little steps one after the other so you couldn't help but watch her. She had black hair cut off short at the bottom of her ears and wore a yellow silk dress with a V-neck, buttons all the way down the front. Sam shook his head and stubbed his cigarette out in the ashtray. Best thing he'd seen all day.

When he got back to the office he walked over to the tape deck. Put *Planet Waves* on to try and change his consciousness. Did a little dance to the opening bars of 'On a Night Like This' as he walked back to his desk. Barney nearly got out of his basket, but changed his mind when Sam sat in his chair and put his feet up on the desk.

The Bluesman had moved on to 'Something There is About You' by the time Norman Brown arrived. One knock on the door and he was in the office before Sam could get his feet off the table. 'Hey, caught you at it,' Norman said, coming over to the desk, a broad smile on his face.

Dressed all in blue today. Light blue poplin suit, same colour shirt and a matching tie. Little boy blue. He put the hundred down on the desk and sat on the chair. 'Thought I wouldn't show up, didn't you?' he said to Sam.

'You left a hundred yesterday,' Sam said. 'When a man does that I feel like I'm gonna see him again.'

'Too true,' Norman said. 'You make any progress?'

'Haven't really got going yet,' Sam said. 'Things'll start moving tomorrow. You didn't come up with a photograph?'

'No,' Norman said. 'You know as much as I do.' He reached into his pocket and took out a pack of cigarettes. Lit one up and sat back in the chair with his legs crossed. Looked across the desk.

Sam didn't like him. Even while it was happening he wanted to push the guy's money back over the desk, tell him to go find somebody else. If there had been one more job lined up Sam wouldn't have bothered with him. But there were bills to pay, and the guy hadn't done anything obviously wrong. Somewhere inside, buried deep, there was a little voice telling Sam to cut his losses, get rid of the guy. But it was only a small voice, and reason had no difficulty in swamping it. Sam thought he would like to throttle the little runt and steal his cigarettes.

'This's the same you was playing last time,' Norman said, indicating the tape deck. 'Kind of jazzy like.' He drummed his fingers on the desk. He laughed. 'Jazzy but not funky. Know what I mean? Tina Turner, now she can be funky.'

'Yeah?' said Sam.

'All them spades can be funky,' Norman continued. 'Specially the women. The guys can as well, good movers. Know what I mean? But Tina, shit, she's some woman. Every little bit of her.'

Sam sighed hard. 'Yeah,' he said. Then tried even harder. 'I know what you mean.'

'I've got this photo,' Norman told him. 'Tina in a dress made out of beads. Well, hardly a dress at all, jus' a few beads. Might be stuck on her skin for all I know. See her move around in that, man.' He fished around in his pocket, pulled out the cover from a tape and slid it across the top of the desk. 'Feast your eyes on that.'

Sam unfolded it and feasted his eyes on Tina Turner standing with her legs apart in high-heeled shoes. Apart from the beads she was naked, oiled all over, standing with her arms above her head. Her breasts were almost naked, only the nipples covered with a bead or two He pushed it back at Norman. 'Shaves under her arms,' he said.

Norman looked at the photograph. 'Yeah,' he said. Then, almost to himself, 'She's real chocolate. Don't see many about like that.' And looking back at Sam. 'Know what I'd like to do with her?'

Sam shook his head. 'But I get the feeling you're gonna tell me anyway.'

Norman laughed loudly. 'Hey,' he said. 'You're dry, you know that? You got a sense of humour.'

'You're just saying that,' Sam said.

'No, it's true.' Norman stopped and then looked back over the desk. 'Hey, there you go again. Putting me on, man. You're sharp.'

Sam smiled at him, wishing he would go. 'Have to keep the customer happy,' he said. He stood and took the hundred pounds from the desk. 'I'm expecting another client in a moment,' he said. 'If there's nothing else.'

'OK, OK,' Norman said, getting to his feet. He walked to the door and opened it, stood outside in the passage, still talking. When he opened the door Barney left his basket and went out in front of him. 'I'll call round in a couple a days, see how you're getting on,' Norman continued. Then he said, 'Shit, I've let the dog out.'

'Don't worry,' said Sam. 'He won't go far. I'll get him.'

'Stay cool,' Norman said as he left.

Sam gave the guy a minute to get clear then went out of the office to look for Barney. He went down the stairs to the square, trying to give that little whistle Geordie used when he wanted Barney to follow him. When he got down to the outer door he saw Norman going towards the corner, walking with that characteristic swagger, ogling all the women as though they were wearing bead dresses. There was no sign of Barney, but Geordie and Gus were coming across the square from Betty's.

'Much on, boss?' Geordie asked.

'Not a lot,' said Sam. 'The guy in blue,' he indicated Norman, who was now only a few paces from the corner. 'Calls himself Norman Brown, and doesn't want us to know where he lives.'

'Say no more,' said Geordie.

Gus nodded, and the two of them took off after Norman, who had now disappeared from sight.

Sam went back up the stairs and found Barney in the arms

of the woman in the yellow dress. She was standing there in the anteroom, and when Sam opened the door she turned and said, 'Oh, hello. Does this little fellow belong to you?'

'Yeah,' Sam said. 'Well, he doesn't exactly belong to me. I'm his minder for the moment. Not making a very good job of it.' From a distance she'd looked neat, up close she was really something. Maybe a little older than he'd first thought, past her mid thirties. Approaching forty, but along an elegant route. She was as tall as Sam, and with flat shoes. Her face was open and she looked straight into his eyes, listening carefully as he spoke. There was a touch of eye shadow, but no make-up on her face, nothing on her lips. As she held Barney to her breast Sam noticed her hands, long elegant fingers, and a fine down on her arms. Her neck would have made Modigliani reach for his brush. 'Where'd you find him?'

'He came into the ladies.' She smiled and stroked Barney's ear.

'That's typical,' Sam told her. 'He's done it before. Bit of a perve deep down.'

'I don't think so,' she said. 'He was just looking for company.' She transferred Barney to her left arm and offered Sam her right hand. 'Jennie Cosgrave,' she said. 'I work in that little cupboard over the corridor. And I think my aunt works in here.'

Sam took her hand, cool and slightly moist. 'Sam,' he said. 'Sam Turner. Yeah, Celia told me you would be around. Me and Barney are supposed to work in here, but there's not much doing at the moment. Thought we'd go to the seaside this afternoon.'

'Oh, I thought you had a client. I heard someone talking.' Sam forgot to let go of her hand, but she prised it free with a smile.

'That's right,' he said. 'He was just leaving."

Jennie Cosgrave did something with her face, either an attempt at a frown, or maybe she was just wrinkling her forehead. 'I thought I recognized his voice,' she said.

'Calls himself Norman Brown,' Sam said. 'In this business you never know if the client's on the level.'

She shook her head. 'The name doesn't mean anything. I just thought . . .' Her voice trailed off. 'Never mind.' She looked down at Barney. 'Do you want to take him?'

Sam opened the door to the inner office. 'Put him down,' he said. 'He'll go to his basket and be asleep in two winks.'

'Well, it was good to meet you,' she said. 'And Barney. I work over there, you know, I hear sounds, people moving about. It's good to be able to put a face to the voice. Plus I've heard lots about you from Aunt Celia.'

'Yeah?' Sam said, walking back to the corridor with her. 'We only moved in a couple a days ago ourselves. You're the first person I've met.'

Jennie opened the door to her room and turned back to face him. 'It's really hot in here,' she said. 'I can't seem to open the window.'

'I've got a guy coming to fix our windows,' Sam said. 'I'll send him over.' He looked past her into the tiny room. There was one small window and only enough room for a desk and a chair. The desk had a portable computer on it. By the side of the computer and under the desk were about a hundred books, white paper bookmarks sticking out of them. 'What do you do in here?'

'I'm a psychologist,' she said. 'I'm doing some work at Askham Grange.'

'Oh, yeah, Celia said. The women's prison.'

'Still at the preparation stage. Start in about a fortnight.'

'We work with the same kind of people,' Sam said. 'Should compare notes some time.'

'Yes, it would be interesting.'

There was a long silence. Sam couldn't think of anything else to say. 'Well,' he said, taking a step back.

Jennie smiled. 'Yes,' she said. 'Back to the grindstone.'

'Thanks,' he said. 'For Barney . . .'

She smiled again and closed the door. Sam walked back to his office. The Bluesman was on the last track. Barney was curled up in his basket. Sam picked up the kettle and went to fill it at the sink, then changed his mind and sat down at the desk. 'You're a good dog, Barney,' he said. 'You know that? You're a real good dog.'

When the tape switched itself off, Sam looked over at Barney again. 'She looked at me really weird,' he said. 'As if she knew my face, but couldn't place it.' He shook his head. 'She was probably thinking of Gene Hackman.'

chapter 12

Geordie fell in behind the guy Sam'd said was called Norman Brown, kept himself about twenty paces behind, like they'd done in training sessions. While he walked he pinned his radio microphone to the lapel of his jacket and fitted the Walkman earphones on his head. Gus had adapted the Walkman cases so they acted as receivers as well as playing tapes. Gus could do things like that, build computers, put a transmitter into the body of a pen, anything with electronics. He was a whizz. Recently he'd been talking about a video camera so small it could fit in a matchbox. But something that small, Geordie couldn't imagine how you'd work it, where the knobs and buttons would be.

'You there?' Geordie asked, speaking in the general direction of the microphone but trying not to look at it.

'Check,' Gus said, because he knew and understood the right things to say when you had somebody under surveillance. 'I'm on the other side of the road, 'bout ten yards behind you. Don't look.'

'I know that,' said Geordie. 'What you want to tell me that for?'

'Over and out,' said Gus, and the earpiece went dead.

'Fuckin' check,' said Geordie. *Over and out*? Christ, that didn't sound right. *Check* was something else. Fitted in with the whole scene. But *Over and out* . . . That was something those pilots in fighter planes said, like in those old movies about the war. Biggles, guys like that. *Chaps* like that. The Brylcreem boys.

Norman Brown cut down New Street to get into Coney

Street, and Geordie dropped back another couple of paces as the volume of pedestrians thinned out. 'Don't lose him,' Gus's voice said in his ear. 'Drop back and wait; I'll stay with him.'

'Check,' said Geordie. He stopped for a moment and gazed into the window of an estate agent. Then he crossed the road and took over Gus's former position as the anchor man.

This was more like proper detective work, like in those books Sam was always reading, stacked up in his room. And like the Humphrey Bogart films. Usual detective work wasn't like in the books and the films. It was boring, put you to sleep. Consisted of waiting around in stationary cars, or standing on the corner of the street, maybe hours at a time. You got cramp. You froze to death in winter. Baked in summer.

In the books and the films they made it romantic and exciting all the time, but that was a lie to keep you turning the pages or watching the box. In real life when you met somebody and they found out you was a private investigator, they always said, Oh, how exciting, tell me all about it. And you had to really rack your brains to think of anything to say about it. *Oh, well, today I stood on a corner for seven hours. Nothing happened. Then I went home . . .*

But then, occasionally, it came alive. Like now. Things moved. Geordie knew nothing about Norman Brown, not even if it was the guy's real name. Didn't know where he'd come from, or where he was going. Only that Sam wanted an address for him. Jesus, the guy could be dangerous. Like the mad guy Geordie heard about on the news, one who killed an old couple in Haxby.

Norman Brown went into W. H. Smith's and Gus went in after him. Geordie waited on the opposite pavement, chatted for a while to Tombo who was in his usual spot selling *The Big Issue*. 'Lot of people in town,' Tombo told him. 'More women and girls sleeping in the parks. Waiting for the end of the world. Lot of coke about, too. Every other person you meet has a busted nose.'

'What about you?' Geordie asked.

A smile passed over Tombo's battered face. Then he touched his nose briefly with the fingers of his left hand.

'Yeah,' he said. 'Me too.' The smile stayed put. It had taken a while to get there, as if it had pushed itself through his crusty skin, used a lot of effort to get to the surface, and now it had made it it didn't want to give up too soon. Geordie wanted to hug him for the smile, but didn't know him well enough. There was something in the unwritten code about not hugging the guy you get your newspaper off. He didn't understand it, but he'd talk to Sam about it later, or Gus, or Celia. One of them would know. Between them they knew just about everything. Like the other night they'd all sat around talking about invisibility. Yeah, it was true: infuck-invisibility. Geordie couldn't believe it. Thought it must be a joke at first, but they was serious. Celia had started them off saying women began becoming invisible when they got to be forty years old. Oh, yeah, Celia? Keep it coming. Like she's finally blown the last gasket. By morning she'll be barking.

'But then around, well, sometimes after sixty or between sixty and seventy they start coming back again,' she said.

'You sure about this one, Celia?' asked Gus.

'Absolutely,' she said. 'No doubt whatsoever. I became invisible on my thirty-seventh birthday, and I stayed completely out of sight until I was sixty-two.'

'You're out of sight, anyway,' said Sam. And he looked over at her to check she knew what he meant, and she did. Geordie had noticed that before, the glances Sam and Celia gave each other from time to time. The glance always said something like, Do you read me? And whichever one of them asked the question the other one always seemed to say Yes. This was odd, because if Gus or Geordie or maybe anyone else in the world had used the expression *out of sight*, Celia wouldn't have understood what it meant. But when Sam used it she knew right away.

Anyway, that was another story. In this story Sam had asked her what happened to men, and Celia explained that men hung on a bit longer than women, not becoming invisible until they were in their middle or late fifties, but that once they disappeared they were gone for ever. Men didn't come back again. 'That's why,' she said, 'when you walk through the town you see lots and lots of old ladies, but no old men at all.'

'Where are they?' Geordie asked. 'What's happened to them?'

'Oh, they're there,' Celia said. 'You just don't see them.'

Christ. Invisible.

'Coming out,' said the voice in Geordie's earpiece. 'Over to you.' Norman Brown came out of W. H. Smith's, walked along the pavement and went into Woolworths. Geordie tapped Tombo's arm, said, 'See you,' and trotted over the road and through the swing doors behind Norman. Geordie wished he was invisible. Be great in a job like this. You could do it single-handed, like in that film on the box, *The Invisible Man*. Old Geordie there, unwinding the bandages, stashing his shirt and trilby and tailing Norman Brown in the nude.

Bit parky in the winter, but weather like this, running round Woolworths in the nude, yeah, why not. Nobody would see him. He'd thought about it before, not in relation to the job, but just for the fun of it, being able to see people without them seeing him. Following girls into the ladies. Being in all the places he wasn't supposed to be. Wandering into a restaurant when he was hungry, helping himself to a chicken leg. Chicken breast actually. The whole chicken if he wanted. The waiter walking by with one of those silver salvers on his shoulder. Geordie lifting the lid and running off with the chicken, gravy dripping all over the floor. But Geordie completely invisible, so the chicken looks like it's had enough and flying away. Maybe he'd make the wings flap, do a loud cock-a-doodle-doo, and then pause for a moment at the door to do a final wave.

He smiled, imagining having all that power.

Norman Brown was watching a girl at the make-up counter. The girl pocketed a lipstick and went out the door, with Norman on her heels. 'He's coming out,' Geordie reported into his microphone.

'Check,' said Gus's voice.

chapter 13

Jennie Cosgrave sat at her desk and looked at the blank screen of her computer. Seemed like a nice man, she thought. Had a nice dog, if that was anything to go by. You can judge a man by looking at his shoes, her father had said, how many years ago? Funny, the things you remembered. The way to a man's heart is through his stomach. Clothes maketh the man. You can't judge a book by the cover.

She wondered if she'd closed the door too soon, whether if she'd kept it open he would have said something else. She wondered why she was thinking about him instead of pressing on with the work she had to do. She got up from the chair and moved over to the window, sat on the edge of the desk and looked out at the square below.

She told herself it was the weather. It was too hot to work, too hot to think properly. Then she smiled, knowing it was an excuse. Thinking about the excuses criminals give after they've been caught. The classic ones: *It was the others did the job, I just hung about outside. If she'd done what I said she wouldn't have got hurt. They kept needling me; what did they expect?*

She looked back at the blank screen of the computer and sighed. She had to prepare a tick test to measure the motivation for change in a group of violent female prisoners. It meant eliciting from them the factors which they saw as positive in a life of crime, and then measuring them against the factors which they saw as negative. She had done a similar test with a group of male prisoners at Dartmoor, finding that the most significant factor for a life of crime in that group was that it got them female attention. After that particular result she had not expected the Home Office to continue its grant. But here she was, still working. Not with

87

as many resources as the job merited, but beggars can't be choosers.

Jennie had another go at the window, but it was jammed with several coats of paint. The effort made her hotter and more uncomfortable than before. She was wiping her brow with the back of her hand when there was a knock on the door and Sam Turner's head appeared. The door opened wider and he came in with Barney on a lead.

'We're going to the seaside,' he said. 'D'you wanna come?'

Breeding, modesty and natural reserve all conspired together, telling her to shake her head, send him packing with his dog between his legs. She had to swallow really deeply to make herself say, 'Yes. I'd love to.'

'Car's just round the corner,' he said when they got outside. 'Over the bridge.'

'I haven't got anything with me,' she said. She had a small shoulder bag with a purse inside, the keys to Celia's house. Nothing else. 'I feel naked.'

He glanced across at her. 'It's all right,' he said. 'Everything's covered.' Her hair kept falling over her right eye, so she changed position, walking behind him and over to his right. All the better to see you, Mr Turner.

Jennie was not used to making impulsive decisions like this. She didn't want to change her mind, felt good about leaving the office behind, but somehow the whole thing would have felt better if she had more money with her. And it would have been perfect if she had her big straw bag with a swimming costume, a towel, perhaps a few sandwiches and a flask of coffee.

'Where are we going?' she asked as he opened the door of the Volvo for her.

'You know Filey Brigg?' he answered.

Jennie got into the passenger seat. She waited until he came around and got behind the wheel. 'I don't know the east coast at all,' she said.

Sam looked over at her before reversing the Volvo out of the parking space. She caught his eyes for a moment and something inside her settled down. In her work Jennie came across all kinds of men, on both sides of the bars. Some of them were incapable of negotiation in a one-to-one situation. But this man was not like that. He was not straightforward, far from it. But he would listen, and he would try to understand. In fact, she thought, if the day was going to be good or bad it was not possible to foretell. But it would certainly be interesting.

'You'll like the Brigg,' he said. 'It's wild.'

Now why should he think I'll like something wild? she thought. She didn't doubt that he was right, that he'd discovered something in her she was not conscious of projecting. Only she could not help but be interested in the mechanism. Jennie was careful about the signals she sent out to the world. She studied and understood body language, but was often reminded that she read the body language of others much better than she understood her own. Especially with men. You could tell a man one thing, quite categorically, and very soon discover that he'd heard the opposite. You could say, listen, I'm being polite, I find what you're saying interesting, but I'm not at all interested in you physically. And before you'd turned around the man would be saying, Hey, we're getting on really well, shall we go to bed?

Arrogant.

She hoped he wouldn't be. But it was too soon to tell.

'Do you want to talk about your work?' he asked. 'I'm not entirely sure what it is you do.'

'I'm mainly interested in education,' she told him.

'Educating cons?'

'There're different approaches,' she explained. 'People used to believe that a criminal was evil. You just had to punish him. You had to drive the evil spirit out of him.' The man was listening. He drove his car and he listened, didn't interrupt. 'For a while after that it was fashionable to think he wasn't evil, he was sick. You had to treat him, make him well again so that he could rejoin normal society. Nowadays people working in the field believe that it's possible to educate criminals. What I do is research around the possibilities. See if convicted criminals respond to education.'

'And do they?' Sam asked.

'Yes. If you can find the right way of introducing it.'

89

'And what is that?'

Jennie shook her head. 'That's what I'm trying to find out,' she said. 'It's quite a complex set of circumstances, first what it is that makes someone turn to crime, and then what it is that makes them stop offending.'

'Probably as many reasons as there are criminals,' said Sam.

'Yes.' she agreed. 'There's a woman in Askham Grange,' she said. 'Well, not now, she's been out for a time. But she went in when she was twenty, served something like fourteen years for murder. They let her out on licence, and six months later she was back again for GBH. Did another seven years, was released for ten months and then went back in for another six years, threatening behaviour, she threatened to kill someone. In all she's served over thirty years. Every time they let her out she never lasted more than a few months.'

'Jesus,' said Sam.

'I was talking to her,' Jennie said. 'She's sixty years old, and she's been out of prison and out of trouble for nearly five years. When I asked her what had changed, why she wasn't still being violent, you know what she said?'

'Tell me,' said Sam.

'She's got a dog,' Jennie said. 'She's worried what'll happen to the dog if she goes back in prison. She's so worried about it she stays out of trouble.'

Sam smiled and shook his head. He took his eyes off the road for a moment to look over at Jennie. 'You think we should all have one?' he asked. 'A dog?'

'I think we've all got one,' Jennie said. 'We've all got something like that, something that keeps us out of trouble. Most of the cons I've met have lost theirs, or they never had one. If we can help them find it, they might stop re-offending.'

'You're an idealist,' Sam said.

She looked over at him to see if it was an insult. No, just an observation. He didn't disapprove. 'Aren't you?' she asked.

He nodded assent. 'A cynical one,' he said. 'Social theories are interesting, but there've been quite a few since Lazarus finished his nap. None of them ever stopped a psychopath with a persecution complex.'

Jennie smiled. A very cynical one. 'Where's the idealism in a statement like that?'

'We'll find the answer one day,' he said, glancing over at her. 'Maybe tomorrow. Just because we haven't been so clever up to now, doesn't mean we should give up.'

'Prison itself is a big problem,' said Jennie. 'Especially in this country. At any one time we have more than fifty thousand people locked up. We have more people in prison than any other major European country, including Turkey. And the government just goes on building more prisons. In a few years we'll be locking up more than seventy thousand.'

'You think we should let 'em all out?'

'For all the good it does, yes. Most of them anyway. One in five of them has not been convicted of any offence, a quarter are teenagers, and at least two thirds of them are non-violent. The vast majority of the prison population could be handled more economically and more humanely by extending hostel options, and expanding the probation service.'

'You feel passionately about all this, don't you?' Sam said.

'Sorry,' she said. 'I'm getting on my hobby-horse. But it's such a terrible waste. The largest section of the criminal population are fifteen-year-olds. Kids of that age don't *have* to be anti-social. With the right policies we could turn them around. If we lock them away they just turn into professional criminals.' She shuffled down in the seat, suddenly feeling uncomfortable. Spouting away at this man she'd only known for half an hour. Could be a right wing hang-'em-and-whip-'em-and-lock-'em-up-and-throw-away-the-key campaigner for all she knew. 'I'm sorry,' she said. 'I'll shut up.'

He didn't say anything. Jennie bit her bottom lip and waited. She wasn't going to say anything else, feeling she'd exposed herself enough. Now it was his turn.

She wound down her window a fraction more, feeling the breeze on her face, breathing deeply, wondering if she could actually smell the sea, or if it was her imagination. They turned off the main road, following a sign towards Filey, and

Sam laughed. She looked over at him, and he glanced back at her. 'I was just thinking about your woman with the dog,' he said.

'That's funny?' she asked.

'No,' he said. 'But some of the guys I meet in this job, you give them a dog thinking, you know, it'd keep them out of trouble. Next time you go round they'd have eaten it.'

Jennie didn't laugh. When the car pulled to a stop at the top of the cliff and the ocean spread out before them, she was already beginning to think this trip was a mistake.

When they'd climbed down the cliff and were walking along the edge of the sea he said, 'I said the wrong thing back there.'

'Say what you like,' she said, wishing it hadn't come out so sharply. 'I mean, I'm not the police. I don't want to control your opinions.'

'I was just following a train of thought,' he said. 'I found something funny. It doesn't mean I don't take you seriously.'

Jennie shrugged. She'd been in this position before. Sometimes, especially when she got on to her pet subject, she lost her sense of humour. She tried a half smile on him. 'Shall we drop it?' she said. 'Go back to where we were before.'

'OK,' Sam said. 'But just so it's straight, you didn't say anything I'd disagree with. I hate the system as much as you do, only I don't think it should stop me having a laugh every so often.'

That touched a nerve in her somewhere. She took her shoes off and let the water run over her feet. 'I needed to meet someone like you,' she told him. 'I know too many people who are politically correct, and I appreciate them, even admire them for standing up to be counted. But we don't do a lot of laughing.'

Sam took his shoes off and joined her in the water. 'Hell,' he said. 'I used to be in with that crowd.'

Jennie kicked sea water at him.

chapter 14

Norman met Janet in Woolworths. He watched her steal a lipstick from the cosmetic counter, then followed her out the door and took her by the arm when she hit the street. She froze, then started shaking, so tense he thought she might snap in two. She opened her hand and offered Norman the lipstick. He took it from her, pocketed it, then, still gripping her arm, walked her away from the store entrance.

There was nothing to her arm, just a thin bone with a covering of skin. She was like that all over, seemed about twelve years old wearing a white longline tunic buttoned down the front with flared cuffs, and a pair of blue lycra leggings. On her head she wore a blue and white cap. Round her throat was a leather collar studded with different coloured glass jewels.

She struggled half-heartedly, without a hope of breaking Norman's grip, and she said, 'I din't mean it. Honestly. I jus' forgot to pay for it.'

'Liar,' Norman said. 'Fucking little liar.'

She twisted her thin body to get a look at his face. 'You're not a cop,' she said.

'The Brain of Britain,' he said.

She twisted around some more, but made no impression on Norman's grip. 'Lemme go,' she said, then, striking a hopeless note that was followed by a tear dripping down her cheek. 'What's it to you?' she said, brushing the tear from her face. 'You're not a cop. It didn't hurt you.'

'I'm a citizen,' he told her. 'I got a duty.'

She looked away from him and shook her head. 'This is not real,' she said. Then she turned back to him and said. 'Would you please let go of my arm?'

Norman shook his head. 'I'm making a citizen's arrest,' he said. 'Taking you down the cop shop.'

'Jesus,' she said. 'What do you want? Have I gotta pay you?'

Norman smiled. 'You take your time,' he said. 'But you get there in the end.'

'I haven't got any money,' she said. 'I'm broke.'

'What's your name?'

'Janet.'

'Janet,' Norman echoed. 'How old are you?'

'Nineteen,' said Janet. 'Don't say I only look fifteen. I'm nineteen.'

'You look twelve,' he said. 'But if you say you're nineteen I believe you. After all, I got no reason to think you'd tell me a lie. In the first place, all I know about you so far is you're a thief, and you did tell me a little porkie when you said you meant to pay for the lipstick, but that don't mean every time you open your mouth another lie's gonna come rolling out. And in the second place, just because I happen to know you once stoled one thing, that doesn't mean I'm not gonna be able to trust you, so every time you make a move I think you're gonna steal something else. I'm not that kinda guy, who gives a dog a bad name, and then for ever after that I'm looking for a way to prove I was right in the first place. That's not how I work.

'Now, in a minute I'm gonna let go of your arm, and I hope you won't run off down the street and try to get away from me. Because, and now I'm talking in the third place, which you should listen to, because it could save you having a smack in the eye. If you do, run off down the street, that is, then I, and my name's Norman, will take a deep breath and come running after you, and before you've got a dozen or more steps I'll have caught you and smacked you and you'll have been down on the pavement and I'll have picked you up, and I'll have you by the arm again and we'll all be right back in the first position.

'Now you could scream at that point and kick up a fuss, and a cop or somebody might come along to make enquiries and when that happens I'll be taking this lipstick out of my pocket and putting in a claim for a medal from the authorities.

'Do you understand me?'

Janet nodded.

Norman let go of her arm and they walked along the street next to each other.

After a while Janet asked, 'What do you want me to do?'

Norman said, 'I haven't made up my mind yet.'

They walked for a while longer. 'The thing is,' he told her, 'when I do make my mind up and tell you, some of the things I'll want you'll already have thought of. You might like them, or you might not like them. Either way, it won't hurt much. You'll just do it. But some of the things won't be like that at all. You won't have thought of 'em. You prolly won't even have heard of 'em.'

He left it at that. Hanging in the air. They walked some more. Janet thought a couple of times of making a break for it, but she decided not to be stupid. 'OK,' she said, eventually. 'OK, Norman.'

Janet had a three-room flat in Tang Hall. On the first floor, you walked into a sitting room with an open fireplace and the smell of damp mingled with the smell of cat, after that was a tiny kitchen with a table and a gas cooker, and finally there was a dark and windowless bedroom with a huge unmade bed. This last room had had a window until eighteen months previously, but that window had been broken and the landlord had decided the best way to deal with the repair was to board it up.

On the second floor was a bathroom which was shared between Janet and the girls in the remaining flats who occupied the rest of the building, though the girls and some of their more regular boyfriends had stopped referring to it as a bathroom and called it, instead, the penicillin factory. There was an antique shower fitted over the bath.

'You're all working girls, right?' said Norman.

'Sometimes,' she said. 'When it's the only way to feed the cats.'

Norman followed Janet back down to the sitting room. There were three cats in there, each occupying a chair.

'This is Tabitha, Venus and Orchid,' she said. The cats looked at Norman but remained seated. Norman looked back. Orchid, the last cat Janet had introduced, got to her feet and sidled over to Norman. She was black. She rubbed herself up against his leg. He pushed her away but she came back again. He looked briefly at the poster of some pop star or male pin-up over the fireplace, knowing he should know who it was, but not being able to get it for a moment. Then it came to him in a flash. 'John Lennon,' he said.

Janet smiled. 'Yeah,' she said. 'Imagine.'

Norman looked at her, somehow thinking she had begun to say something, then broken off. But she'd finished. 'Imagine what?' he asked.

'John Lennon,' she said. 'He's dead. He was killed.'

'I know that,' Norman said. 'Some guy blew him away. One minute he was there, the next minute he was coughing up blood. Few minutes later he couldn't even do that. What's to imagine?' Orchid moved over to Norman's leg again and nuzzled against it. Norman picked the cat up by the scruff of its neck and dropped it on to a chair.

Janet began crying. She flopped down into a chair and let large tears roll down her cheeks.

'What's wrong now?' Norman asked.

'I'm pissed off,' she said, between the tears. 'You get so angry, and I haven't done anything. For a minute there, I thought we were getting on OK. Talking about John Lennon. Really communicating. Then you start getting mad. I haven't done anything. I was trying to be nice to you.'

Norman took her by her hands and pulled her to her feet. He put his arms around her and held her tight. 'It's OK,' he said, using his quiet voice. 'You just thought I was mad, but it's only the way I sound. I had a pretty bad day, all told. And I get tired.' He held her at arm's length and looked at her. She tried to smile through her tears.

'I bet you're not used to women, either?' she said.

Norman shook his head. 'No,' he said. 'I'm not used to any of that.' He let go of her arms and took the lipstick from his pocket. Handed it over to her.

'You look a bit like him,' she said. Glancing from Norman to the poster and back again. 'Round the eyes.'

Norman let a smirk spread itself over his face. 'You reckon?' he said as modestly as he could.

'He knew he was gonna die,' Janet continued. 'He talked about it the day before, even knew the name of the guy who was gonna shoot him. Must have had predestination, whatever it's called, you know, before the fact? I have that sometimes, lots of women do, before their period. It just comes over me, something'll happen, anything really. Like I'm gonna get a letter, or someone'll drop a twenty-pound note and I'll find it. And next thing the postman comes round and there's the letter.

'He was called John Winston Ono Lennon, because of Yoko, his wife, he took her name, and he baked bread and looked after his son.'

'No shit,' said Norman. 'I thought he was the Beatles.'

'That was before,' Janet said. 'Something happened. But he was a lovely man.'

'This period of yours,' Norman said. 'You got it now?'

'No,' said Janet. 'I don't have periods. Ain't had one for years.' She didn't say anything for a while after that, seemed to drift off into her own thoughts. 'Are you hungry?' she asked eventually. 'Do you want me to make you something to eat?'

'Later,' he told her. 'First I want to fuck you.'

chapter 15

Geordie came out of Woolworths through another door, avoiding the one Norman Brown used. That was because Norman Brown was still standing outside the door he had used, being heavy with the girl he had followed out. Norman had the girl by the arm. A tight grip, and she was struggling, trying to get away from him. Norman's face was set and grim, and there was no way he was going to release her. The girl didn't call out, but she was clearly not at all pleased with the way Norman was handling her. Geordie looked across the street and saw Gus take a step or two forward. The voice through his earpiece said, 'What the . . .?', and Geordie moved along the pavement away from Norman Brown and the girl, wondering if he should go back and try to hear what was going on between them.

'Stay there,' Gus said through the earpiece. 'Don't get involved.' Gus reading Geordie's mind, as usual.

Geordie had no real thoughts of interfering in the dispute between Norman Brown and the girl. His most urgent impulse, as always when faced with potential violence, was to run. Get as much distance between Geordie and the violence as possible. When he thought about the past, Geordie could not remember anything *except* violence. He thought about the past often, because it was there like a solid weight, dragging him back. The future seemed like a dream with no substance. The present an unreality. The present was like a weekend break, the kind in the advertisements. Like all those companies wanted to give away. But the past was violence for as far back as he could go inside his head. From his mother and her boyfriends. From the neighbours and the local police during his early childhood. From the Social Services and, after his mother disappeared, from the staff at the orphanage. After he got away from that place, the violence was the violence of the streets.

Geordie didn't think of the violence as compartmentalized, from his mother, from the police, from the street. It was not like that at all inside his head. It was simply a solid block. He could not comprehend it. It stretched from here to the horizon. It went on for ever, like leg irons.

The only break in the continuing saga was when Sam picked him up that night and took him home. And later, when Sam introduced him to Celia. After that, with Sam and Celia, the violence ceased to be a solid block. It differentiated itself into patches. After Sam and Celia entered the equation there were only periods of violence. And between the periods of violence there were periods of peace, periods of music, periods of solitude, periods of laughter. Even periods of gentleness.

Celia said that was called life.

Geordie didn't know what it was he had had before. He just knew he didn't want no more violence.

Sam said you couldn't have life without violence.

Geordie usually wanted Sam to be right. Sam usually was right. But this was one of the things that Geordie hoped he was wrong about.

Although Geordie's most urgent impulse was to put distance between himself and the violence, there was a secondary impulse which directly contradicted the first one. It came pushing itself up from the region of his solar plexus, and was capable of turning him into a screaming rage, a kind of fireball of energy. Geordie would find himself off his feet, hurtling towards and into the fray, a scratching, punching, tearing, biting whirlpool of distilled aggression.

When he was in prison for a while, before Sam came along, between the orphanage and the street, he very soon got himself known for kicking off. For a time in that place he would punch the first person he saw. Punch them in the throat. Punch them between the eyes. Whoever was passing, screw or con, a visitor or social worker. He punched a priest one time. Then the Governor would say, 'Put him down on chokey for a while.'

When he was back on the main cell block he was still known as the little psychopath who might lay into you with his boots and his fists and his knees and his elbows. He'd go at you with anything that moved. You'd be head-butted or given two straight fingers – one in each eye. He was a walking barrel of dynamite and you'd never know when he was gonna go off. It worked as well. Geordie would pick on a big guy, walk right up to him and say, 'You think you can just look at me, and get away with it?'

'Me? No way, pal. I'm not looking for trouble.' Faced with a fracas between them and Geordie, even the biggest and toughest cons would inexplicably take up a new religion, known to everyone behind bars as Devout Cowardice.

But Geordie *was* broken by the system. First off he acted

tough, let them see they were not gonna break him, that he'd keep his integrity, never bend the knee. But he discovered that you don't waste time in prison, you spend it. You throw your table against the wall and drag your bed up against the door and barricade yourself in. You refuse your food. You realize sooner or later that prison hurts.

Inside you it hurts. Right down deep inside of you, it hurts. When Geordie left the door of his cell to go down to the canteen, no one saw him. All they saw was a con with a smile on his face, walking along swinging his arms. *Hi Sid. Hi Chass.* That was the Geordie they saw, the outside, but inside of him was a hole, a big hollow empty hole, that's all, a big big hurt. Eating him away, shrinking him smaller and smaller, inch by inch, depriving him more and more of what was left of his personality and feelings, every shred of his individuality. By the time he got out, there was nothing left.

Except for now. Except for what Sam and Celia had helped him regain. Somehow. He didn't know how. Maybe he'd never know how.

'Where are you?' The voice in his ear crackled.

'Uh?'

'I can't see you,' Gus said. 'It's time to change over.'

Geordie looked around. He'd walked away from Norman and the girl and Woolworths and was almost back at the office. 'Dunno,' he said. 'I wasn't thinking. Where are you?'

'Jesus,' said Gus. 'Jesus Christ.'

Geordie waited. But Gus didn't say anything else.

'Check,' said Geordie.

Gus's voice came back into Geordie's ear, but he wasn't talking to Geordie. Not really. Geordie could tell. This was one of the times Gus was talking to himself. 'Stroll on,' he said. 'Jesus Christ. If you want a job doing, do it yourself.'

Maybe he was talking into his dictaphone? Gus had a dictaphone that he used like a diary and a notebook. He never wrote anything down these days, except his final report for a client, and Celia usually typed that up. Geordie thought he might get himself a dictaphone one of these days. Much easier than writing everything down. Specially when you couldn't find a pen.

Geordie took the headphones off and went upstairs to the office.

Deserted. A note from Sam saying he'd gone to the seaside. No sign of Barney anywhere. Probably be paddling by now.

chapter 16

The following morning Sam set off for Leicester at seven thirty. Go look for Snow White. See if she wanted to be found.

The news was full of the double murder. A couple had been found in Haxby, on the outskirts of York, she bound and gagged and suffocated and he shot through the back of the head. There had been a clumsy attempt to make it look as though the man had shot himself. But he would have had to be a contortionist. A large quantity of firearms was missing from the man's place of work, a local gun club. Sam knew the gun club. He'd never been inside, but remembered the site. Police were following several leads, but no one had been detained.

Sam smiled at that. In his experience the York police couldn't investigate a head-on collision between two skate-boards and come up with a result. Sounded heavy though, the murders, like the work of somebody really dedicated.

But for the rest of the trip along the M1 his thoughts were occupied by Jennie Cosgrave. The previous day had turned out quite interesting in the end, though it had been punctured constantly by small misunderstandings. Each of them had felt forced occasionally into defensive positions, and though they'd worked their way through every one of them, that didn't stop them coming up against another one at the next corner.

He thinking: *Hell, let's just relax and have fun.* Her

thinking: *I need to know who you are, where you're coming from before I can relax*. Tying themselves up in knots. At the end of the day he couldn't help feeling she'd enjoyed it more than him. She seemed to thrive on conflict, taking everything on board, all the time asking for more, then going into long analyses of his contribution, acknowledging her own failings. Finally saying something that led to another misunderstanding and beginning the whole process over again. She was intelligent, clever, bright, talking all the time, and incapable of being dull. But Sam just wanted to smell her, get up real close and have a good sniff.

Should have told her so, he said to himself. Then we could have had a long conversation about that, and finally she might have let him do it.

'I really enjoyed it,' she said when he left her at her door. 'Just what I needed. I feel as if I've laid a ghost.'

Sam couldn't help himself. 'Cheers,' he said.

Next time they were going to talk about women, feminism, all that. God knows when they would get around to the sniffing. First he'd have to prove he wasn't a misogynist.

There had been a time when that question never arose. But now it was always there, with every woman you met. Like a hurdle you had to get over. Sam had argued it and won, and he'd argued it and lost. Sometimes he didn't know if he was a misogynist or not. It was so complicated, the processes and denials you went through if you *were* a misogynist, that you might be the last one to hear about it. The only thing Sam was sure of was that he didn't want to be a misogynist. But more than one woman had told him that was because he couldn't face up to the fact that he was one.

Christ, when they started getting into that he wondered why he hadn't become a monk. And it wasn't any easier for all the younger guys at the men's group, emasculating themselves. If anything it was more difficult for them. They couldn't remember the time before the question came up, the good old days when a man could depend on a modicum of certainty.

But he shook his head. He didn't want to go back. Painful as it all was, it was for the best. Who knows, there might come a time when a generation of women are not discriminated against? Anything's possible.

In the Leicester library he turned up the record of Selina White's birth. She was born on 24 June 1964. He made a note of the names of her mother and father, together with their address. They were no longer listed in the electoral roll.

Sam took Barney with him when he called at the address on the birth certificate. 'I'm looking for Mr and Mrs White,' he told the woman who answered his knock.

She opened the door only a crack. Sam could see both of her eyes, her nose, but only part of her mouth. The woman looked down at Barney and seemed reassured, opened the door another inch. 'He's dead, I think,' she said. 'The wife, I don't know. She was in hospital. Something like that. With her nerves.' She closed the door back to its original position. 'You a relative?'

'I'm trying to find their daughter,' he told her. 'Selina.'

'Don't think she's called that,' the woman told him. 'There was a daughter, but that's not her name. Try next door but one,' she said. 'They used to know them. More than me, anyhow.' The woman looked down at Barney again and made a clicking sound with her tongue. Barney looked up at her but she was gone, the door closed tight.

Sam knocked on the door of next door but one and a man of around sixty opened it. 'We don't want any,' he said. He had a soft little pot belly and his head came level with Sam's shoulders.

'Don't blame you,' Sam told him. 'I'm trying to trace Mrs White.'

'You'd better talk to the missus,' he said. He disappeared back into the house, leaving the door open. A moment later his wife appeared, a small wiry woman about the same age as her husband.

'You looking for Joan White?' she asked.

'D'you know where I can find her?'

'She's in the mental home,' the woman said. 'Couldn't cope when George died.'

'I really want to contact her daughter,' Sam said. 'Is she called Selina?'

'Selina? I don't know anything about her. Louise, the youngest one, she's still around.' The woman scratched her chin. 'Selina,' she said, 'I'd forgotten about her. Right pretty little thing. Went to London they said. She was only a kid.'

'Louise, then,' Sam said. 'Do you know where she lives?'

The woman shook her head. 'See her sometimes in the town. She's got a couple of bairns. But she doesn't remember me.'

'You don't know any way I could contact her?' Sam said. 'A married name? Anything would help.'

The woman shook her head. 'I'd recognize him as well,' she said. 'Tall bloke with ginger hair. But I don't know what he's called.'

The woman's husband appeared behind her. 'It's starting,' he said, then disappeared again. A moment later Sam heard the signature tune of *Neighbours*.

'I've got to go,' she said.

'The hospital,' Sam said. 'The home? What's it called?'

The woman became agitated. The signature tune of the soap was coming to an end. 'Bentley Cross.' She began closing the door.

Sam took out one of his cards and waved it towards her. 'In case you remember anything else,' he said. 'I'd appreciate it.' He pushed the card through the remaining crack in the door, felt the old woman grab it. Then he got his fingers out just before the door closed on them.

'Jesus, Barney,' he said to the dog, looking at his fingers. 'We're gonna need danger money on this job.'

The Bentley Cross Nursing Home was in a leafy northern suburb of the town. 'Sorry,' Sam told Barney, 'you'll have to wait in the car.' The dog looked neither surprised nor happy.

Sam walked along the pebbled drive to the house, a large Georgian mansion with a huge oak door set in a mock gothic porch. The door was ajar and he pushed it open and went inside to a reception area with two teenage girls at a desk. They had well-trained reception smiles, sparkling eyes and identical make-up. 'Good afternoon. Can I help you?' said the one on the left. The other one sparkled supportively. If the first one couldn't help, she was ready to jump into the breach.

'I'm here to see Mrs White,' Sam said. 'Mrs Joan White.'

'Are you a relative?' asked the girl.

Sam shook his head. 'A friend.'

The receptionist pushed a ledger towards him. 'Sign the book,' she said. 'I'll take you down to see her.'

Down, Sam thought. They keep her in a cellar? He signed the book and followed the receptionist along a corridor to a room with four beds, all empty. A small frail-looking woman sitting next to one of the beds. She wore a dressing gown, and when Sam and the receptionist entered the room she looked away from them, as if the sound of their entry was coming from behind her.

'You've got a visitor, Mrs White,' the receptionist said. She turned to Sam. 'Would you like a cup of tea?'

Sam said, 'No,' and the girl left him with the old lady. He pulled a chair over from one of the other beds and sat next to Mrs White. She looked straight ahead, occasionally making some nervous movement with her hand. Her head shook rhythmically from side to side. Her face was a mask.

'I've been talking to a neighbour of yours,' Sam said.

No response. It was as if he wasn't there.

'I'm trying to contact Selina,' he tried.

Nothing. The rhythmical shaking of the head continued without a break.

'Or Louise?'

The old lady's head turned towards him. She said, 'Don't eat the bread. There's maggots in it.'

There was someone at home but she wasn't answering the door. Whoever it was in there was sitting in the dark, the curtains closed tight against the world. She was playing solitaire with what remained of a full deck, maybe a dozen cards out of the original pack.

Sam sat with her for another ten minutes. There was no further exchange. Once she looked at the door and pointed at it, becoming agitated for a moment or two. But whatever she saw there must have evaporated because the next moment she had gone back to her immobile stare. Without moving her lips she grouped a few notes together in the back of her throat. She left it and then a minute later returned to the same group of notes, like the beginning of a song. It was barely recognizable. Sam knew what it was, only he couldn't think of the title or how it continued. He stood and smoothed her hair lightly. 'Jesus,' he said quietly. Then loud enough for her to hear he said, 'My bonnie lies over the ocean.'

Back at reception only one of the girls remained, the one who hadn't spoken when Sam arrived. 'She's in a bad way,' Sam said.

The smile never left the girl's face. 'Mrs White?' she said. 'Sometimes you can reach her. Not very often.'

'Look,' Sam said. 'I need to contact her daughter, but I don't have an address.'

'We're not allowed to give personal details,' she said.

'How about if you ring her and ask if it's all right?'

She shook her head. 'Sorry.'

'I've come a long way,' said Sam. 'It's quite important.'

The girl sighed, looked at the door, and then came back to him. 'I'm sorry,' she said. 'I'm not allowed to.'

Sam pulled a twenty-pound note out of his top pocket and put it on the desk.

The girl's eyes fixed on it for a moment. The smile was still there when she looked back at Sam. She shook her head. 'I could get into trouble,' she said. But she said it with a hint of uncertainty.

'No one's gonna know,' he said, taking another twenty from the same pocket and placing it on the desk alongside the first one.

The girl quickly looked around and picked up the notes. 'I get off in about fifteen minutes,' she said.

'There's a maroon Volvo in the car park,' Sam told her. 'I'll be there.'

Louise White was a tall woman, twenty-eight years old, and a dog lover. Barney recognized her immediately, did that little walk on his hind legs Geordie had taught him, and got himself and Sam into the house almost before Sam had explained why they were there.

But she shook her head when Sam asked the question. 'Selina,' she said. 'No, I haven't seen her for years. Last time I heard she was moving to York.' When she spoke the name of the town she looked away from Sam. 'Terrible murder there yesterday,' she said. 'A couple. It was on the news. Made me think of Selina.'

She had long fair hair tied up in a bun, reminded Sam of a schoolteacher. And she had a long narrow face which was not unattractive, though it gave the impression of a fish, a dolphin perhaps? She sat opposite Sam on a huge sofa, Barney at her feet. She stroked the dog's head from time to time. When she stopped Barney would nudge her leg with his nose until she started again. Then she would say, 'Oh, you want some more, do you? You're beautiful, you know that? You're a beautiful dog.'

Sam sat in a matching armchair, up to his ankles in the pile of the carpet. The rest of the room was furnished sparsely, though there seemed to be a preponderance of mirrors and clocks. There was a traditional wooden alpine cuckoo clock over the fireplace, and on the opposite wall a pendulum clock in a long case. On a bookcase by the side of Sam's chair was a ceramic mantle clock, and by the door on a small table was another with a picture of a Harley Davidson on it, and a legend underneath which read: JOHN'S DREAM MACHINE.

'When would that be?' Sam asked. 'How long ago did she leave?'

'Six, seven years. She rang to say she was getting married and moving to York. She said she'd send us the address, but she never did.'

'So you don't know how to contact her?'

Louise White shook her head. 'When she was in London she never wrote. I haven't seen her since I was fifteen.' She pushed herself out of the sofa and took a box of photographs from a cupboard. She riffled through them and handed one to Sam. 'That's what she looked like then.' She went back to

Barney. 'Oh, you're a fussy little chap,' she said. Then to Sam, 'When did you know her?'

'I don't,' he said. 'I'm trying to find her for someone else. Man called Norman Brown.' He waved the photograph at her. 'Do you mind if I hang on to this?'

'Take it,' she said. 'I'd like it back, though, when you've finished with it.' Louise shook her head. 'She's only my sister,' she said ironically. 'I don't know anything about her.'

'What about her husband?' Sam asked. 'You don't know what he's called?'

'Oh, yes I do,' said Louise. 'I asked her when she rang. He's called Crumble.' She laughed and the fishy look disappeared. 'Not a name you'd be likely to forget,' she said. 'Mr Crumble. So she's Mrs Selina Crumble. Can you trace her with that?'

'Probably,' said Sam. 'At least it's somewhere to start. You don't know what he does, Mr Crumble?'

'He's a solicitor,' she said. 'I remember we sometimes used to fantasize about it. You know, Crumble, Crumble and Crumble.' She laughed again. 'Is that enough?'

'Yeah,' said Sam. 'It should be easy now.'

She saw him to the door, said goodbye to Barney ten times. To Sam she said, 'When you find her, remind her she's got a family.'

chapter 17

Sam arrived home just after six in the evening. Traffic was held up on the ring road by police blocks on the exit roads. He sat with the photograph of Snow White when she was fifteen. A blurred black and white image of a scrap of a girl standing next to a garden shed with a broken window. She had her mouth open and was obviously shouting something at whoever it was taking the photograph. Telling them to stop, maybe.

She was at that age when it's not possible to see the child, because she's gone, and yet still not possible to see the woman, because she hasn't arrived yet. Invisible. File the thought away and tell Geordie and Celia about it later. Especially Geordie. He was obsessed with invisibility at the moment. Had talked of nothing else since Celia had brought the subject up. Sam found himself thinking about Bronte again, his own daughter, and what she would have been like at the age of the girl in the photograph, had she lived a few more years. She would have been like Donna, he thought. A scrap of nothing bursting with energy. A handful and a half, as Donna's family had always said about her.

And what would Donna have been like now?

But no, hell. He stopped himself. He'd been down that road so many times before. It led nowhere. It led to a steep cliff with a drop into nothingness.

Sam walked over to the phone and punched the numbers. After a moment he said, 'How're you doing?'

'Oh, Sam, is it you?' said the voice of Jennie Cosgrave.

'Yeah,' he said. 'Did you eat yet?'

'No. I was going to have a sandwich.' She was silent for a moment, then said, 'I missed you today. Where've you been?'

'I was in Leicester,' he said. 'Detecting.'

'Did you find whatever it was you were looking for?'

'Tell you later,' he said. 'I'll come round. There's a Mexican-type place I was gonna try. Loud music and hot taco. Keeps your mind off things.'

'Sounds terrible,' she said.

Earlier in the year, 16 March, the anniversary of Donna's death, she had come back so strong Sam had bought a bottle of whisky and drunk it during the course of a slack afternoon. The same evening with Donna's ghost still at his shoulder he'd gone out and bought another one and spent the night with it. Geordie, living in the flat above, but still using Sam's flat as much as his own, did not understand what was happening. He thought it was party time at first and had a few slugs himself.

Only when Sam started screaming, hallucinating a kind of white hell in the early hours of the morning, did Geordie realize what was happening. He called Celia and Gus, and the two of them sat on Sam through the next couple of days to see him through.

Since then he'd been straight. He occasionally took out the empty bottle and had a swig of air. If he was going to slip again, he'd go away to do it. Get lost for the duration.

She wore a white T-shirt outside a pair of blue jeans which were turned up at the bottom, white canvas shoes, and a small shoulder bag. She was standing at the window and watched him arrive and she had left the house and closed the door behind her before he got to the gate.

'Done a lot of travelling today,' he told her. 'If I'd known I was gonna end up here I'd have travelled faster.'

She laughed. 'Thank you kindly, sir, she said.'

'We can walk,' Sam told her. 'El Mexicana's just down the road.'

A group of people were talking on a street corner. One woman said she was afraid to go out. 'But you are out,' her neighbour said.

'The murder,' Sam said. 'It's getting to people.'

'It's such a strange feeling,' she said. 'To know it happened close by. What, three miles away? I can't stop thinking about that poor woman suffocating.'

'Unique,' said Sam.

'What do you mean?'

'Murder,' he said. 'It's always unique. It's gone on for all time. Somebody's murdered every day, but when we talk about it, even after all this time, it's like a unique event. As though it's never happened before.'

'You think we should be used to it?'

'No,' he said. 'I wonder about the mechanism. What keeps us so clean, so naïve? So that we're never prepared, always so surprised.'

'It's too terrible to contemplate,' she said. 'Things we can't face, we distance them, put them to the back of our mind. We refuse to face them. Then when someone's murdered, especially if it's someone we know or it happens nearby, we have to face it. And we're surprised because we've never thought about it before. It's forced on us.'

'Is that the professional talking?'

She smiled. 'Yes. It's my job.'

'Through here,' he said, turning left into a short driveway, the entrance to the El Mexicana restaurant. They walked into a huge room with a circular bar, tables lining the walls, the air hot with spice. An adolescent boy dressed in jeans and a white apron took them to a table behind the bar and said something inaudible because of the amplified music. Two locals with American accents were harmonizing a Neil Young song on a small stage. Behind them was a floodlit graphic stolen from the set of *The Good, the Bad, and the Ugly*. Despite the level of amplification there was a constant buzz of conversation from the sixty or seventy tables in the room.

'Would you like a drink?' the young waiter asked.

Sam raised his eyes at Jennie.

'A glass of white wine?' she said.

'And lemonade for me,' he told the waiter.

When the boy left to get their drinks Jennie said, 'Lemonade?'

'I'm an alcoholic,' he told her. 'But I'm being good.'

She had the same surprised look on her face that everyone had when you told them. Look that said, *What? How?* Look that had so many questions behind it you almost wanted to cry off and have a drink. She would either say something about it now or come back to it later. He just hoped she wouldn't say something about it now *and* come back to it later, and then keep coming back to it for ever more. Some people never wanted to talk about anything else.

'You're looking at me,' she said, 'and giving nothing away. You're completely inscrutable. I don't know where you want me to go from here.'

He shrugged, held the eye contact. 'I've stopped smoking,' he said. 'Absolutely. Don't think I'll have another.'

She shook her head and leaned towards him over the table. 'You probably think you're leaving me free,' she said. 'But in reality it's intimidating.'

'If I start drinking I don't stop,' he said. 'I'm an addict. When I'm dry I make an effort with people. At least with people I like. When I drink, the only effort I make is with my elbow.'

Jennie smiled. 'My mother was an alcoholic,' she said. 'Not like you. She would never admit it. And in a way she could control it. She drank every day for as long as I can remember. Even the day she died.'

'I used to be like that,' Sam said. 'But I can't control it when I'm drinking. I drink until nothing works. I drink myself unconscious. I lose control of everything. Become like blubber.'

The boy waiter returned with their drinks, gave the white wine to Sam and the lemonade to Jennie. Sam pushed the wine over to her. 'You wanna swap?' he asked.

'Yes.' She took the wine and passed the lemonade to him. 'I think I'll handle it better than you.'

In the short silence that followed they both overheard a conversation at the next table. The people there were talking about a local couple, a gun dealer and his wife, who had been murdered the previous day.

chapter 18

That evening Norman left Janet's flat and returned to the Station Hotel. It was a good deal and he was pleased with himself. A bit like fucking a boy, being with her. Reminded him of being back in prison again. But she'd serve a purpose. Living with her would be safer than living in a hotel. And when the time came it would be easy enough to get rid of her. She didn't have any friends, so no one would miss her. Maybe the security people in Woolworths; they might miss her. These firms, clinics, whatever they're called, that do the silicone breast implants; they might miss her. But nobody real would miss her. Nobody in the real world.

Norman watched television in his room until late. Then he got to thinking about Squishsquash. He put his gun in his shoulder holster and went out into the night. He followed the city wall until he came to the house on Lord Mayor's Walk. The house was in darkness, no lights at any of the windows. Norman looked at it from the grassy knoll on the other side of the street. She would be in there. She would be in bed. Naked, probably, in this heat. Squishsquash. Unsuspecting. Not knowing what was watching her window.

There were two ways of doing this. He could knock on the front door, wait till she comes down to open it and then just push his way in. Surprise, surprise. Or he could get round to the back of the house, do a break-in, quietly, then find her still sleeping in her bed. Whisper in her ear: 'Squishsquash, wakey, wakey.' Watch her face as it slowly dawns on her what she's gonna get.

No choice, really, when you think about it. Go round the back and do the break-in.

But before Norman got to his feet to cross over the road, they came round the corner. Squishsquash and her boyfriend. Holding hands. She wore a white T-shirt with blue jeans, white shoes, and with her free hand she was swinging a shoulder bag. She was laughing. And the guy, he was familiar. As they drew closer Norman realized how familiar the guy was. It was Mr Detective. Sam Turner, the guy Norman had hired to find Snow White.

That wasn't right. Not right at all. It was true that Norman had seen Squishsquash come out of Mr Detective's building, but he had not imagined that they had any connection. The way they were clinging on to each other here, pawing each other and making the eyes, they were definitely an item. He watched as Squishsquash opened her bag and took out a key to the door. Then she went inside and Mr Detective followed her, closing the door behind him.

Norman shifted on the grass and realized that the night dampness had seeped through his trousers. For a moment he thought of going over there and sorting the two of them out, but what he did was get to his feet and follow the wall back round to his hotel. He needed to think this one through.

Maybe watch them some more. She turned him on, this woman, this Squishsquash. He wanted her. He wanted her all to himself.

The next day Norman moved out of the Station Hotel and drove with his four suitcases full of guns to Janet's flat in Tang Hall. He paid cash for the room in the Station Hotel, and left a large tip for the porter who helped him with the suitcases. He used an old Bedford van for the trip, one of those with sliding doors, got you way up above the road, so you looked down on the silly fuckers in cars. But the cars could always go faster than the van. The ideal vehicle, Norman thought, would be some kind of supercharged van. Something heavy but with a lot of power under the bonnet, and power that sounded like power as well, not one of these silent things like a Rolls or a Bentley, like you couldn't hear them coming. No, Norman would rather have something that roared. Everybody on the street would look round, say, *Shit, here comes Norm with his ENGINE. Better get out the fucking way, man. Like, move over.*

Oh, yeah, and one of those crash bars on the front, big heavy set, bull bars, so you could ram your way through a shop window if you felt like you were getting short on the readies. Maybe have the same on the back as well. Save you turning round sometimes.

One day Norman would have a vehicle like that. And it would be painted bright gold. Just simple bright gold all over, none of your red stars on it, zaps of blue lightning, shit like that. No clutter, man. Jus' simple and tasty.

Maybe mount a gun on it?

Norman drove through Tang Hall and parked outside Janet's flat. He humped two of the suitcases to the door of the flat and dropped them on the bare boards of the passage. As he walked back out to the van to collect the others he heard a peal of female laughter erupt inside the flat. Sounded like a hen party going on in there.

Norman brought the rest of his luggage and kicked at the door with the toe of his shoe to get Janet's attention. She came to the door and helped him in with the luggage, then turned and introduced him to two women sitting next to the open fireplace. 'This is Margaret and Trudie,' she said. 'Friends of mine, from upstairs.' And to the women, 'This is Norman,' she said. 'My boyfriend.'

Margaret, the tall one with the cigarette, got to her feet and came over to Norman, extending her hand, and Trudie, who was smaller and dumpier, with bleached hair and dark roots, followed suit. Trudie had Janet's cat, Orchid, in her arms. 'Heard so much about you,' said Margaret, and Trudie giggled shrilly and looked down at Norman's crotch. 'Oh, excuse Trudie,' Margaret continued. 'She's a bit tiddly.' She turned to Janet. 'We'll be off, then, love,' she said. 'Leave you to it.' She walked towards the door, but then remembered something and came back. 'Better take the newspaper,' she said, picking it up from the arm of the chair. 'Read about the murder.'

Trudie let go with another shrill giggle, and followed her friend out of the door. She put Orchid carefully down on the carpet. 'Ooh, I don't know how you can read about murder, Margaret,' she said. 'Gives me the willies just to think about it.'

Janet closed the door behind them as they made their way up the stairs.

'You been talking about my balls?' Norman asked.

Janet didn't reply, hung her head a little.

'You did didn't you?' Norman said. 'You've been discussing my balls with those two. Having a good laugh. Taking the piss.'

'Can I open your cases?' Janet said, half carrying one of them, half dragging it towards the bedroom.

'Janet,' Norman said. 'Leave the case where it is and answer me what I'm fucking asking you. Have you been talking 'bout my balls to them two slags from upstairs?'

Janet let go of the suitcase. 'I might have mentioned it,' she said. 'I din't think you'd mind.'

'Well, I do,' he said. 'Mind, that is. It's not exactly a state secret, but I like to be the one that does the telling. OK?'

'It's interesting,' Janet said, 'when somebody's got four instead of two. It's just the kind of thing I like telling people about. Specially Margaret and Trudie. Everybody thinks it's interesting. Like John Lennon.'

'Did he have four?'

'No, I mean he was an interesting person because of things he did, and what he looked like. And you're the same,' she said. 'You know, because of having the four.' She giggled quickly and then stopped. Orchid jumped silently into her lap and she immediately began stroking her.

'What you laughing at?' he asked.

'Trudie,' she said. 'Trudie said we were a funny couple with you having four balls and me having no tits.'

'What's funny? I don't see nothing funny.'

'Do you mind, though? Me not having any?'

Norman shrugged, picked up a suitcase and walked into the bedroom. 'Most women've got them,' he said. 'If I need tits some time, I'll prolly find a pair.'

chapter 19

Gus stayed on the guy. He followed him and the girl to Tang Hall and stood outside the house for four hours until the guy left. Looked like separate occupants on the two floors, but you couldn't tell for sure. Then he followed the guy back into town and watched him go into the Station Hotel and collect the keys to his room.

There were more police about in the town than usual. Looked like the local force had recruited more manpower to help with the murder investigation. The news hoardings were splashed with just two words: DOUBLE MURDER.

Gus ordered himself a coffee in the hotel lounge, positioned himself so he could see the lift and the stairs, and waited again. Normally he didn't like this aspect of the job, the interminable waiting. But today it was OK. Gave him a chance to reflect on his relationships, with his partner Marie, with his girlfriend Karen, with Sam, Geordie, Celia. He wanted to spend as much time as possible in his head. He didn't want to go home, or to talk to anyone.

He was prepared to stay on Norman Brown's tail for as long as it took. Even longer. As long as it kept him away from real life. Gus would follow the man for ever.

Although the sound on the television was turned down, he could still make out most of the action offered by Christine and Mary Beth, and before dropping off to sleep he wondered idly how they managed to keep up the pace.

The night porter shook his shoulder again, and Gus opened his eyes wide and tried to dislodge his tongue from the roof of his mouth. 'What's-a-time?' he asked.

The porter pointed to a wall clock, which said it was 12.45 a.m. 'Didn't wanna wake you,' the porter said. 'But if I leave you there it costs me another job.'

Gus struggled to his feet and walked home through the town. Marie was sleeping soundly, and he managed to slip into the bed without waking her. He pretended to be asleep in the morning when she crawled out of bed to get ready for the early shift at the hospital.

By 7 a.m. he was back at the Station Hotel, on a coffee drip, waiting for Norman Brown to come down for breakfast. His eyes kept closing. This is unprofessional, he thought. Every time he forced his eyes open he was aware of the checked shirt he had worn yesterday, and was still wearing today. It was a lightweight shirt Marie had given him last summer, and a more unsuitable garment for a surveillance job would have been possible only in Day-glo colours. When you're tailing someone you want to fade into the background. You need to be invisible, like Celia's old men. Yesterday, Gus had been aware of the shirt, but had put up with it because he hadn't known he was going to be tailing someone. But today he *had* known, and he had still put it on.

Why?

He put it down to fatigue. There were only two other possible answers, and he didn't see himself fitting either of them. One was that he didn't care. The other was that he wanted to be discovered.

The more he thought about the shirt, the more Gus realized there was something else about it which was even more disturbing. It was beginning to stink.

Norman Brown came out of the lift at eight forty-five and walked to the breakfast room. Still swaggering. He wore a lightweight suit, kind of beige colour which was fashionable that summer, and under the jacket a plum-coloured shirt with a white collar and white buttons. On his feet he had tennis shoes with no socks. The air conditioning in the hotel kept the temperature cool and comfortable, but outside the windows the sun was already high, and the day was setting itself up to be another scorcher.

While Norman ate breakfast, Gus toyed with the idea of running into the town and buying a fresh shirt, but he didn't actually get to his feet. There was the fear that he would lose his quarry, but the real reason was fatigue. So he would move through the day in a haze of body odour? Tough.

When the movement happens it comes all at once. You wait for hours and hours. Your ass gets numb, your feet get cold, your brain seizes up completely. And then, when you're least ready, the guy you're tailing gets to his feet and strides purposefully off into the world. Norman Brown didn't go back to his room, he left the breakfast room still nibbling at a piece of toast and went straight to the front doors of the hotel. As he passed the reception desk he inclined his head towards the receptionist. Gus wasn't able to see his face, but whatever was on it stopped the woman in her tracks. She was about to answer the phone before Norman walked past, but when he did she just looked at it, let it ring. By the time Gus got to the door, Norman was striding across the front of the station towards the car park.

Gus had to hang back a long way, but he watched Norman open up an old Bedford van and drive it out of the car park and round to the entrance of the hotel. Looked completely incongruous, the van, which had been hand-painted in a kind of ultramarine, and the hotel which had a modern commercial frontage. Like Norman's suit and shirt. The guy seemed to have a talent for bringing things together which should never have been.

Lack of taste. Or lack of good taste, maybe. And yet, in a way that was all his own, Norman's lack of good taste didn't matter at all. Over and above his taste or his lack of it, he had a natural magnetism that was somehow encapsulated in every movement he made. It was there all the time in his swagger, the way he walked, but it was also there in small movements of his head. The way he had looked down and sideways at the girl outside Woolworths yesterday, and almost the same movement he had made this morning, to the receptionist at the hotel desk. It was as if both women had been physically stunned, not knocked out or manhandled in any way, but with something much subtler – they had both been subdued, touched in a way that left them looking round to find out what happened. But whatever it was touched them was out of sight, invisible.

Norman disappeared into the hotel, and after a few minutes he emerged again with a porter and several suitcases, his camera swinging from his neck. Gus got a taxi from the front of the railway station and told the driver to follow the blue van. 'Where's it going?' the cabbie asked.

Gus waited half a minute, give the guy time to think it through, maybe answer the question out of his own resources. But it didn't work.

'Where's it going?' he asked again.

'That's why I want you to follow it,' Gus told him. 'I don't know where it's going. I want to find out.'

The cabbie thought about that. 'Does he know? The guy who's driving it, does he know we're following him?'

'No. He doesn't know.'

'Because you could ask him,' the driver said. 'In case we lose him. You could ask him where he's going, then if we lose him, we can still both end up in the same place.'

'I don't want him to know,' Gus said patiently. 'I want you to stay back as far as possible without losing him. Then when he stops I want you to drive past and go round a corner, then stop and let me out.'

The driver thought again. Let out the clutch when the blue Bedford passed him, and eased his way into the stream of traffic. 'I get it now,' he said. 'Kind of a surprise.'

Norman stopped at the girl's house in Tang Hall, unloaded his suitcases. In all he spent maybe half an hour there, then he came back out and got in the van. As he got back in the van he looked at Gus on the other side of the street. For a moment Gus thought he'd been rumbled, but then the van pulled away from the kerb and headed back towards town. Gus scooted for the corner, retrieved his taxi, and took off after the van.

'What do you think about the murder?' the taxi driver asked.

'Sounded more brutal than it needed to be,' Gus said. 'For a robbery, I mean.'

'Be one of those cults, probably,' the taxi driver said. 'Charlie Manson types. They'll end up making a film about it.'

'Plenty of cops around,' Gus said, feeling that he was expected to keep the conversation going.

'Oh, God, yes,' the driver said. 'Clogging up the system.'

Norman dumped the van in the Lord Mayor's Walk car park and walked up towards the traffic lights. But he stopped outside Celia's house, on the other side of the street, under the city wall. Sat down on the grass with his camera around his neck, and looked over the road at the house. Even squinted at it through his camera. Could have taken a photograph. Gus couldn't be sure.

Gus walked on by. He didn't trust his senses. There was no reason that he could think of why this guy would stop outside Celia's house. There was no way he could even know of Celia's existence. He walked up to the traffic lights, crossed over the road, then walked back the way he had come. Passing the guy again so soon, and especially wearing this stupid checked shirt, was not at all a good idea. But Gus couldn't think of any other way of handling it. Lack of sleep and the sheer surprise of Norman sitting outside Celia's house combined to dull his thought processes.

Norman watched him approach, and he kept his eyes on him as he walked past. For the rest of his journey along the walk, Gus could feel Norman's eyes boring into his back. Gus didn't look behind him. He simply kept on walking until he got into town. He'd definitely blown it, and decided to call it a day.

As he walked he took out his dictaphone and spoke into it. He said: 'Norman Brown is sitting outside Celia's house at the moment. He knows it is Celia's house. He knows the house is connected with us. How? Why?'

He called his girlfriend, Karen, to confirm she was home, then walked out towards Blossom Street where she had a flat.

Karen, looking faintly old-fashioned in a long Indian silk skirt and beads round her neck, made him some coffee, and he had just finished telling her about his morning when the doorbell sounded.

chapter 20

Norman pulled all the papers out of the desk and slung them across the room. He was getting nowhere and he was getting mad.

The adrenalin was flowing now, he could feel it coming at him in a constant stream. How he liked it best. When he'd first noticed the guy was following him, the guy with the checked shirt, then it had come in spurts. Each spurt getting longer as he'd slowly turned the tables around. And now he was on top again, it was a constant stream.

The hippy woman stirred over in the corner, but she was well wrapped up in the curtain, and Norman had ripped her shirt off and stuffed it into her mouth. She wasn't going anywhere, and she didn't have a lot to say about it. She'd bit him as well, while he was stuffing her with the shirt, drawn blood, probably given him AIDS. Norman had looked at his hand then, at the teeth marks and the thin red line of blood, and he'd wondered what to do.

A bite was a bite, and if that's all it was he'd know what to do, probably smack her around a little, maybe cut her face, so she'd remember another time. But AIDS? What did you do to somebody who gave you AIDS? Norman didn't know. He didn't even know where the question came from. It was probably metaphysical, something like that. The name Aristotle flashed through his mind, swiftly followed by Freud.

In the top drawer of the desk he found a First Aid box and stemmed the flow of blood with a plaster. The hippy woman was kicking the curtains away from her. Her skirt had ridden up to her waist and one of her legs had dark and prominent veins protruding from the calf. Norman walked across the room towards her. She had hard skin on her feet. And on her thigh, high up, almost as far as her hip, there was a coffee-coloured birth mark that ran down to her knee. Or was it a bruise?

Norman stuck the gun in her ear. He made eye contact. Then he removed the gun and with his free hand he took hold of the small bunch of varicose veins in her calf. He had a vague idea of pulling the veins out, of somehow unravelling them, of causing pain to the woman in this way. But he couldn't do it. He was already somewhat nauseous from the bite to his hand, and the texture of the varicose veins repelled him. He let go. He stuck the gun under her chin. He established eye contact with her again. Saw the terror. Smiled so she could see his teeth.

Then he slowly squeezed the trigger and blew a hole through her head.

He watched Janet at the table in the tiny kitchen. She had an old pair of scales, the kind with individual weights, and she was weighing out the ingredients for dinner. You could tell right off she was going to be a hopeless cook, the kind who takes forever to produce a meal the cat would turn its back on. Except these cats turned their backs on nothing. You put something into their bowls and it disappeared immediately.

She had a packet of lentils, an onion, two tomatoes, one egg, a packet of butter, and some salt. She'd already put rice into a pan with water, and she kept leaving the table to go to the cooker and stir the rice. Norman couldn't imagine why she wanted to stir the rice. He'd never seen anyone stirring rice before. But there must be a reason. Maybe she'd bought stirring rice.

'What we having?' he asked.

'Lentil risotto,' Janet said.

Norman didn't interfere. He watched her. She was his woman and she was doing her best. No one could do more than that. He imagined her serving it up eventually, with candles and a couple of bottles of posh beer. She looking at him in trepidation, waiting for his verdict on the first mouthful. He tasting it, rolling it around in his mouth, letting his palate soak up the juices. Eventually he'd swallow it and tell her it was delicious, and Janet, she'd smile coyly, look away from him briefly, down at her plate, and when she lifted her eyes back to him again they'd be sparkling.

Norman shook his head. He looked at Janet surrounded by her ingredients. Well, he thought, it might be like that, or what'd probably happen, she'd make a hopeless mess of it and they'd get something from the Chinese.

He left her there and wandered away into the sitting room. He took the gun from the waistband of his trousers, unscrewed the silencer, unloaded, and proceeded to dismantle and clean the parts.

Orchid came over and leapt up on to his knee, and Norman shoved her back to the floor. She leapt to the arm of the chair and tried to push under his arm, an essentially friendly gesture. Norman punched her in the head, hard, and she leapt to the floor and scampered through to the kitchen.

The guy had been obvious, stupid. Now he came to think about it he had noticed the guy the day before. He couldn't remember where, but when he noticed him today it certainly wasn't for the first time. Norman had just opened the blue Bedford van when he saw the checked shirt on the other side of the car park. After that there was a checked shirt behind him every time he moved, at the entrance to the hotel, outside Janet's flat in Tang Hall. Norman had deliberately sat down on the grass outside the house Squishsquash used, and by that time the guy must have realized he'd blown it. So

Norman turned the tables on him, followed him through the town and out to that flat near the cinema.

Norman had kicked his heels for a few minutes, then walked into the entrance and knocked on the door. He had taken the gun out of his holster for insurance purposes. He didn't intend using it, except maybe to scare the guy. He only wanted to know what was going on, why he was being followed. But when the guy opened the door he looked like he was gonna start shouting.

The situation wasn't right. The guy didn't move right, maybe that was it, or look right, or act right? It wasn't clear what was wrong. There were some long unexplained silences, where the guy had looked at Norman, and Norman had looked back, then the guy had turned his head and seemed like he was gonna start shouting, yelling for the police, maybe. Norman couldn't remember all the things that had happened. But he knew the situation wasn't right, so he lifted the gun and shot the checked-shirt guy in the face.

And the blast of it lifted the checked-shirt guy right off his feet and took him back against the wall in the passage, pasted him up there for a few moments, until he came unglued from the wall and fell to the floor. That was when the hippy woman came out of another door and ran along the passage howling. Norman's first impulse was to shoot her too, shut her up.

But he restrained himself, took hold of her by the upper arm and chopped her around the head a couple of times with the gun.

Then he dragged her along the passage into a living area, pulled the curtains down from the window and wrapped them around her arms and legs. When she started moaning again he pulled her shirt off and stuffed as much of it as he could down her throat. Then he clubbed her again with the barrel of the gun.

What he had intended to do was ask her who the guy was, the checked-shirt guy, but because she was so much trouble he forgot all about it until she was unconscious. So he went through the desk, looking for clues. But there weren't any clues because what it looked like was that this was the hippy

124

woman's flat and the checked-shirt guy was just a visitor. There were no men's clothes in the cupboards, no shaving gear in the bathroom, and the guy didn't have a wallet or any documents in his pockets. Just a ten-pound note and some coins. He had a Walkman, though, which Norman took along with him, thinking it would be useful to play his Tina Turner tape on. Norman dug the Walkman out of his jacket pocket and pressed the Stop/Eject button. But what was in there was not a normal-sized tape, but one of those mini tapes, MC-30, whatever they called them. And there were no earphones on the machine. Norman shoved the tape back in and pressed the Play button, but no sound came out. Nothing at all. He put the machine on the table and sighed. You think you've scored a Walkman, then you find you're right back where you started. Nowheres.

Orchid returned to the sitting room and curled up at Norman's feet. Norman stuck the barrel of the gun in her ear and pulled the trigger. The gun wasn't loaded. Norman smiled down at the cat. 'One day,' he said, 'you're not gonna be so lucky.'

There was still the question of Squishsquash and Mr Detective to sort out. Norman hadn't thought about that yet. It was difficult to know what to think about it. A guy could start to get paranoid with things like this happening around him. Like, people following you. And the guy you hire to find Snow White, you find out he's got another woman you thought was yours for the taking.

Norman finished cleaning the gun and loaded it. He stood and tried to stamp on Orchid's paw as he moved away from the chair. But the cat saw it coming and got out of the way. Norman nodded at the picture of John Lennon above the fireplace and went back into the kitchen to watch Janet some more. She had a timer on the kitchen table and when it rang she lifted the lid off the pan of rice and stirred it with a wooden spoon. Then she put the lid back on the pan and reset the timer for another two minutes. She brushed a wisp of hair from her eyes, glanced nervously at Norman, and then returned to the recipe book, running her finger along the text as she read. 'These are supposed to be Egyptian lentils,' she said. 'But the people in the shop didn't know where they were from. They're not very helpful. If they know the answer then they're helpful and pleasant, but if they don't know the answer, or they're not sure, they get edgy and make out as though you're being fussy.' She weighed out exactly four ounces of lentils. 'I hate that,' she said, returning to the recipe book. 'One onion. How're you supposed to know if it means a small onion or a gigantic onion? Even when it says one small onion, or one large onion it's a problem, because you don't know if what they mean by a large onion is the same as what you mean by a large onion. So it just confuses you.'

'You got any beer?' Norman asked.

Janet shook her head. 'This is health food,' she said.

Norman sat on a kitchen chair and sighed. 'Listen, Janet,' he said. 'Beer *is* health food. In the medieval ages, 'fore the industrial revolution, if we'd been alive then, like peasants, running round in rags, covered in sores, all that stuff. You know why we'd be covered in sores? Have great boils on your face, maybe half your nose eaten away? You know why that was? Because you didn't have a balanced diet. Not enough vitamins and minerals and traces. Not enough of anything. Plenty of meat, I think they had that, but you can't live healthy on meat, you gotta have the fresh fruit and the vegetables. Otherwise, scurvy, like in the pirate films. You end up going out of your skull, turning into a howling psychopath.

'So the only thing they ate or drank in those days that actually contained all the proteins and vitamins and all the stuff which you now call health food, you know what that was? It was beer. That's why everybody drank beer, made beer and drank it. 'Cause it was full of good stuff. I think the average lifespan in those days, maybe it was twenty or twenty-five, thirty years, if you lived to be thirty you'd be like an old woman. You'd be a grandma by then. Teeth falling out, bald, half blind. You'd be a real fucking mess.'

Janet looked up from her recipe book and stared at him. 'Even with the beer?' she asked.

'Yeah, they were,' he said. 'I've seen pictures.'

'So the beer couldn't have been that healthy, then,' Janet said. 'I mean if people were falling apart by the time they was thirty.'

Norman sighed. 'Jesus,' he said. 'Why don't people listen? I'm explaining two different points to you here. First point is about the beer being like health food, that is full of healthy ingredients. That's one thing, that's complete in itself, without having to say anything else about it. I mean, it's easy enough to understand, even for a pinhead like you. Am I right? Can you understand that?'

'Yes, Norman.'

'Good. And the second point I'm trying to make here, is that people didn't last long in those days, like if they lived to thirty, to be thirty years old, they would already be toothless old crones, old hags. Jesus, Janet, there was sabre-toothed tigers and great mammoths wandering round, specially in the north here. Just think about the walls round the city, here, round York. You know why they built these walls all the way round the city? Why they built them at all, and why they built them so thick? No? Well, I'm gonna tell you if you wanna get educated. It was to keep the fucking wild animals out, stop people being eaten alive. 'Cause that was what happened then, people were being eaten alive both inside and outside. Inside they was being eaten by lack of nutrition (except for the beer), that's why they might have only half a nose, or be going blind, all the boils and warts and stuff. And outside they was being eaten by wild animals, wolves, you name it, that prowled around in the night. There was wild cats as well, lots of them. They'd eat the little kids. And during the day as well. Loads of people got taken during the day.

'And if they didn't drink the beer they wouldn't live to be any age at all. Probably by the time they were fifteen, sixteen years old they'd already be dead.' Norman got out of the chair and walked round the table to Janet. He stood in front of her and rapped on her forehead with his knuckles. 'Anybody at home?' he asked. 'Can you understand what I'm saying?'

Janet half smiled. 'I don't have any beer,' she said. 'If you want beer, you'll have to go out for it.'

chapter 21

A few days earlier Sam had jerked off in the shower first thing in the morning. Today was different. The day he jerked off he worked out that it was nearly seven months since he'd been with a woman, and it was that recollection which had led to what was known in his youth as self-abuse. Today it was more than seven months since he'd been with a woman, but the way things were shaping up with Jennie, perhaps it wouldn't be long before the abstinence came to a sticky end. The thought put a smile on his face.

The day he'd jerked off in the shower he'd woken up feeling much the same as he felt today, but then he'd got into a warm shower and done the business. He was older now, and had learned that maturity consists of the ability to defer gratification. Today he got into a cold shower. Colder'n a witch's tit, he thought as he immediately leapt out of it again. He turned up the heat to lukewarm, and stepped back inside the rain. OK, there had been a time when he would have stood the cold shower. Even now, if he had had to, he could have stood it. Gritted his teeth and stood there. Anything he had to do, he could do it.

'In the shower?' Gus had said. 'Bit crude, isn't it?'

A marked difference, Sam reflected at the time, to the reaction such a revelation would have elicited from the members of the men's group. Masturbation, in the men's group, was regarded as a norm. A natural release. Some members regarded it as close to an art form.

'Crude,' Sam had said to Gus. 'Not as crude as if I'd done it in the bath? I mean are there circumstances where it would be more or less crude? Come on, Gus. Let's hear it.'

But by now Gus wanted to turn the issue into a joke. The

trouble with Gus was that he'd put his erection anywhere: in, on, or near a woman. It didn't seem to matter if the woman was tall or short, thin or fat, sick or healthy. Perhaps she had to be alive? Sam had never actually witnessed Gus giving his erection to a dead woman, so he wouldn't swear to the fact. But he was a fair man, and to be fair, he thought, perhaps Gus would draw the line at a dead woman.

But what did Gus know? He had a permanent partner. Not only did he have a permanent partner but he was also having an affair with someone else. In a position like that it might easily appear that jerking off in the shower first thing in the morning was crude. The guy couldn't begin to imagine what it might be like to have an erection with nowhere to go.

He wondered briefly if Gene Hackman ever jerked off in the shower. Probably not, film stars paid people to do it for them.

When Sam had been married or had a more or less permanent partner he hadn't been troubled in this way. Except with Brenda, his second wife, who'd used sex as a weapon. She'd withdrawn all privileges after the first month, but at the same time ensured that Sam was in the room when she dressed or undressed, which she did with great frequency. She'd parade around the house in a cloud of Body Shop perfume, wisps of lace and satin, flashes of forbidden flesh. Miss Integrity. Subtlety was her middle name. But Brenda and her ways were all now in the past. Thank you, Jesus.

It was like having a missionary on the doorstep. A real dedicated pro, a Mormon, say, one of those. You couldn't get rid of either of them. The hard-on and the missionary on the doorstep both had God on their side. Why should they listen to you?

It wasn't as if you could reason with a hard-on, say, 'Look, I'm sorry, but this is just not convenient at the moment. Do you wanna come back tomorrow? Or maybe next week some time? Yeah, that would be altogether better. Come back next week.'

It was like a submarine. Lurking about there in the unfathomable depths. Out of sight, out of mind. But suddenly it wants to surface. There are no warnings, or maybe there have been some warnings, but you haven't paid them any heed. Now, suddenly, the thing wants to surface, like it's run out of oxygen or something. Anyway, it's coming up. And it's coming up fast. What it wants, what would be oxygen to it, is straight sexual intercourse. But there's no way it can have that because it's dependent on Sam to furnish a woman with the same desires and expectations, and he hasn't got one. So what this erection wants and expects is a complete no-no.

Sam could also ignore it. Pretend that it isn't there. So he'll walk funny all day, be damned uncomfortable, and people'll be watching him.

And the only other possibility, the third possibility, is to jerk off in the shower. Which is crude. It's not crude to walk around with a big lump in the front of your trousers, walking with your knees bent. That's not crude. Oh, no. That's really sophisticated. Guys who do that have really got their act together. They wouldn't even think of jerking off, let alone jerking off in the shower. If you really concentrate on it, you can ignore the erection altogether, and you can use a jock strap, tie the bastard down, whatever, flay it to death. At the end of the day you can walk down the street almost normal. No one would even know you were in pain.

Geordie came downstairs with Barney while Sam was cooking breakfast. Whenever he lived alone Sam ate muesli for breakfast, or sometimes just rolled oats in milk. When Geordie moved into the flat upstairs and they started eating breakfast together, Sam had got into the habit of cooking bacon and eggs, and occasionally more, like fried bread, sometimes mushrooms or tomatoes or beans. Since the news about his blood pressure, Sam had continued cooking the fry-up for Geordie, because without it Geordie started on what he called his withdrawal symptoms, but Sam only made himself a couple of slices of toast, and ate it with a smear of marmalade. He still made up around a pint and a half of coffee, which the two of them drank in the hour before leaving for the office.

While Sam put the food on the table, Geordie took a tape

out of a recently acquired wall unit, and slipped it into the deck. He pushed the Play button and stood watching it until Paul Simon's voice came from the speaker. Sam stopped by the table and cocked his head a little to one side. He narrowed his eyes to concentrate, then smiled when he recognized the song, and sang along with the chorus, 'Still crazy . . .'

'Jesus,' he said. 'Haven't played it for years.'

'It's been invisible,' Geordie said. 'Every time you get a tape out of there, that tape is staring you in the face. But you don't see it, 'cause it's invisible.' He opened a can of dog food and spooned it into Barney's bowl, then he sat down at the table and attacked the egg and bacon.

Sam reached for the marmalade and pulled it over to him. 'Why is that, oh maestro?' he said.

Geordie spoke through bacon. 'Because,' he said, 'it's not in your head. Other things are in your head, like the tape you might be looking for, or what you're gonna do tomorrow, or sex, or food, or whatever, your granny, or the state of the world. But not this tape, this particular tape. It's not in your head, and therefore you can't see it. It's invisible.'

'So,' said Sam, 'it's not possible to see anything unless it exists as a concept?'

Geordie looked confused. 'Dunno. I haven't thought that far.'

'But that's what you just said,' said Sam.

'What I was thinking,' Geordie explained, 'is how sometimes things are so visible, so much part of the landscape, that you can't see anything else. And then other times, it could be the same thing that blocked out everything else, *that* thing becomes invisible. You lose sight of it, and it becomes invisible. Know what I mean?'

'Yeah.' Sam nodded and chewed toast and marmalade. Donna, Sam's first wife, had been like that, so visible he couldn't see anything else. Then when she was hit by the car she disappeared for ever. He looked over the table at Geordie, and Geordie looked back at him as if he understood, but no words passed between them.

'My mother was like that,' Geordie said. 'When I was little

131

she was always there.' He shook his head and speared what remained of an egg with his fork. 'I went back to Sunderland once,' he said. 'Did I tell you that? I found the house where we used to live, me and my mother and brother, before she did her disappearing act. There was a family in the house. Little kids, one boy and lots of girls. I watched them for a while.' He looked down at his plate, and over by the sink Barney finished up his meal and walked over to where Geordie was sitting at the table. He nuzzled against the boy's leg, and Geordie reached down and patted the dog's head. Then Geordie looked up at Sam again and gave him a false smile. 'There was no sign of my mother,' he said. 'It was really disappointing. There was no indication that she, or me, or any of us had ever been there, or anywhere near the place. Know what I mean? It was like we'd never happened.'

'You'll have me in tears in a minute,' Sam said.

Geordie smiled, and Sam thought he looked like a biker who'd just had his Harley repossessed. He hung on to the eye contact.

Eventually Geordie gave in, and his smile softened into something genuine. 'Go to hell,' he said.

'I'm on my way,' Sam told him.

'I don't feel like that about my mother any more,' Geordie said. 'I know I used to, well, I used to blame her for running off and leaving us behind. But I don't feel like that any more. I can still remember times before, when I was very small. Must've been a toddler. And I know she loved me then. And I've got pictures in my head, I know this sounds stupid, but I've got these pictures in my head of her looking at me, or of her bending down to tend me. If I'd fallen down and cut my knee, say, or if I was ill. And her face was right up close to mine, so close I couldn't tell where I ended and she began. And in the picture I'm her and she's me, there's no separation between us. Together we're an *it*.

'I talked to Celia about it,' he continued, 'and she said that's what love is. She said it sounded like religious love to her. Sufism or Pantheism, something like that.

'Anyway, so when she went away, I don't think it was because she didn't love us any more. She probably thought we'd be better off without her.' He reached down and patted Barney's head again.

'And what do you think?' Sam asked.

'I think she was wrong,' Geordie said. 'If it was up to me there'd've been no choice. I'd rather have had her under any circumstances than not have her.' He shook his head. 'And you know what else I think?' He paused for congratulation on being able to. 'I think she's trying to find us now. I mean, not all the time, she's not like desperately trying to find us, like tramping the streets of Sunderland. But she's sorry she went away, and she'd really like to turn the clock back. And I bet she's been back to that house, and asked the people there, that family, if they know where I am.'

'Did you leave a message with them?'

'No,' Geordie said. 'I didn't have a message.' He laughed, realizing the stupidity of his remark. 'I didn't have an address then. I couldn't leave an address or anything, you know, like a telephone number or somebody she could contact. But I can now, and I'm gonna do it.'

'What would you do?' Sam said. 'What would you do if she walked in here? Or if you were walking along the road and you bumped into her?'

'What, now?'

'Yeah, today.'

He smiled at the thought. 'I'd be really excited,' he said. 'But I'd stay cool. At first I'd stay really cool, and like, feel it out.' He stood and walked round the table. Barney followed him, maybe thinking it was time for his walk, but Geordie was distracted with the idea of his mother. 'I'd put my arms round her,' he said. 'And my cheek next to hers. And I'd squeeze her gently at first, then a little harder.' He began acting it out as he spoke. Sam watched him manipulating the invisible woman. 'Then I'd kiss her on the forehead, maybe on the eyes. I don't know, but I'd hold her at arm's length and have a good look at her. Then I'd hug her again, really hard this time, and swing her off her feet. And I'd say that word, that name, *Mum*, and I'd say it over and over again. *Mum, mum, mum.*' Geordie closed his eyes to get closer to his images. 'We'd probably go for a walk,' he said. 'All of us

133

together, with Barney. And I'd show her round the town, all the places I know. Then we'd come back here and I'd make her a cup of tea, play her some tapes, show her some of the books I've read.' He turned to the older man and said, 'Hell, Sam, it'd be magic.'

Geordie did the driving. Sam sat next to him and made fists out of both hands, felt his face and neck tense up and become immovable. 'Just relax,' he told Geordie. 'Take it easy. We're in no hurry.'

The kid was wearing his leather jacket with the bullet hole in the back. Both Sam and Celia on separate occasions had offered to have it mended, but Geordie refused. 'I don't mind having a bullet hole in it,' he said. 'It's fine by me.' Didn't mind! He loved it. Told everyone he met. Took the jacket off and showed them the hole. 'Went right through,' he would say. 'Nearly fuckin' killed me.'

Apart from the bullet hole it was a nice jacket. Made somewhere special by a tailor who knew what he was doing. It hadn't been made for Geordie, but it suited him better than the original owner. Soft brown leather, fingertip length, just about a perfect fit. Geordie wore it with the collar turned up, hands thrust deep into the pockets, and it made him walk with a little swagger, his head and shoulders going from side to side rhythmically like a singer with real cool.

Geordie engaged first gear and pulled away from the kerb in a series of small leaps. He glanced over at Sam and gave him a reassuring smile, then snapped quickly back to the road. He sat bolt upright, his chin almost touching the steering wheel. He glanced in the mirror, quickly changed through second and third, and took off. Sam had dispensed with prayer several years before, except in emergencies. He began this one with the word *please*. If supernatural intervention was at all possible, he wanted to see it happen now.

It was only a short journey to the office and the roads were remarkably free of traffic. Geordie kept the speed between twenty-eight and thirty-two miles an hour on the straight patches, gunning the Volvo forward to corners and traffic lights. He still had to grasp the concept of pedestrian crossings, and today for the first time he had hit on the idea of approaching these with his horn blaring. Tourists and commuters clung to the edge of the road and the pavement, trying to make themselves invisible, only growing in stature and boldness when the Volvo had passed. Then they came out into the rearview mirror, shaking their fists and mouthing obscenities.

Sam thought the car with the flashing blue light wanted to get past them, and he sat up higher in his seat and said, 'Geordie.'

'It's OK.' Geordie said, and indicated left. 'I'll get out of his way.'

'No,' Sam said, but it was too late. Geordie was committed to the left turn by now. The car with the blue flashing light tucked in tightly behind the Volvo, and turned left with it.

'Christ,' said Sam. 'Pull over. Just stop.'

'No,' said Geordie. 'He wants to get past.'

Sam touched his arm. 'Stop,' he said.

Geordie hit the brake.

The car with the flashing blue light hit the Volvo.

Sam hit the windscreen.

There was a period of time which had Sam and Geordie together rubbing their noses. Both were bleeding. It must have taken only a few seconds for this period to pass, because the next thing Sam remembered was a tap on the front of the windscreen. He looked up to find a lump of dough wearing a policeman's uniform standing in front of the car. There was another one off to the side of the car, and they seemed to want Sam and Geordie to get out. Neither of the policemen looked happy.

Sam felt in his pocket for tobacco. Then remembered he'd given it up. This was not the right time to stop smoking. He wound the window down and the policeman at the windscreen asked him to step out of the car. As he was getting out he heard the other policeman ask Geordie if he was Sam Turner. Geordie said, 'No. I'm just the driver. That's Mr Turner.'

'I hope you've got a driving licence and insurance,' the policeman said.

'I'm a learner,' Geordie told him. 'That's why I've got the Ls on the front and back of the car.'

'Well, do yourself a favour,' said the policeman. 'Don't apply for the test yet. You'll fail it.'

'Must say something about your driving as well,' Geordie said. 'It was you drove into us.'

The other cop asked Sam for some ID, and when he'd seen it he asked Sam to accompany him to the police station.

They jumped the cars apart and Sam went with the lump of dough in the police car, while Geordie and the other cop followed in the Volvo. As soon as they arrived Sam was shown into a small interview room and left sitting at a bare desk. They posted a tall, gangly and ridiculously young policeman at the door. He didn't speak. Sam assumed that he was there to stop Sam committing suicide, so he smiled and asked him, 'Are you here to stop me committing suicide?' The policeman still didn't speak. For the first five minutes Sam half expected Geordie to arrive, but then realized that they were keeping them separate.

But why? Geordie's driving skills hadn't been exactly spectacular this morning, but splitting them up and giving them the cold isolation bit seemed like a slight over-reaction. Sam shrugged and settled himself to wait even longer. There was little point in trying to figure how a cop's mind works. That day, long ago, when God was handing out the brains, the cops in the world weren't even in line; they came the next day, some of them, the ones who could find their way.

The two who came in next, Chief Inspector Delany and his sidekick Sergeant Thomson, were old adversaries of Sam Turner. On several occasions Sam had had to explain to them that they were the dumbest people he had met in his life, even by cop standards. But they didn't listen. Delany especially didn't listen. He was a talker.

'Do you know Angus Scott?' he asked.

'Gus? You know I do,' said Sam. Why were they asking him about Gus? Sam suddenly felt uncomfortable. Cold. But he couldn't make the connection. 'What's he done?' he asked.

Delany smiled. 'I think we should be asking the questions, Mr Turner.' He was a weasel of a man. Looking not unlike Charlie Chaplin in the role of *The Great Dictator*. He had that same floppy bit of hair as Hitler, the bit at the front, and it was the same colour. His moustache was different, thinner, meaner. The look he cultivated was thin and mean, the image he tried to project; but what came across was the clown.

'Do you know Karen Ludendorff?' Delany asked.

Sam shook his head. 'No. What's Gus supposed to have done?'

'German young lady?' Delany continued. 'Lives in a flat in Blossom Street?'

'I don't know her,' said Sam, thinking back to the phone call. *A sweet voice, a low voice, a voice that had waited and thought about it before picking up the telephone and dialling the number. Something else as well, a barely concealed Teutonic accent.* Karen Ludendorff. Gus's girlfriend. It must be her.

Delany half looked behind him at Sergeant Thomson, and Thomson came forward and sat on the edge of the desk. He placed a photograph of a blonde girl on the desk and span it round so Sam could see it the right way up. 'To jog your memory, sir. Mr Turner, sir,' he said.

There was little in it, but if anything, Sam disliked Thomson more than Delany. Thomson was a head taller than Delany, and was in the habit of wearing suits with pin-stripes and wide turn-ups. He believed in procedure. Statistically, he liked to say, statistically, plodding gets you there in the end, more often than other methods. And he used the word 'sir' like a cosh. Women he called 'ma'am', and unless they were completely insensitive they felt soiled afterwards.

Sam looked at the photograph and remembered the voice again. Yes, that would be her, Gus's type. The kind of girl he was a sucker for. The kind of girl who always looked like a virgin, but never was, and never had been. The kind of girl who needed men, rather than a man. There had been a succession of girls like this in Gus's past. Sam had met some of them, and others he had only heard about. But this one, the girl in the photograph, she would have fitted the description of almost any of them. They'd all of them been looking for Gus. And Gus, he'd been waiting for them. Born for them.

'It doesn't jog my memory,' Sam told Thomson. 'I've never seen her before. She's pretty. I'd remember.'

'What about the man who ran the gun club?' said Delany. 'And his wife. Did you know them?'

'The couple who were killed?' said Sam. 'The couple in Haxby? What's going on, Delany? How's Gus mixed up with that? What are you trying to pull?'

Delany smiled at Sam and counted on his fingers. 'Five questions,' he said. 'And all in a row.' The smile withered. 'We ask,' he said. 'And you answer. OK?'

'Your counting's coming on a treat,' Sam told him. 'Keep this up and you'll be into double figures before you know it.'

Delany ignored him. 'Your associate,' he said, 'Angus Scott. What's he working on at the moment?'

'I'm not answering any more questions without my solicitor,' said Sam. 'You've got something slimy up your sleeve, and I'm not giving you anything till I know what it is.'

'Please yourself,' said Delany. 'Sergeant Thomson, take Mr Turner to the telephone and let him make his call, will you?'

Sam dialled Celia's number and breathed a sigh of relief when she picked up the phone. 'Any possibility of bringing me some tobacco into the police station?' he asked.

'I don't think I should encourage you to smoke, Sam,' Celia told him.

'OK, forget it. But I still seem to have a little problem here, Celia,' he said. 'You got a minute?'

'I'm not going anywhere,' she said.

Sam knew the feeling well.

chapter 22

Marie Dickens had finished the medicine round. There were seven patients on the ward waiting for BP and temperature checks. She had done the first one when she noticed the police. Two of them, a tall male PC and a shorter WPC, walking along the corridor in that way policemen walk, like they can't help but be in charge.

The stethoscope was not working properly again, and Marie was having difficulty reading the BP of one of her male patients. Everything was falling apart in the health service. There was no money to replace anything. Tiles fell off the wall and were swept up and thrown away. The hole in the wall remained. Equipment of all kinds died and disappeared. Went to heaven. It certainly went somewhere. Was never seen again. Never replaced. They were low on blankets at the moment, and were thankful for the hot weather. The winter was going to be bad, though. A fight against hypothermia. People told her it was even worse in education. Marie didn't see how it could be. She couldn't understand why the government were still in power. She never met anyone who supported them. Everyone thought they were sleazy and disreputable. Yet they were still there.

She tapped the stethoscope and tried again, then threw it to one side. She smiled at her patient, a man who had seen better days and would not see them again. 'No good,' she told him. 'I'll see if I can find another one. Back in a minute.' She left the room and made her way to the nurses' station to get another stethoscope that also worked only occasionally.

As she approached along the corridor the WPC turned her head slightly, and something in Marie knew that they'd come for her. The movement of the WPC's head was so slight most people would have missed it completely, and yet there was a whole world in it. It left Marie in no doubt whatsoever. In her mind she repeated the last words she had spoken to her patient, *Back in a minute*, and even as the words were passing through her mind she knew that she wouldn't be back in a minute at all. She didn't know when she would be back.

It was at that moment, when the WPC's head made the slight turn, that time began slipping away. There were certain key words that enabled her somehow to hang on to a semblance of reality. Angus Scott was not even a name she recognized. Not at first. She never thought of Gus as Angus. He wasn't an Angus to her. So when they asked her, Do you know Angus Scott? she had shaken her head and said no before realizing that she did know him, that she lived with him.

Then they said they'd found a body, and there was the word *accident*, and the name of the woman, Karen Ludendorff, though they wouldn't be drawn on Gus's connection with her. When they arrived at the police station there were others who mentioned Sam and Geordie and the gun dealer in Haxby who had been murdered with his wife. And Marie thought they were keeping her conscious on sound bytes (or was it bites? She didn't know). She thought maybe she'd lost her mind. She was the only one here dressed as a nurse, and she hadn't had time to cry.

There seemed to be some reality to the fact that Gus was dead. Though she hadn't seen him. Hadn't seen his body. When she thought about it she hadn't seen his body for some time. Over the last weeks the thought had come to her that he was having another affair. But every time that thought occurred she brushed it to one side. Bought a bar of chocolate.

They talked to her for hours, what seemed like hours. They asked her the same questions over and over again. From time to time one or the other of them would put his face very close to hers. So close she would see the emerging blue stubble of beard, the tiny pores and stress lines. They were nearly all male – more or less. Usually a token woman in the room, somewhere near the corner. They didn't believe that she didn't know the answers. Her mind wandered away by itself. In the corridor outside the room where they talked to her a tile had come away from the wall and disappeared, leaving a hole. A perfectly tiled wall with a hole in it. The tile had come off and gone to heaven.

And Marie smiled when she thought about their handcuffs, about what happened when they became faulty, or someone lost a key. Did they use rope instead?

Everything happened at once when they told her she could go. She walked through a door and Celia came forward and put her arms round her, and Marie's face was suddenly wet, her eyes streaming. Celia was saying, 'There, there. You poor thing. What have they done to you?' Celia's arms didn't reach all the way around Marie. Marie wished she wasn't carrying so much weight. She'd really have to do something about it.

Marie was trying to brush the tears away from her face and regulate her breathing. It seemed like her lungs were too small and they couldn't contain enough oxygen to enable her to get through the immediate little tasks, like crying and breathing and looking at Celia and walking a few steps to the wooden bench against the wall.

And when she got to the bench and sat down with Celia next to her she knew her life had changed for ever and Gus was dead and with him had gone all the dreams and plans of a lifetime. And in one way her life up to this point had been a complete lie, because nothing that had been dreamed in it would ever now come to fruition. And then in another way, in lots of ways, more than she could think of, her life had not even begun, never begun. Not until now. On this small wooden bench in the police station she was born.

Then Geordie came through the door in his leather jacket with the bullet hole in the back, and he looked confused as well. And shortly after him came Sam, with the man who was a solicitor, whose name Marie couldn't remember, but thought might be Forester.

And Sam came over to the bench and went down on his knees in front of her, and his face was also wet with tears.

141

Sam Turner, the big constant. Crying like a man.

Marie was a nurse and knew pain and tears. Men didn't know how to cry. When they lost control they felt guilty and the original motivation for the tears got lost. That's why they made a noise about it. And that's why it was such a job to get them to stop.

chapter 23

Norman was still sleeping. Janet was sore and she went to the penicillin factory and rubbed more cream into both her front and back bottom. Men with four balls seemed to need twice as much sex as other men. She hoped the soreness would pass. She thought it would as she adjusted to Norman's demands. You had to get used to a man. To his particular ways. None of them were angels.

Except maybe for John Lennon.

He would be an angel now. But there was no real way of knowing if he was an angel when he was alive. It seemed like he was, from what she'd heard, what she'd read. And she loved his voice on those songs, the way it reached right inside you, way down there where babies lived before they were born. In the womb.

Janet liked to think about John Lennon. It was comforting to conjure him up and to imagine all the nice things he could be and was capable of being. But she knew he wasn't real. That he was dead. That he would never really be with her. Not like Norman.

If she had to choose. If she really had to choose and there was no way of getting out of it, she'd choose Norman. She'd prefer John Lennon, and she was sure, absolutely sure that John Lennon would be kinder to her. But Norman was real. Janet thought she must be a realist.

She also knew something else. John Lennon looked like a much better prospect since she'd met Norman. Before

Norman came along John Lennon had been just a voice on some records and a poster on the wall. He had been present in fragments of dreams. But now that Norman had arrived in her life John Lennon had fleshed out, become more real. Janet knew why that was. It was because Norman wasn't perfect. He wasn't exactly what she had dreamed of when she thought about a man. So she used the image of John Lennon to fill out the parts that Norman couldn't reach.

She touched some of the cream to her nipples. One of them had bled earlier. It was not bleeding now, but still raw. She shrugged and smiled. It was homoeopathic cream, so it would heal in twice the time.

She went back down to the flat and looked through her recipe book for inspiration. There were several possibilities but she kept returning to the rice and lentil roll. She had not cooked it before, but she had all the ingredients apart from the parsley. She could nip out for that now, while Norman was still sleeping. He wouldn't even know she'd been out. Then by the time he awoke she'd have the thing under way, that good aroma you always get when the onions start cooking. Put him in a real good mood. The man opens his eyes, sniffs that cooking going on, his woman's in the kitchen wearing a little apron. He knows he's got a good thing going.

Janet went out for the parsley. When she talked about Norman, if, for example, someone some time were to ask her about him – or if she met someone in a shop, or someone she knew vaguely asked her if she had a man – she wouldn't tell them he was a gun salesman, even though that was the truth. Well, he even had the samples. Though he didn't take the samples out with him when he went selling. Sometimes he took one or the other, but not the whole case. Anyway, what Janet would do when the question came up, she'd just say he was a salesman, or maybe a sales manager. That wouldn't be a lie, just missing out the bit about the guns.

She wasn't sure if she liked guns or not now. Before she met Norman she definitely hadn't liked guns. But now that Norman had shown her the guns, and explained to her how some of them worked, she wasn't sure at all. Some of the guns felt nice in your hand, like they'd been made to fit a hand. And they were so slick, so smooth, and the parts worked together so nicely, like when you took them apart or loaded or unloaded them. There was something real nice about a gun. Not the idea of a gun, that wasn't nice at all. But the weight of it, the way it fit so snugly into your hand, that was nice.

Oh, and she would say, later, when they found out he was a gun salesman. *If* they found out. Say if she said he was a sales manager, and then whoever she was talking to said, 'Really. What does he sell?' Then she'd tell them it was guns. And she'd say, 'Oh, yes, Norman's main customers are members of the farming community.'

Because they were, farmers. That's what farmers were, after all, members of the farming community.

When she returned with the parsley she peeled and sliced an onion. Sliced it finely. Then she began cooking it gently in a little butter. She kept poking it with the tip of a knife. The recipe said to cook it until tender. She combined it with the rice and lentils and tomatoes and got it into the oven before Norman opened his eyes.

When he came stumbling through to the kitchen, Janet presented him with a drawing she had made.

'Good smell,' he said, holding the drawing in his hand. 'What's this?'

'It's for business,' Janet told him. 'It's a gun.'

'I can see that,' he said. 'You're a good drawer. Looks just like a gun.'

The drawing of the gun was encircled with double lines, and around the circle were the words: 'Buy a Gun and get a Bang out of life.'

'What, like an advert?'

'Yes,' she said. 'I didn't make it up. It's like a real advert. Mark Chapman, he was the man who shot John Lennon. He lived in Honolulu, and the gun he used, he bought it from a shop which had this sign above the door.'

'Is this true?' Norman said.

'Yes. It's the truth. I've read all about it. He bought a five-shot two-inch-barrel Charter Arms Undercover .38 Special revolver, but no ammunition. And he killed John

Lennon outside the entrance to the Dakota, in New York, on 8 December 1980. He waited for him and when John Lennon arrived with his wife he shot him dead.'

'A five-shot two-inch-barrel . . .' Norman struggled to remember what she said.

'Charter Arms Undercover .38 Special revolver. That's what he used,' she said.

'That's not the best gun in the world,' Norman said. 'It's just a cheap gun.'

'It's small, though,' Janet said. 'Good gun for a murderer.'

'Maybe,' said Norman. 'And he didn't buy any ammo?'

'No.'

Norman laughed. 'So what did he shoot him with? Peanuts?'

'No,' Janet said. 'He got some dum-dums from a policeman.'

'You're kidding me.'

'It's true,' Janet said. 'He knew this guy in the police force. And he got the dum-dums from him so he could shoot John Lennon.'

Norman shook his head and turned a full circle on one foot. Where did she get it all from?

'So, anyway,' Janet said, 'I did that drawing, that advert, because of this double murder the other day. They said on the radio that everyone's afraid to go out. And if they're afraid to go out, that'll be real good for your business. You'll have all the farming community ringing up to buy more guns, because they're too afraid to go out, and their wives are too afraid to go out. Do you see what I mean? It'll mean you'll be really busy.'

'What we eating?' Norman asked her. 'And when's it ready?'

'It's a surprise,' Janet told him. 'It'll be ready in exactly,' she looked at the clock, 'forty-five minutes.'

'That long? I'll be dead by then. I'll have starved to death.'

'You want to listen to some John Lennon songs?' She led him through to the sitting room and pushed him down on to the couch. 'You just sit there and rest,' she told him. 'I'll give you a shout when it's ready.' She put her copy of *Rubber*

Soul on the turntable and lifted the arm past the first track. 'First track's Ringo,' she said. 'This's John.' Lennon's voice filled the room with the opening lines of 'Girl'.

Orchid, sitting on the chair opposite Norman, opened her eyes and looked at him. Norman stared back, turned up his nose.

Janet handed the record sleeve to Norman, and he looked at it about half a minute before placing it on the floor. 'They look like dinosaurs,' he said. 'But it's a good song.'

Janet retrieved the sleeve from the floor and placed it next to her turntable. She smiled to herself as she looked down at it. 'They're not dinosaurs,' she said. ' Just need a haircut.'

'After we've eaten,' Norman told her, 'we could go out. Go to a pub in the town. Somewhere with music, things going on. You could put on a nice dress, get done up a bit. We could have a skinful.'

Janet smiled at him. 'Like a couple,' she said. 'We'll be like a couple.'

'Yeah,' Norman said. 'There'll be two of us.'

'No, Norman. You don't understand. I mean we'll be like a couple. A proper couple.'

'I heard you,' he told her. 'I heard you the first time. There's nothing wrong with my ears.'

She went back to her kitchen, leaving Norman tapping his fingers to the rhythm. A few minutes later he appeared in the doorway to the kitchen. 'He got – what's his name, the guy who shot him?'

'Mark Chapman,' she said.

'Yeah, him,' said Norman. 'Mark Chapman. He got dum-dums from a cop?'

Janet closed the oven door. 'It's true, Norman,' she said. 'Dum-dums, that's when they drill the end of the bullet, so the bullets explode when they hit the target? Is that right?'

'Yeah.' Norman shook his head. 'Fucking cops,' he said. 'Never trust 'em.'

He returned to the sitting room and crept up on Orchid. He grabbed her with both hands and threw her across the room. She landed on all fours and scrambled through to the kitchen with a shriek. 'Orchid,' Janet said, 'what's the matter

146

with you?' She appeared in the door to the sitting room. 'Something's wrong with Orchid lately,' she said. 'She keeps freaking.'

'Yeah,' said Norman. 'I noticed.'

chapter 24

Geordie was the only one didn't cry that day. When he woke in the morning he didn't even know it had started. He had begun the night in his own bed, but neither he nor Barney had slept, so he had fished Sam's old sleeping bag out of the cupboard under the stairs and crawled into that on the floor in Sam's sitting room. Sam wasn't sleeping either. He was listening to the kid creeping around in the dark, slamming cupboard doors, stubbing his toe and swearing about it.

One point during the night Sam got out of bed and made himself a cup of tea. Geordie was snoring in the sleeping bag, Barney curled up on his feet. Sam had intended drinking the tea and going back to bed, but the sound of Geordie's rhythmical breathing, the proximity and relative peace of having someone else in the room, had lulled him into a secure and even restful sleep, though he was sitting upright in a chair. Barney swapped position during the night, but Geordie didn't notice he'd gone and Sam didn't hear or feel him leap up on to his knee.

Sam opened his eyes when Geordie drew the curtains. He didn't move from the chair. He watched as Geordie stumbled round the room, clearing away the sleeping bag, opening a can of dog food for Barney, filling the kettle with water and putting it on to boil. It was after he'd filled the kettle that Sam noticed his face glistening in the early morning light.

'You're crying,' he said.

'Uh-uh?' said Geordie. His hand went to his face and came away wet. He looked at his fingers, then rubbed around his eyes. He smiled through the tears and shook his head. 'I didn't know,' he said. He walked over to Sam and knelt in front of him, and Sam pulled the boy's face down into his lap and stroked his hair.

'You know what I thought?' Geordie asked.

Sam nodded his head, but in reality he had been lost in his own thoughts. He had no idea what Geordie thought.

''S'really dangerous job,' Geordie said. 'What we do. I mean, I knew that before, but then when something like this happens it moves the goalposts. When I got shot that time, I knew then how dangerous it was. But now I have to think it's even more dangerous than that. And like, life is really good at creeping up on you. You go on for ages thinking nothing ever happens, then one day it all happens at once, and we all say, oh, no, like it's too much.'

Sam smiled at him, and reached out to touch his arm. But Geordie had moved out of reach. He didn't come forward to meet Sam's outstretched hand, not realizing how important the touch would have been.

'And I thought something else last night,' Geordie said. 'How did they know it was Gus? The police? If he didn't have any ID on him, how did they know it was him?'

'It was luck,' said Sam. 'The first patrol car at the scene, the cop recognized him. He'd come across him on one or two jobs. And he looked at him for some reason. Usually people don't look at dead bodies. I mean they see a dead body, that's all. They don't see who the dead body used to be. But for some reason this cop noticed it was Gus.'

'Was he screwing her, Sam?'

Sam nodded absently. 'Yeah,' he said. 'I don't know how much Marie knows, so go carefully when you talk to her. I don't think it would have gone on much longer, with the Ludendorff girl, he might even have been there to finish it.'

'You think that guy killed him? That Norman guy?'

'He's got to be the favourite,' said Sam. 'But I don't know why.'

'So we have to find him,' said Geordie. 'Track him down.'

'I think he'll show himself,' said Sam. 'Specially if he thinks we've got something he wants.'

'You want me to hang out in the town?' Geordie asked. 'I

can only keep my eyes skinned. If I come across him follow him wherever he goes? What do you say?'

'That's all we can do at the moment,' said Sam. 'But be careful, Geordie. If he's the one killed Gus and the German woman, he's not an easy man to deal with.'

'Neither am I,' Geordie said. 'People think I'm stupid, but I've never been sussed on surveillance. I'm a natch. I work in the guy's blind spot.' He knelt to rub Barney's coat against the grain. 'You take the dog, though,' he said. 'Barney's sad about Gus as well. But people don't take him into account 'cause he's a dog.'

'Yeah,' said Sam. 'I'll take him.'

'Where to? Where you going?'

'First to Marie,' said Sam. 'Spend some time with her. Then, if there's any of the day left, I wanna see Jennie.'

Geordie stood in thought for a moment, then reached for his jacket. 'So you won't be drinking,' he said. And he walked to the door and went through it, outside, and closed it behind him.

'No,' Sam said, alone now except for Barney. 'I won't be drinking.'

She wore a black dress, more like a smock which finished just above her knees. She wore soft black pumps on her feet. She wore no socks or tights and the flesh of her legs was white and placid in contrast to the blackness of her clothes. Her face was lined and streaked with the tread marks of old tears, and behind this was a deeper disfigurement carved out of grief. Her eyes were dark and bruised and unsure of any fluctuations in the light, of quick movements. The pupils were small and black. The room was dark, the curtains were drawn tightly against the day. When Sam knocked she opened the door a crack, a diminished figure, smaller than the Marie he knew and recognized by several inches. She stood aside and opened the door wider so he could pass through into her domain.

He touched her arm as he passed through, hesitating briefly by the door. Remembering absolutely sweet Marie, wondering where she'd gone.

He sat in the chair he always used in this room. The upholstery on the right arm was torn and some of the stuffing was peeking out, tempting him to defy it. Marie crossed silently in front of him and sat on the edge of the couch by the window with the curtains blocking out the day. You looked at her and you would never know she was a nurse. You thought of something artistic, or holistic, a healer of some kind, or a painter. You could believe she painted pictures. But not a nurse. You could never imagine she'd fit into a uniform with anything starched. And the hygiene of a hospital, the sterility, somehow simply didn't fit her.

'How is it?' he asked quietly.

She raised her hands, palm upwards, and shook her head from side to side. 'Fucking awful,' she said. She never swore. In fifteen years Sam had never heard her use a swear word. She wasn't a prude, Gus swore in the house, and she never objected. Sam realized that he hadn't known she didn't swear until now, when she swore.

She pulled on one of the loose strands of hair that hung in front of her ear. 'I must look terrible,' she said.

'Yeah.' Sam confirmed it. Then wondered if she'd wanted him to deny it. 'You do,' he said. Mr Integrity. Rubbing it in.

Marie smiled. 'You're no oil painting yourself,' she said.

Sam got out of the chair and joined her on the couch. He put his arms round her and she put her arms round him. And they sat together like that, their heads together, their muscles tense, whatever strength each retained passing back and forth between them. She was a big woman. Big-boned but with a real surplus of flesh on her hips, her behind. Her breasts really did heave. Gus used to say that when Marie was in town no bar of chocolate was safe.

They rocked slightly, swayed from side to side, holding the contact as they slowly warmed each other. When the warmth turned to real heat and he felt a rivulet of sweat trickle down his chest, Sam slowly released her and let her rest against the back of the couch. 'I'm gonna make a drink,' he said. 'Something to eat.'

He went to the kitchen and prepared some crackers with

cheese, two mugs of coffee, black for him, white with no sugar for Marie. When he brought it through she had pulled out a small table and they sat and talked together, eating and drinking like a couple of survivors. The only thing missing for Sam was a cigarette.

'What are you going to do?' he asked.

'When you've gone I'm going to wash up,' she said. 'Then I've got a list in my head. I'm going to get Gus's body released so I can arrange a funeral. After that I'll go through the house and bundle up his clothes. I'm handing in notice at the hospital. I should have done that before, anyway, the state of the health service. Then I'm coming to work with you. Take over where Gus left off. I'm going to find whoever it was shot him.'

Sam waited until she looked directly at him. 'Revenge?' he said.

She shook her head. 'I don't believe in that. But if you need to put a word to it, revenge'll do just as well as any other. I'm going to get up early every morning and run six miles. Blow away all the cobwebs in my head. What I feel at the moment is confusion and regret and grief. I feel physically and emotionally drained, like if it was possible to sleep at all I could sleep for a hundred years. But what I feel as well is something more permanent, a sense of apprehension, and something else, I think the word is ennui. Is that right? Ennui? I need to clean it out of my system. The way to do that is to hunt him down and face him. That's what I need.'

Sam pursed his lips together and shook his head from side to side. 'Me too,' he said. 'I want to hunt him down and face him. I want to look into his eyes.' Then he had another thought. 'The longer I'm here,' he said. 'On the earth, I mean, living my life. It's been half a century now, and I'm beginning to realize that I'll never discover who I really am. I'll never really know. The best I can hope for is that I see myself occasionally reflected in someone else's eyes, or some-one else's consciousness. And this guy, the one who killed Gus, or the one I think killed Gus, facing up to him is not just facing up to someone who's external to me. It's me I've got to face, Marie, and it'll be the same for you, when you

151

finally get him in your sights, it won't be a man, another being out there you've suddenly caught up with. It'll be the you that is searching for him. That's where the apprehension comes from.'

'Before you asked me what I was going to do,' she said, 'I didn't know. I hadn't thought about it. But when you asked me I knew immediately, without thinking. And that's what I want to do now. That's the way I want to do it. Without thinking, without reflection, without any kind of philosophical searching. Do you understand?'

'No,' Sam said. 'But I never let a little thing like that stop me.'

Barney looked up at Sam and gave him the old one-eye, which was his way of saying, 'Are you gonna leave me in the car again, or can I get out and have a stretch this time?' Sam said, 'Come on,' and the dog was up and out of the car in a flash.

The town centre was crawling with police and their vehicles. On the whole they had it to themselves, because residents were staying in the safety of their own homes, and tourists were cancelling their reservations and going to Edinburgh and London instead. The only people coming to York were those who thought they might see a dead or mutilated body, or people who actually wanted murdering themselves.

Jennie and Celia were not at home. He took the key from under the dustbin and let himself in. Barney followed, wagging his tail. Marie had surprised Sam, and he shook his head at the thought, because it had always been like that. Marie had been surprising him for as long as he'd known her. He had been surprised when she'd taken up with Gus in the first place, and even more surprised when they'd moved in together. Every time he visited them and saw that they were still together he was surprised all over again. And now that Gus was dead and Marie had committed herself to hunting down his killer, guess what? Old Sammy boy was shaking his head and wondering if he really knew who this woman was.

He sat in Celia's chair, the one with the lace headpiece and the old lady smell, and repeated Marie's word over to himself a couple of times. *Ennui . . . ennui . . .* And he knew it would send him to sleep if he said it one more time. *Ennui . . .*

It began as one of those anxiety dreams when you're travelling east and needing to get west. You have no compass, you just know you're going in the wrong direction and you can't seem to do anything about it. You know you're dreaming but you can't stop worrying. Makes you want to open your eyes and start all over again.

Then all that anxiety drained away. Quite suddenly there was the body of Gus and the realization that it was not an anxiety dream, but a real nightmare. Because the body of Gus, the body of anyone in a dream like this, was going to metamorphose. It was a dead body, and there would soon be two dead bodies and neither of them would be Gus. He tried to look away, to tear himself free of this dream and its dreaded landscape.

But his eyes were drawn back to where Gus was stretched out on the ground and he saw it was already too late, because Gus had been replaced by Donna, and she wasn't dead. Her eyes were closed but her breast was rising and falling, rising and falling with the breath of life. She was going to live. But as long as she lived she would never open her eyes. She was going to live, but as long as she lived she would never hear a word he had to say, and she would never reply.

And behind her was the beech hedge, and in the hedge was a freshly painted cottage-type gate with a latch and a blackbird. And Sam didn't want to go through the gate because he knew very well that the body of his daughter, Bronte, would be lying on the other side. But there was no choice involved, because as much as he didn't want to go, his legs were already carrying him up to and through the gate. And the whole bloody pity of it all was in a small crumpled heap on the grass before him.

The world was full of healers. The world was full of priests of one brand or another. It was full of other people's miracles; of wondrous and life-affirming tales and legends.

Everything was possible. You only had to believe. You had to believe and you had to pray, and it would all come right.

Sam prayed.

He buried his daughter. He left Donna in a coma in the hospital and he walked behind the hearse with the tiny coffin and he buried Bronte. And he left the cemetery and returned to the hospital and sat by the bed of his wife and took her hand and he prayed.

Sometimes in the night his praying would become fervoured, he would sweat freely and slowly realize that he was not praying at all any more; he was begging. At first he begged for everything, he wanted both of them back. He wanted them alive and by his side. Then he realized that Bronte would never return, and he begged only for Donna. For her full recovery.

But in the end, in the days before he asked them to switch off the life-support, he begged only that she open her eyes. She wouldn't have to say anything. Only open her eyes for a few seconds, maybe a minute, so that they could say a final goodbye.

But God wasn't at home. He wasn't listening. No one anywhere was listening, because no one anywhere could help. Bronte was dead and gone, buried in the ground, and Donna was never going to blink, let alone open her eyes and say goodbye. There was no future for either of them. There was a future only for Sam.

He was being crucified now. His right shoulder was pinned to the cross and they were hammering the stake through it. He opened his eyes and saw Jennie's face close to his. She was shaking his right shoulder, and behind her Celia was saying, 'Leave him, Jennie. He probably didn't sleep last night.'

Jennie smiled and planted a kiss on his forehead. 'You were crying,' she whispered. 'Fast asleep and crying your eyes out. Thought you might drown.'

Celia pulled Jennie aside and looked down at Sam. She shook her head. 'What a sight,' she said. 'You look like I feel.' She turned to Jennie. 'You could make him a cup of tea,' she said. 'Or he prefers coffee. I'm going to have to rest a while.' She glanced at Sam again. 'You ought to think about sleeping in a proper bed,' she said.

Sam got to his feet. 'I was dreaming about cigarettes,' he lied. 'I haven't thought about cigarettes all day, then I go and dream about them. You go and have your rest, Celia,' he said. 'I'll take Jennie out for a coffee. Then I'll rest.'

Celia put her hands on her hips.

'Promise,' said Sam. 'Honest Injun.'

'What happened?' Jennie Cosgrave put a lump of brown sugar into her coffee and leaned on the table with one elbow. 'Do you have any idea who shot Gus?'

'The day before he was tailing a guy with Geordie. But Geordie got lost. Gus could have still been tailing the guy. We don't know for sure.'

Jennie shook her head. 'It doesn't sound very professional,' she said. 'Surely someone ought to have known exactly where Gus was.'

'There were reasons,' he said. 'Gus was involved with the German girl. We weren't exactly communicating.'

'So, really, you have no idea who killed them. It could have been the German girl's husband, boyfriend? Was she married?'

Sam showed her his palms. 'You're right,' he said. 'We don't know.'

Jennie reached over the table and took his hand. 'I don't think it was anything to do with the German girl,' she said. 'It looks to me as if it was the same person who killed the gun dealer and his wife.'

'Is this a professional opinion?' Sam asked.

'I've never done any real psychological profiling,' Jennie said. 'But I have read around the current ideas. I know the procedure. Yeah, it's as professional as you're going to get. I'd put money on it being the same man.'

'Man?' said Sam.

She smiled. 'Oh, undoubtedly. I wouldn't say a woman couldn't commit a crime like that. But in this case it's got macho written all over it.'

'What else do you see?'

155

'He's not a first time killer. I would think he's done it before, more than once, and the odds are that he's been caught and served some time in prison.'

'The guy Gus was tailing's been in prison,' Sam said. 'I don't know for sure, but I have a strong hunch about him.'

'Who is he?' Jennie asked. 'Why was Gus following him?'

'Calls himself Norman Brown,' Sam told her. 'I don't think it's his real name. We don't have an address, so I put Gus and Geordie on him to see where he was living. He hired us to find a woman, Selina White. He calls her Snow White.'

'Snow White?' said Jennie. 'That rings a bell.'

'She lived with her stepmother,' Sam said. 'Really got off on little guys.'

Jennie put his hand down on the table. 'Fool,' she said. 'No, I mean it really rings a bell. I've heard it before. Someone called Snow White.'

'You know her?' said Sam.

'I don't think so. I don't know. Just when you said the name, I know I've come across it before. Not in the fairy story. In life, someone's mentioned it to me, or I've met her. I can't remember. A woman called Snow White.'

'I've been getting close to her,' Sam said. 'She's living in York, and I've got her married name. It shouldn't actually take long to find her. Once I've run her down I'm sure she'll know who Norman Brown really is.'

'I know that name as well,' said Jennie. 'Norman Brown, or Norman something.'

'Maybe I mentioned it to you,' Sam said. 'Didn't you see him that day when Barney went into the ladies? I thought we talked about him.'

'I remember,' she said. 'No, I didn't see him. But I heard him speaking. There was something about his voice. I bet I know this man. If he is the one, the most probable thing is that I met him in prison. And if I met him in prison he's liable to have been serving a long sentence, and have a history of violence.'

'I could see him fitting all those categories,' said Sam. 'He's a real slimeball. You spend a few minutes with him, he doesn't touch you, but you get contaminated. From right over the desk. When he's gone you feel like you want to go home and have a shower, change your clothes.'

'I think I know who he is,' she said. 'In fact I do. He's called Norman Bunce, not Norman Brown. And I heard the Snow White story from him.' She was speaking quietly at first, dragging it up out of memory, but her voice was rising in crescendo as she spoke. 'He was one of the ones in the prison break. You remember the Isaac Bova break, when they used artillery on the prison transport? Norman Bunce was one of the prisoners that got away.'

'What was he in for?' Sam asked. 'What did he do?'

'Can't remember,' she said. 'Something to do with animals. People and animals. I'll have it on my computer.'

'People and animals,' Sam said. 'What's that supposed to mean?'

'He killed them,' she said. 'He tortured them and killed them.'

chapter 25

The day after the check-shirt guy and the hippy woman died Norman went to the private detective's office twice. Both times the door was locked, and nobody answered his knocks.

Two thoughts occurred to Norman: one, that the guy was out tracing Snow White, hot on the heels of the bitch; or two, and this would be just his luck, that the recession had caught up with the detective and he'd gone into voluntary redundancy, or that somebody had foreclosed on him and the bailiffs had come in and hauled him off to debtors' prison, which in the south they didn't have any more, but up here in the frozen north they probably still needed.

He mentioned both these thoughts to Janet and he said, 'If it's the second, that the bastard has gone broke, then I'm one of his legitimate claimants. I gave him two hundred pounds up front, no questions asked, and without a fucking receipt.

157

And when I gave him the money he didn't even blink. Took it out of my hand and put it in his pocket, knowing, probably, at the time, that it was robbing Peter to pay Paul. You see what I mean about the state of the country, the way people's morals have been undermined? I went to that man in the first place in good faith because I had been ripped off by an unscrupulous woman, and he must have thought it was his birthday when he saw me coming up the street. Because he hears about my hard luck and immediately thinks that it might be his good luck, and then watches wide eyed while I actually give him my hard-earned money. Take it out of my pocket and place it in his hand.

'There was something about the guy,' he said. 'I noticed it almost immediately. He was sly, sizing me up. I wouldn't be surprised if he wasn't a private detective at all. I wouldn't be surprised if he was a con artist, set up like a private detective's office so poor unsuspecting and innocent mugs like yours truly would unload their cash on him.'

Janet didn't have much to say about it. She was having one of her quiet days. It wasn't that she was uninterested or unconcerned. It was more like her mind was fogged up. She got like that sometimes, where everything fogged over and she just wanted to be by herself with her thoughts about John Lennon. Kind of dozy. Where she had thoughts but she couldn't put them into words. Like she was sleepwalking.

Norman got changed and went out into the town. He went to a jewellery shop and bought himself a snake ring and a puzzle ring. He came out of the shop wearing both of them, and then turned round and went back inside and bought another ring with his initials inscribed on it, and wore it on his pinkie.

He trawled the other jewellery shops in the centre of town and bought himself two identity bracelets, one for each wrist, and a thick gold chain with nothing on it to wear round his neck. They had thick gold chains with gold bars on, some with nuggets on, even one with a miniature gold piano. But Norman thought these were tasteless. The one he bought was not ostentatious. You had to look at it, but as you looked at it, slowly it would dawn on you that it was better than the other stuff. Like the guy who sold it said, well, only a teenager, but bright with it: 'It's simple. What more can you say? Simple. Expensive. Gold.'

He bought a steak in a tourist restaurant and left half of it. He found he preferred Janet's vegetarian cooking. Trouble was it always left him feeling hungry, and he had this craving for meat. But then when he got the meat it made him feel sick. He tried another piece of the steak but just moved it around in his mouth. He took it out of his mouth and put it on the side of the plate. When the waitress came to collect his plate and asked him if he'd finished, looking critically at the remains of the steak, Norman told her, 'Yeah. I'd have eaten it. But it had more saturated fat than I'm used to.' She looked at him for a good long time, so he spelt it out for her. 'We eat polyunsaturates at home.'

A teenage girl at the next table watched him, and nudged her friend and whispered to her. The friend stole a glance at Norman. He rattled his identity chains and thought what it would be like if he locked them both in a cellar somewhere and used them as sex slaves. Those two, and Squishsquash, and over time he could get a few more. He'd have the cellar fitted out like one of those Arab harems, central heating, carpets, hot showers. And when he was there he'd dress in robes, like a king. Make the fuckers worship him.

He waited until the teenagers left, then followed them through the town. They kept glancing behind to see if he was still there. Whispering and pushing and giggling. When they went into Boots he walked on past. Let them go.

He found a shop that sold good silk ties and bought one with two naked women on it. A black woman and a white woman. Tina and Janet he called them. He told the woman who sold him it to keep the bag. He'd wear the tie.

Then he walked to Squishsquash's house and sat on the grass opposite, under the city wall, and waited.

If he did have AIDS now, since the hippy woman had bitten him, he didn't care. In prison nearly everyone had AIDS and it didn't do them no harm. If you were straight and got AIDS it wasn't the same as if you were a fag and got AIDS. There was different strains of it. Straight AIDS and fag AIDS. And if you had straight AIDS it didn't develop for maybe fifteen years, which would mean he'd be fifty. And the way Norman looked at it, if you were fifty you might as well be dead anyway.

On the other hand, if you had AIDS, it wasn't the end of the world. There were advantages because it was like you had a concealed weapon. You could leave it behind you everywhere you went. And it would spread itself out behind you like the wake of a ship. It was perfect. No one could see it happening. But you could change the world.

Perfect. Simple. Expensive.

Squishsquash went into the house with an old woman. The way she walked was burned into Norman's skull. He could live to be a hundred, except for the AIDS, and he'd never forget that walk. *Squishsquash, squishsquash*. There are some things a man never forgets. Formative experiences stay with you for ever and ever. The first kiss, the first kill, rock and roll and being sick after drinking cider. Getting out and hearing the prison door close behind you. Yeah, all that, and the way Squishsquash walks.

He didn't know who the old woman was. He had imagined Squishsquash living alone, and he smiled to himself and lit up a cigarette, shading the flame on his gold lighter from a tiny breeze. It was wishful thinking that she lived alone. He had hoped she lived alone, because then it would be straightforward to go in there one night and play with her like a cat plays with a mouse. Now he knew it would not be straightforward. He'd have to watch and wait until the old woman was out, or he'd have to go in prepared to deal with the old woman. It was never easy when there were two people, especially two women. With guys you knew what they'd do, how they'd react. But with women anything could happen. They start bawling, or even piss in their knickers like that one last week. Jesus, people start pissing themselves, you just want to pack up and go home.

Still, Norman the optimist came rushing to the fore, always ready to look on the bright side. It's only an old woman. It's not like she's married to one of these Arnold Schwarzenegger types, or living with three steroid-sucking brothers, Eye-talians or something like that, want her to stay a virgin for ever.

Squishsquash came out of the house again, half an hour later. She came out by herself and walked back into the town. She went into Newgate Market and Norman followed, once getting so close to her he could touch her bottom in the crush. He did it too, let his hand lightly brush against her rump. She didn't flinch. If she felt it at all she must've assumed it was par for the course.

Norman thought of speaking to her. Just stand in front of her when she'd finished buying mushrooms, say: 'Hello, Squishsquash. I want your body.' Something like that. One of the problems with York was there was nowhere you could actually attack someone during the day. Tourists everywhere. At night it would be easy. Maybe he should come back one night, follow her and jump her in one of these narrow streets.

But the best bet still seemed to be his earlier idea. Call round on her and the old biddy. Get the old biddy out of the way, and then he'd have Squishsquash all to himself. No interruptions. Could take all night over it if he felt like it.

And he did feel like it. The more he thought about it the more he felt like it.

The headline said: SECOND DOUBLE SHOOTING and Norman bought the newspaper because he wanted to know who the guy was, the dead guy, and why the guy had been following him.

He read the article twice and still didn't understand it. This guy, this Gus Scott, was a partner of the detective, Sam Turner. That's what it said in the newspaper. But Norman had hired Sam Turner to find Snow White. So why was Sam Turner having him tailed?

Could it be that Norman had made a mistake? Was this Gus character following him to give him some news about Snow White?

It was all very confusing. Really did your head in the more you thought about it.

Norman had not even thought about Snow White these last few days. He had some money in his pocket now, and soon he'd have a whole lot more. And he had Janet as well, so why did he need to waste his time with Snow White? Oh, yeah, he'd really like to give her a good slapping if he ever got the chance, even cut her up some. Well, you didn't let women work you over and get away with it. And, in any case, all that time in prison he'd come up with some pretty good fantasies about what he'd do with the bitch. It would be a pity to waste them.

But in reality she was no longer on the urgent list.

He could always work Janet over if he got into a state. If it happened, like it used to do in prison, that his head became so full of Snow White that he had to have her. Then he could pretend Janet was Snow White. Make her squeal. Or he could use Squishsquash. Either of them. Any woman actually. Put a bag over their head, after a minute or two even Norman'd believe it was Snow White.

One thing, Norman realized, he'd have to stay out of the way of Sam Turner. Which was a pity, because he'd given Sam Turner that cash. But if Gus Scott was Sam Turner's partner, then Sam Turner would have a fairly good idea who topped the guy. It didn't say anything like that in the newspaper, but Norman wasn't stupid. He could put two and two together and cut his losses.

Who needed Snow White, anyway? What did she amount to? A ten-quid ass and a five-pence brain.

Norman went home and took Janet to bed, imagined she was Squishsquash walking home along that street. Did it doggie fashion. Janet said he was a brute and that he didn't consider her feelings, and Norman told her she shouldn't be so particular.

'Look at it this way, Janet,' he said. 'Sometimes I think I'm doing it to Tina Turner' (he didn't tell her about Squishsquash) 'and it gives me that extra oomph. But that's all that happens, I get an extra inch of oomph out of it. It's not like Tina Turner's getting something that belongs to you. Not like I'm giving it to her and you're being left out of the equation. Know what I mean? It's probably, what's probably happening is that because I've got a head full of Tina you're actually getting a bit more as well. Because if I was just thinking about you, you'd only be getting your share, right? But because I'm thinking about her while I'm actually having you, then in fact you're getting a double dose when you should only be expecting a single.

'Don't you think that's right?'

'Listen, how do I know, or how does anybody know if, when they're getting you, you might be thinking about John Lennon? I bet you do, sometimes. Like I'm coming on a bit and you're there thinking you're Yoko Ono or some broad he's been sniffing round. And me, as far as you're concerned, I'm not there at all. Like I've got four balls, but I might as well have eighty-four for all you care, because I'm not even me, I'm a guy on a poster in the living room, used to get into bags with people. And when that happens, do you hear me complaining? Am I like saying you don't think about my feelings? All that shit. No, Janet, you don't hear that from me, because I'm sensible enough to know that if you're thinking about some pop star instead of me, then what's actually happening is that you're getting a little extra, and if you're getting a little extra, then so am I. I'm getting the you that I went after in the first place, and I'm getting the you that imagines she's getting John Lennon.

'Now, add to that the Tina that I imagine I'm getting, and add it all up, and whichever way you look at it there's got to be four of us in the fucking bed. Jesus Christ. Care about your feelings! I'm actually broadening your experience here. Most chicks like you, the best they could expect is a quick shag in the afternoon. That's the very best thing could happen. Mostly nothing happens. They sit at home and read a book, or they smoke cigarettes and finger themselves. You listening to me? Nothing happens for these women. But because you've got me, you don't just get me coming home and taking you to bed, giving you the time of your life. You get a whole international orgy of pop stars, film stars, whatever you want. Listen, Janet, for what you just had, there're women'd give their right arm.'

He swung his legs over the side of the bed and pulled on his trousers. Janet sat up and riffled among the covers for her T-shirt. She didn't have much to say. Norman looked over his shoulder at her, wondering if he should say something else. But she looked as though she was in another world. Sometimes he wondered if she actually listened to what he said, or if she just switched off altogether. Left him talking to the wall.

He put his shoes on and walked out of the room. Left her there, kneeling on the bed, looking like she was gonna say her prayers. He filled the kettle with water and put it on to boil. Then he went back into the bedroom, kicking Orchid on the way. He placed a small handgun on the bed. 'I'm going away for a couple of days,' he said. 'Got to meet some people in the Midlands. Business.'

'What's this?' she asked, picking up the gun. It was sleek, small and snub-nosed.

'Careful,' he said. 'It's loaded. With dum-dums.'

Janet turned the gun in her hand. She looked up at Norman with wide eyes. 'Is it . . .?'

'Yeah,' he said. 'A Charter Arms Undercover .38 Special. It's a present. So I know you'll be safe while I'm away.'

'When are you going? Today?'

'No. Tomorrow. You gonna be a good girl?'

'What does *that* mean?' She threw the gun on to the bed.

'It means, Janet, are you gonna be a good girl.'

'I know what it means, Norman. It means, I am so sex mad, I am so horny and man crazy that as soon as you've gone out the door I'm gonna be going out and looking for a dick. That's what it means.'

Norman shrugged his shoulders and went back into the kitchen. 'Jesus,' he said, smacking his forehead with the palm of his hand. 'Jesus Christ.' Who could understand them? You say one thing, just one little thing. You don't mean anything by it. It's just like passing the time of day. And what do you get? A load of garbage. Like you set off a volcano or something. For nothing. You do nothing. It doesn't matter. You must've touched a hormone or some-thing. A whole warehouse full of hormones. It's like they have hormones stacked up in pyramids like cans of beans in a supermarket. You're trundling your trolley along and you don't even want any beans. You don't like beans. But one of the wheels on the trolley knocks one of the cans off the bottom row of the pyramid. Next thing you know the whole lot is coming down round your ears.

You're being battered to death.

And you only went in there in the first place to buy a pack of cigarettes.

For somebody else. The cigarettes weren't even for you.

You were doing somebody a *favour*.

chapter 26

Marie began collecting together Gus's bits and pieces. There must have been three hundred copies of *Practical Electronics*, dozens of textbooks on computer technology, as well as half-completed kits and projects, and, under the bed, four cardboard boxes of assorted silicon chips and discarded printed circuit boards. She put them all out for the dustman to collect.

Geordie called round while she was going through Gus's wardrobe. He tried on a couple of shirts, but they were at least two sizes too large for him, and he packed them in a suitcase and offered to take them to the Cancer Research shop.

'BHF,' she said.

'What?'

'British Heart Foundation,' she said. 'Their shop. I prefer to give it to them.'

'Oh, yeah. OK,' he said. But he hovered in the doorway. Came back into the house and stood at the foot of the stairs. 'He was a good man, Gus,' he said. 'He didn't talk about his feelings much, but I think he thought about things a lot. I don't know if you think he loved you, but I think he did.'

165

Geordie kicked his heels, looked down at his Reeboks, then stole a short glance at Marie. He looked naff, and what he had to say sounded naff, but Marie felt a tear plough a small channel in her cheek. Her eyes misted over, and when she looked up again there were two Geordies, both of them in soft focus, stereo images with arms outstretched like a pose she associated with Jesus. A card she'd collected from Sunday School twenty years before, the text under the image of the man saying, *Suffer little children* . . .

She dropped the armful of Gus's clothing and went over the short divide between her and Geordie and let him put his arms around her. His body was hard and angular, in complete contrast to her own soft and gentle curves. Bone and muscle meet deposits of fat, she thought, while at the same time recognizing that there was no real substance to Geordie. He was physically there, but he was youth. His strength and weight came from innocence rather than experience. What he had to offer was a gesture. And Marie, in a kind of despair that she had not yet allowed herself to recognize, clung to it.

'I think he loved you very much,' Geordie said again. 'I'm sure he did.'

Marie took a step back and put her index finger to Geordie's lips. 'I know,' she said. 'You don't have to convince me.' She took Geordie by the hand and led him through into the kitchen. 'Oh,' she said, rubbing at her eyes with the heels of both hands. 'I was going to make us a drink, but what I'd really like to do is go out. How about if I fill up another couple of bags with clothes and we go to the BHF shop together. Then go to Betty's and have coffee and cake? Chocolate cake?'

'Yeah,' Geordie said. 'I don't have any money but . . .'

'. . . I do,' said Marie.

And she watched him put away two huge slices of chocolate gâteau, both of them swimming in cream, while she delicately picked at one. He also consumed two large coffees with sugar and cream while she sipped at a small black one. And even while she watched she knew that by tomorrow she would have put on at least three pounds in weight because

166

of it, while he would probably be lighter than he was today. That's how the world was organized. There was no God, only chaos.

'I hate thin people,' she told him.

'It's not my fault,' Geordie protested. 'I can't help being thin.'

'Neither can I,' she said. 'Help it, that is. I hate you.' She laughed and paid the bill, and realized finally and irrevocably that she would always be at least a little overweight. There were some things in nature you couldn't alter. Or if you did alter them they lasted only a short time. Finally they reverted back to whatever they were to start with. In Marie's case, fat.

She left Geordie on the corner of Coney Street and doubled back into Church Street where she knew a shop that sold cut-price sweets. She bought a stock of Mars bars, fourteen of them. A quarter of sugared almonds. A packet of chocolate biscuits. A giant Toblerone. And, as an afterthought, a small box of Mint Thins.

'You having a party?' the woman behind the counter asked, popping the Toblerone into the plastic bag. She had adenoids, and spoke only occasionally because of it. You knew if she spoke more than one word she must really like you.

'No,' Marie told her. 'I'm gonna eat myself into a sideshow.'

'Nice,' the woman said, handing the bag over the counter. 'Very nice.' When Marie got to the door the woman was still saying it, elaborating freely now, like if she had wings she'd be flying: 'Very nice indeed.'

Betty's had been only half full. And Betty's was always packed. The sweet shop always had a queue; but not today. There was a real sense of fear in the town. A tension that was carried by the people, but was so tangible it felt as though it was in the walls of the buildings. York had seen a lot of violence and terror in its long history, but violence in a historical context is acceptable. This was now, and it felt very different.

So it was fixed. She'd work with Geordie. They'd comb the town together. Looking for the man. A sharp dresser. Preferred his clothes tight. Had a small beard. She looked at the sketch Geordie had made in Betty's. 'There's something missing,' Geordie had said. 'I mean, that's what he looks like, something like that. But there's something else about him, a kind of aura, something electric. You feel it coming off him when you get up close, or if he looks at you. Most people don't have that, or if they have it it's only weak. This guy has it real strong. You wouldn't want to be alone with him, not if it was dark. Do you know what I mean? Electric.'

Marie didn't know what Geordie meant. She assumed he was talking about magnetism. And in a way he was, because Norman was charismatic. But what Geordie failed to recognize was that Norman's electricity was connected with a deep sexuality. A deep sexuality and an almost unending capacity for violence.

Marie watched television until late. Got a small headache at the back of her skull and thought she would sleep. At one thirty in the morning she rang Celia because she thought she would go mad if she didn't talk to someone. Celia answered the phone immediately.

Celia listened quietly while Marie told her she was sorry but she needed someone to talk to. Then she said, 'I feel exactly the same, my dear. I tried to sleep and kept thinking about Gus, and for the last half hour I've been thinking about you. I was just saying a little prayer, then I was going to try again. Do you want to come round?'

'Is that all right?' said Marie.

'I'll put the kettle on,' Celia told her. 'Make a nice cup of tea. I'll have it ready when you get here.'

Marie put the phone down and grabbed a coat. She went in the toilet and poured bleach into the bowl, something to combat the stench of vomit. Then she checked she had a key and went outside. A little prayer? she thought. Why not? Nothing else had worked.

Celia was white faced, without any kind of make-up, and as with many elderly people the night had taken some of her

168

corporality, left her looking slight, weakened and wraith-like. She pecked Marie on the cheek and led her into the centre of the house. Around Celia's chair were several books, a couple of paperback novels but three other volumes with seriously religious jackets, at least one of them a Bible. There was a tall standing lamp behind Celia's chair, but on the dining table a candle burned, and it was to the table that Celia went, and Marie followed. They sat on either side of a corner of the table and Celia reached across and took hold of both of Marie's hands. She smiled warmly.

'It's a brute when you can't sleep,' she said. 'The night goes on for ever.'

'Never ends,' Marie agreed. 'As long as a bad novel.'

Celia squeezed her hand. 'You can always come to me,' she said. 'When you get to my age you don't sleep well anyway. Too many past sins to contend with.' She laughed at that because it was a joke. 'Seriously, though, there will be times in the coming nights when you need somebody. Don't even think about it, give me a ring and come straight round. I know what it's like to be on your own.'

Celia had never married. She had lived with and cared for her mother until the old lady died, and since that time she had lived alone. She didn't call it living alone. She had her books, and her music, and for much of the time she was a Quaker. She had her friends, and her involvement with Sam and Geordie constantly reminded her that there was a fantasy element to life, something which had been sadly missing from much of her early experience, but for which she was determined to make up lost time.

'I can muddle through the day,' Marie said. 'The night has a different quality to it. I become a different person as soon as it gets dark. I don't have the same kind of resistance. My father was like that. When he worked the night shift he was miserable all the time, made my mother miserable, and me and my sister. When he worked days we were a really happy family, but when he was on nights it was hell.'

'Do you see them much,' Celia asked, 'your family?'

Marie shook her head. 'Dad died when I was seventeen,' she said. 'A particularly aggressive cancer, tore him apart in about three weeks. Reduced him to nothing. My mother died the following year. I don't think she ever really got over the shock of his death. The way he died. And I never see my sister.'

'I'm sorry,' Celia said. 'You don't have to talk about it.'

Marie shook her head. 'It's OK,' she said. 'I don't mind. Julia, that's my sister, she married a black man. He was English, I think his parents were Jamaican, but he had been born and brought up in Leeds. Anyway, Julia met him and they had this kind of whirlwind romance. They fell in love and before they turned round they were married. They came to visit me. I didn't know anything about it, I didn't know she'd met a man, let alone that she was married and pregnant. And I was surprised. It took me a while to get used to the idea. Also, her husband, he was very black and small, but with long dreadlocks. It was a lot to digest at once.

'The result was,' Marie said, 'they didn't come back again. They thought I was prejudiced. That I disapproved. But I didn't, Celia. I was just socially inadequate. If they'd given me another chance it would have been all right. But as it was I blew it. When I tried to contact them again, a few months later, they'd gone. I found her husband's family, and they had gone through the same experience as me. They hadn't adjusted to the idea immediately, and so Julia and her husband had walked off into the world alone, thinking that the people closest to them had rejected them. But we hadn't. I hadn't rejected Julia, and I'm sure his family had not rejected him. But no one's heard a word from them since. In eight years.'

Celia shook her head. 'You've no idea where they are?'

'Brixton, we think,' said Marie. 'A friend of his in Leeds said they went to Brixton. But he didn't have an address. We've never heard a word from them. I don't even know if she's still alive. Anything could have happened. And it seems much worse now, now that Gus's gone. It's as if there's no one left at all. Just me, getting fatter every day.'

'Marie . . .' Celia said.

'No, Celia, don't tell me I'm not fat. I might very well be on my own, and feeling sick and sorry for myself, but I don't

170

want to avoid reality altogether. If I have to choose between you and my scales, I'd believe the scales every time.'

'I wasn't going to say that,' Celia told her. 'I wouldn't argue with your scales, Marie. I'm sure they understand you better than I do. But I think it would be better if you listened to them less, let them be the master less, and put yourself in charge. If you really want to be brave you could throw the blessed things out of the window. No one in their right mind would say that you weren't overweight, Marie. Goodness, if you carry on like this, you're going to make yourself ill. But it's up to you. If you really want to do something about it you can. You can lose the weight, or you can decide to keep it and not worry about it. Whichever decision you make will be the right decision for you. It won't make any difference to me, or to Sam, or to anyone else who loves you. We love you with or without the fat. Do you understand?'

'Yes,' said Marie, the tear in her eye glinting in the candlelight.

'But the self-pity,' Celia continued, 'that's something else altogether. You're going to have to do something about that.'

chapter 27

Sam opened the door and let Jennie into his flat. Geordie grabbed his coat and his dog and said, 'Goodbye,' and Sam ushered him closer to the door. 'Sorry,' Geordie said still pulling his coat on, and Sam whispered, 'I told you she'd be here. Jesus, Geordie, why d'you always leave everything till the last minute?' Then Geordie turned on the doorstep and said something else and Sam quickly turned to Jennie, who was standing in the middle of the floor, and gave her a smile which had been in his family for generations.

Geordie somehow stood on Barney and the dog gave one of those indignant doggie yelps, and Sam's tone changed from indignation to concern, but eventually they decided that Barney was OK and Geordie and the dog trundled off along the street and Sam came back into the flat with his tail between his legs. He cocked his head to one side and said: 'Welcome.'

'I brought this,' she said, handing over a bottle of ginger beer. 'I drank half a bottle of wine before I came out.' She sank into a chair by the table.

'Dutch courage?' he asked.

'Yeah,' she said. 'Get through all the police in the town. There's TV crews out there now. Police and TV crews, journalists. That's about all there is out there. No people. The TV crews are filming other TV crews, and the journalists are interviewing other journalists, and the police are chasing the police. It's ridiculous. Norman Bunce must be watching it all on TV and laughing up his sleeve.'

'How was it at the police station?' Sam asked.

Jennie sighed. 'They didn't believe me.'

'Is that what they said?'

'Not in so many words,' she said. 'But they didn't take me seriously. They wrote it all down. I signed a statement. But they think he's in London. There've been several sightings of him in the south. They're so busy with the killings, interviewing neighbours and relatives, following up sightings of various vehicles. Hoaxers, as well. It was busier in the police station than it was in the market yesterday.'

'So they're not even gonna look for him?' Sam asked.

'I don't think so, no,' she said. 'They seemed to be convinced that he'd be picked up in London any minute. They're looking for a madman, but not that particular madman.'

Sam shrugged. 'We'll have to find him ourselves, then,' he said. 'Shouldn't be too difficult, especially if we're not tripping over the fuzz all the time.'

'Frustrating, though,' Jennie said. 'Talking to policemen who you feel are just going through the motions. Can we talk about something else? Try to get them out of my head.'

Sam went to a shelf and brought back two glasses. He unscrewed the top from the ginger beer and poured it into

172

the glasses on the table. 'Your mother liked to drink?' he asked.

'Did I mention that?' she answered. 'Yes. She drank every day. She never got involved in AA or anything like that. But she had a daily and ongoing relationship with alcohol.'

'When did she die?' he asked. He sat on a small hassock at her feet, and she shifted her legs a little to accommodate him.

'Two years ago,' Jennie said. 'She got out of bed in the morning, had a sherry for breakfast then said she didn't feel too good. A neighbour called an ambulance and they took her into hospital. She was dead by midday. My marriage was in deep trouble at the time, and Dad called me at work to tell me what had happened, give me the time of the funeral. I remember thinking it was a relief. She'd been on my mind for the past weeks, since my marriage started slipping away. She'd never have understood if we'd split up while she was alive. Her own marriage had been through so much, she could never imagine how anyone else couldn't manage.

'Anyway,' Jennie continued, 'I felt sad but liberated. It meant I could tell my husband to sod off with his floozie – both of them as it happened – floozies, I mean. One at each end of town. And at the same time I wouldn't be upsetting my mother.

'All psychologists have mother problems,' she said. 'I'm not an exception in my profession. Mother problems or father problems. The best psychologists have both.' She set her lips for a moment, then reached for her glass of ginger beer. 'My dad was clever,' she said. 'He taught me to arm-wrestle. I don't think he ever taught me much of anything else. But he taught me arm-wrestling, just as if I had been a boy. I got very good, we can have a contest later. I'll probably beat you.'

'This I've got to see,' said Sam.

'But later,' she said. 'I know you don't believe me. Men never do. You'll be surprised. Anyway, Dad rang me and I left my husband and got in the car and drove up for the funeral. Dad was at home and I went to the funeral parlour alone. Say my last goodbyes, have a look at her before they put her in the ground. This was the morning of the funeral. The funeral was mid afternoon.

'And it wasn't her.

'They showed me into this room, with the casket raised up from the ground – must be on some kind of plinth, but it looks as though it's free-floating, nothing supporting it, flowers everywhere. You know how they arrange everything? And there was a woman in the casket, the body of a woman about twice the size of my mother, twice the size she'd been when she was alive.' Jennie laughed, an odd nervous laugh like they sometimes do it in films to show that the heroine is neurotic. 'I looked round the room,' she said. 'I remember looking at this big woman and thinking, "Mother? This isn't my mother." Then I looked round the room to see if there were any other coffins, or if there was anywhere else they could have put her. But there was nothing, just this white coffin with silver fittings and an enormous corpse that wasn't anything to do with me.'

'Jesus,' said Sam.

'So I went back to the reception area, there was this woman there a lot younger than me, all in black, a black suit, tight fitting with a short skirt, just a little too short for an undertaker. You know what I mean? There wasn't a lot in it. If the skirt had been maybe half an inch longer you wouldn't have noticed, but as it was, you did. But not all in black, she wore a white blouse with small white roses embroidered on it.'

'Hell, I don't care what she wore,' Sam said. 'What happened about the body?'

That stopped Jennie for a few beats. 'That's what I noticed,' she said. 'What she was wearing. That's what stayed with me since then. The way this woman was dressed.

'I told her that wasn't my mother in there, and she apologized, said she'd find out about it. They had these new chairs, or they looked new to me, really sumptuously stuffed, but with canvas upholstery, some kind of rough material. So when you sat down the first impression was comfort, even luxury, but after a minute or so you began to realize that this particular luxury had a rough edge to it. It was disconcerting when I first realized that, but later, when I'd had time to digest it, I thought that all real luxury does have a rough edge to it. Don't you think?

'Anyway, she left me there so long I was beginning to think I ought to go look for her. I heard one or two doors opening and closing behind the scenes, and at one point someone was shouting, a male voice, but I couldn't hear what he was saying. Then eventually the receptionist came back, and while she'd been away she'd acquired a kind of servility that she certainly hadn't possessed the first time I saw her. And she smiled at me a little like a mouse might smile if it was being polite but really had not found anything amusing. And she said, "Our Managing Director, Mr Burack, will be with you in a moment."

'I didn't want to see a managing director. I wanted to see my mother. That's what I was there for. I had other things to do as well. I was getting behind. I had people I wanted to see, and I thought this trip to the funeral home would have been over by now. It was turning into some kind of wake, where I had envisioned a quick visit, a prayer, even a few tears. It wasn't like the relationship between my mother and me had been idyllic, far from it. For the last few years it had been virtually non-existent.

'So I sat there another five minutes, all the time getting more and more irritable, and eventually the MD plucked up the courage to come through and make his speech. "I'm sorry, Miss Cosgrave," he said, and he had a professional undertaker's face on while he said it. "I'm sorry, but we appear to have misplaced your mother."'

'Misplaced?' said Sam.

'Yeah, that's what I said,' continued Jennie. '"Misplaced!" like Lady Bracknell. It came out like her line in the play: "A handbag!"' Jennie did her nervous laugh again. 'A few lines later when she leaves the stage, Wilde describes her exit as sweeping out in "majestic indignation". That describes what I felt like.

'I actually said to the man, "What the fuck have you done with my mother?" And after a few hesitant starts it came out

175

that another family had buried her that morning, thinking they were burying their mother.

'I could have caused a fuss,' she said. 'I left the MD, Mr Burack, whatever his name was, with no uncertainty about his competence. I told him that I had come across patches of mould smarter than him. But what they did in the end was, they dug up my dear old mother, they transhipped her from the old coffin to the new one. The big woman they took out of the new coffin and put her in the one my mother'd been buried in. Then they buried her, the big woman I mean, and put the flowers back on the mound just as if nothing had happened.

'Then, later in the day, my mother was buried again. All the mourners except me were touched by the coldness of it, being committed to the earth, all that. Everyone except me and mother. For me it was still sad, there was that sadness about it, but it had also become a farce.' Jennie laughed. 'For Mother, though, it was already becoming a habit.'

Sam shook his head. 'Is this true?' he asked.

'Yeah,' she said. 'I know it's unbelievable, but it happened to me. I was just making my way through life and then I entered this surrealistic period, and that was the beginning of it. After that I still had a divorce to get through. That was even more bizarre.'

'I don't think I can take any more tonight,' he said.

'Yeah, I know,' she said. 'I saw you step on the dog.'

'Except maybe the arm-wrestling,' he said. 'That might keep me going.'

'All men are suckers for that,' Jennie said. She moved over to a dining chair by the table. 'Deep down they don't think it's possible for a woman to beat them, but they're not sure about it. So whenever the chance of proving it comes up they want to have a go. Come over here,' she said. 'I'm going to tell you the basic facts. I was the European Champion for two years. And for the last three years I have been either a finalist or semi-finalist. So you won't beat me.'

'You gonna humiliate me?'

'You can pull out if you like,' she said. 'But if we go ahead with it I'll beat you.'

He looked at her. Caught and held her eyes. He'd never liked aggressive women, but he was ready to make an exception. He liked the way her dark hair hung over her eye. He liked her sense of humour. The way she'd told the story about her mother. If she was going to beat him she'd have to be good. He stood and moved towards the bathroom. 'Get yourself psyched up,' he said. 'I'll be right back. Just gonna take a leak.'

chapter 28

Norman loaded the guns and ammo into the boot of a three-year-old Ford with a sunroof. He had the sunroof open. It was a nice car he'd found down by the river, complete with a burglar alarm which had gone off when he broke in. Bleeping away like a stuck pig. He'd fought with it for several minutes before he'd sussed how to quieten the thing down. No one interfered. No one said anything. They weren't interested, the tourists and the people passing by. They didn't like the noise, but they didn't want to get involved. They were wise people.

When he'd piled up the guns and covered them with a rug he went back into the flat and returned with a stack of tapes from Janet's collection. He had his Tina Turner tape, and the one of Janet's that he knew he liked was the Diana Ross *Greatest Hits*. In addition to those he had three John Lennon tapes, one early one from when he was the Beatles, then one called *Rock 'n' Roll*, and one from just before the guy went to have breakfast with Jesus. It had her on as well, Yoko What'sherface? Which Norman definitely didn't like, her being just totally noisy, screaming, out of time and out of tune. Not like music's supposed to be. 'I reckon this guy, Mark Chapman, the guy who shot Lennon, what he was really after was putting *her* away,' Norman had told Janet the previous evening. 'She was there, right? When Lennon bought it? OK, we've cracked it then,' he said. 'Mark Chapman with his gun full of dum-dums, he's not a natural born killer. He's shakin' like a leaf. New York, right? Freezin' cold, and he's been standing there all day. He's aiming at Mrs Yoko, but he's shakin' so hard he can't get a bead on her. And when he finally starts letting go, Johnny boy gets in the way. Old fucking screaming Yoko there, she's scampering up the steps, 'cause she prolly knows the guy's after her, and Lennon's inherited all her karma. He's looking up at Jesus, and Jesus's already got the kettle on, milk in the cups, and he's trying to remember how many sugars John takes. Whadda you say, Janet? Am I a detective or am I a detective?'

She shook her head. 'I think he was after Lennon,' she said. 'He was the Catcher in the Rye.'

'OK,' Norman said. 'But if it was me I'd have been after her.'

Diana Ross and Tina Turner together would keep him fully occupied. He could play both them tapes a couple of times and by that time he'd be in Manchester. If he felt like it once he hit the motorway he could play bits of the John Lennon tapes, fast forward through the tracks where his wife was screeching. Then he would know more about John Lennon, could quote some of the words to Janet when he wanted some finger pie. Plus, the bonus was, he'd stand some chance of understanding what Janet was talking about half the time.

Norman walked round the corner to the barber shop. Take a little time, make sure he looked like a guy who took care of himself. In business, first impressions count. He registered a couple of holes in the glass door as he walked in the place. The barber was sitting in the barber chair with his feet up on the washbasin. He was reading the *Sun*. When Norman came in he got out of the chair and threw the tabloid on to a counter. 'Yeah,' he said. 'They're bullet holes. Check this out.' He walked over to the window to the right of the door. He pointed out another five bullet holes. 'And check this out,' he said. He snapped his fingers and went to the other window, the left of the door. There were another three bullet holes. One of these had cracked the window from top to bottom.

Norman grinned, sat in the barber chair. 'You been having some trouble?' he asked.

The barber threw a black cape around Norman's shoulders. 'It's unbelievable,' he said. 'I don't believe it. I didn't believe it was possible before it happened. When it was happening I couldn't believe it was happening to me. And now it's happened I still don't believe it.' He showed Norman his palms in the mirror, holding them out like a man who was lost. 'What am I doing here?' he said. 'You want a trim? You want to keep the beard?'

'Yeah,' Norman said. 'Jus' tidy me up, OK? I want the beard. But I want the beard short.'

'I have to pay for this,' the barber said. 'Seven hundred quid. That's about four hundred haircuts. Just because some crazy kid shoots the shop up. I have to stand in front of four hundred heads and cut the hair on all of them for nothing. Does that seem fair to you?'

'No,' Norman told him. 'Doesn't seem fair. Not at all. What about insurance?'

'That's what I'm saying,' the barber said. 'There's some clause, they don't tell you this when you pay the premium, which says I should have shutters at the windows. Well, I got shutters at the windows all night long, but in the daytime I don't have shutters at the windows on account of it being a barber shop, and people wanting to look inside and see barber activity going on. Also, I don't have shutters up during the day, because I'm in here cutting people's hair, and if I do it in the dark I'm liable to cut their ears off, mutilate the odd nose, and I'm fairly sure there'll be a clause about that. I told the guy from the insurance, the one who told me about the clause. "Hey," I said, "what d'you mean there's a clause? How can there be a clause? I didn't do nothing. Nothing at all." I'm in here cutting hair. That's what I do. It's Saturday morning, right? The place is full of kids and their mothers. Teeming. They all wait for Saturday morning. Splat. Then again, another splat. Nobody knows what it is for a minute. There's holes appeared in the door, and we're all looking round, looking at each other. They're looking at me, like I might be shooting holes in my own windows. Then there's another one, that window there, with the crack. And, Jesus, one of the women says, "He's got a gun," and we all look out the window. This kid, could only be about ten, maybe twelve years old at the most. He's got a handgun, I don't know what it is, some kind of airgun maybe, but it's loaded with ball bearings. Steel ball bearings. And he's shooting up the shop. He gives us a few more, then he starts shooting up the cars by the side of the road. There's a Volvo out there, holes through the windscreen. After that he's blasting away at the bus shelter. The glass out of that just disintegrated. Then he's gone. He walks away. Five minutes later the shop's empty. It's Saturday morning, the busiest day of the week and I don't have no customers. I'm sitting in here with nothing to do, all my windows is full of holes, and the floor's covered in ball bearings. Whadda you think?'

'I blame the parents,' Norman told him, nodding through the mirror. 'Yeah, that's great,' he said, meaning the back of his head, which he could see reflected through a second mirror the barber was holding behind him.

'So now I don't get no customers,' the barber said. 'You're the first today. Probably the last. They're all saying it was the gunman did it. Even the people who were in here that day. The women who saw the little kid with the gun, even they're saying it was the gunman. This guy who's been doing the murders.' He raised his eyebrows at Norman in the mirror. 'Can you believe it?' he asked. 'People who know who did it are actually saying it was somebody else who did it, which is what's causing me to have no customers, when I've got at least four hundred haircuts coming for which I am doing it free.'

'I can see you're upset about it,' Norman said.

'It's just the neighbourhood,' said the barber, whipping the black cloak away from Norman's shoulders. 'That's the kind of place it's turned into. Never used to be like this. Used to be a good place to live. But not any more.'

He looked at Norman's tie. 'Hey, now that is what I call a nice tie,' he said. 'Where'd you get it?'

Norman couldn't remember the name of the place. 'If I remember I'll come back and tell you,' he said. He let the guy brush the loose hairs off his shoulders, paid him, and walked back round to Janet's flat. The poor sop would still have to do another three hundred and ninety-nine haircuts before he broke even.

She wanted to come, of course, Janet. Didn't want to be left at home all alone. All alone! Jesus, there's three cats in the hall. Two slags upstairs. She gave him a few sniffles and long wistful looks, threatened at one time to break out into a continuous howl. But she gave up on that idea when Norman told her he'd break her neck if she did it. But then he had to spend another half hour at least calming the bitch down, promising that she could come the next time, assuring her that he wouldn't be screwing other women, and that he'd come home safe, and that he'd buy her something expensive.

Which all meant that he didn't get on the road until much later than he'd anticipated, so the chances of getting to Manchester by lunchtime disappeared. When the lunchtime feeling hit him Norman was on top of the Pennines, and he pulled into the car park of a pub which was serving meals, or so it said on the hoarding outside.

Norman opened the boot and let Tabitha out. He'd really wanted to get Orchid in there, but she'd been too fast for him. Tabitha had been easy. Just let him pick her up and dump her in there. Now she could try and find her own way home. Norman had an almost certain feeling that she wasn't gonna make it. Would have put money on it. Tabitha walked slowly away from him, didn't turn for a last look. She wasn't going to plead.

Her ginger coat gave her a certain amount of camouflage, Norman thought. Allowed her to blend into the landscape up here.

Inside the hotel he found a dining room which was deserted apart from a tall hard-faced woman who gave him a menu. Norman ordered a prawn salad and a Pils, and she served him with both immediately. The salad was shrink-wrapped on the plate. When he was halfway through it, wishing he hadn't been so healthy minded and gone for the steak instead, the door opened and a man came in. The man was a head taller than Norman, and he wore a black suit with a faint stripe. Black brogues. He had on a white shirt and a thin grey tie with a Windsor knot. On his head he had a tight-fitting woolly cap, which was pulled down over his ears. He didn't remove it. He stood by the bar and regarded Norman.

Norman wore his new beige lightweight suit, and grey loafers with leather tassels. His shirt was black silk, and he'd pulled the knot of his tie down, and released the top button to display his gold chain. His short beard was freshly trimmed, and dangling from his right earlobe was a new gold ring in the shape of a saxophone.

Out of the corner of his eye Norman saw his own Ford in the car park. But nothing else. No other car. Around the pub or hotel or whatever it was supposed to be there was nothing but moor for as far as the eye could see.

Norman looked back at the guy and noticed that he had a small tuft of black hair growing out of a mole on his lower cheek. Could be he was a farmer, but what it felt like was that the guy was something else altogether. Not a farmer. Nothing at all like a farmer.

Norman pushed the remains of his meal away, got out of the seat and walked slowly to the door. The guy's eyes followed him all the way. Once through the door Norman walked quickly across the car park and got into the Ford. He turned the key in the ignition and threw up stones and grit as he gunned the accelerator and hit the open road again. He didn't stop for petrol before he got into the centre of Manchester.

Norman had to stop twice to ask directions, but he eventually found the Star. Was in the same place he'd left it. He went inside and had a glass of beer. There were a couple of girls in there, but neither was Tina, and there was no sign of the big brother. When he'd finished his drink Norman left the bar and walked around the corner to the house where he had gone with Tina on his previous visit. The door was open, but the place appeared deserted. No music coming from the back room. He stood at the door and knocked. After a while he pushed the door fully open and shouted. There was no response but Norman had been around long enough to know not to go inside.

After a couple of minutes a black teenager on a skateboard stopped on the road. 'They's at the funeral,' he said. Then he was off again.

Norman walked back to the Star and got himself another beer. 'Who's dead?' he asked the barmaid.

'Toby,' she said. 'You know him?'

'Big guy?'

She nodded. 'You know him.'

'What happened?' Norman asked.

The barmaid shrugged. 'Got in a argument,' she said. 'Not here. Somewhere near the station. Shot in his own car. Left him to bleed to death.'

'This is it,' Norman said. 'The state of the nation. This is where two thousand years of civilization has brought us.' He shook his head and gazed into his beer. Anyone could see he was deeply troubled by the world.

The barmaid gave him a wide berth the rest of the day, except to fill his glass when he asked. Norman slowly drank himself into a near coma. Several girls approached him during the early part of the afternoon, when he could still talk, or at least smile. But by early evening he was no longer trying to communicate.

Tina arrived around half-past eight and took him to the room they had shared before. She undressed him and put him in the bed and left him there while she returned to the Star. 'We're having a wake,' she told him. 'I'll see you later.' Norman blinked a couple of times, but she'd gone. He had her standing there, all in black. Large black hat, black tights. Looking like a dream.

He fell asleep and woke up in the dark. Had to get out of bed to piss in the sink. Then he crawled back into the warmth of the sheets.

And he spent the rest of the evening drifting in and out of dreams. He was the only surviving male on the planet. 'All

183

the men had been killed off,' he told Tina the next morning. 'There was only women left.'

'Sounds like one of my dreams,' she told him. 'In fact, it sounds like the dreams of all the women I know.'

'And so they was all crazy about me,' he said. 'Could do what I wanted with them.'

'Oh-oh,' said Tina. 'This is where our dreams start to go different ways.'

Norman couldn't keep up with her. Her mind seemed to be working at twice the speed of his. He'd abused himself last night, drinking, and he wasn't used to it. Janet kept him healthy with regular meals, talking about sesame seeds and pumpkin seeds, all that stuff. Without her he'd fallen into bad ways already. Now he felt like a basket case. And he had the trots, rushing off to the lavatory every five minutes. 'My ringpiece is doing a dance,' he said, coming back for the fifth time. 'It's like it's completely independent of me, working out on its own.'

Tina made a face. 'Ugh,' she said. Making out she was shocked or offended.

'What you wanna be like that for?' Norman said. 'I'm jus' describing a normal biological process.' He slumped down on the bed. 'Try plugging yourself into a piece of compassion, here, Tina. I've got the mother of all hangovers.'

Still feeling shaky, Norman followed Tina downstairs and got into the back of a gleaming black Rolls Garnet Shadow II. There was a black chauffeur up front, and a wraith-like brother with thick-lensed spectacles huddled in the back seat. It took Norman a moment or two to focus on the tiny brother. The car itself was overwhelming. Leaving Tina's room and seeing it on the street had taken his breath away. It had specially fitted chrome wheel-arches, custom hubcaps and whitewall tyres. The interior was soft magnolia leather upholstery, piped in red and with armrest tops. There were headrests, and when Norman put his head against the one behind him he could look up at the sky through the electric sunroof.

'Don't go to sleep,' the figure in the corner warned. His

184

voice was like a hiss. You couldn't tell if it was a hiss for effect or if it reflected a medical condition. Some of the brothers in the prison had talked like that, but not to white men, what they called honkeys. They didn't speak to honkeys at all.

'I talked to the big guy,' Norman said. 'We had a deal.'

The little brother shook his head. Norman couldn't make out his features in the gloom of the corner. 'Don't bullshit,' he said. 'Toby told me you might have cars or dope.'

Norman sighed. 'Or shooters,' he said. 'I told him shooters.'

'Yeah,' breathed the rasping reply. 'Shooters. Is that what you got?'

'I got sixty-eight assorted weapons,' Norman told him. 'I got ammo, the lot. You interested?'

The brother nodded. What light there was caught his spectacles for a moment. 'You heard about Toby,' he said. 'There's gonna be a war here.'

'Sounds like I arrived right on time,' Norman told him. 'We jus' gotta sort out the money.'

'We'll talk money later,' the wraith said. 'First we'll have a look at the goods.'

The Shadow II pulled to a halt and the chauffeur came round to open Norman's door. The wraith didn't speak as Norman left the car, and Norman didn't speak either, didn't turn round and offer his hand. Nothing. He stood on the pavement outside the Star and watched the beautiful car disappear around the corner.

Norman would have gone into the bar, but two brothers came out of there and joined him on the street. They were both a head taller than Norman, and one of them had a knife scar from nose to chin that travelled down through both lips. Norman wondered where and how the guy got it, and what the other guy looked like, but he didn't ask. He watched while the Scar said: 'Let's take a looksee, then, the shooters you got.' The other one, the one without the scar, looked real surprised when the Scar spoke, like he'd never heard the Scar speak before, or maybe he'd never heard language before at all. He looked surprised and puzzled, not unhappy. But confused, certainly confused.

Norman put one hand in his trouser pocket, the other to his head. He turned round on the pavement, a complete circle. He looked at his feet, still holding his head. 'Let me get it right,' he said. 'Two of you want me to take you to where the shooters are? Two of you and one of me?'

''S'right,' said the Scar.

'And does that seem right to you?' Norman asked. 'I mean does it seem fair? You two being so much bigger than me, and twice as many as me?'

The Scar looked at his friend and said: 'The white man's fucking us about.'

'I think,' said the other one, and he paused on the word think and looked as though he expected to be congratulated or even knighted. 'I think so,' he said finally.

'Look,' the Scar said. 'I've gotta drink on the bar. You wanna play, or do I go drink it?'

Norman had actually considered all there was to consider when he had done that histrionic turn on the pavement. This was his only possibility of getting rid of the guns. Maybe he'd get paid for them, maybe he wouldn't. There was even a possibility, a good possibility that they'd take the guns and leave him dead, or try to. Norman didn't care. If they tried anything he'd give as good as he got. He had a loaded gun in his shoulder holster. If there was any trouble he'd blow these two away. Scarface and Dickhead. Who'd miss them?

'OK, let's go,' he said. 'You got wheels?'

They travelled in the Scar's BMW V8 automatic. It sported five-spoke alloys and was finished in Calypso red metallic with a light silver leather trim, air conditioning, and a stacker CD radio cassette. These guys were slicker'n snot on a doorknob.

Norman had left the Ford in a cash-and-flash car park near the station, and the Scar pulled in close behind it. Norman unlocked the boot and opened it, then he stood back while the two brothers inspected the shooters. He loosened the gun in his shoulder holster, listened to the sound of them inspecting the contents of the suitcases, watched their backs and fantasized about them trying to rip him off. Giving themselves the average life expectancy of fruit flies.

They were probably druggies, he thought. Most of the brothers were druggies inside, so they must be the same outside. Addled brains. Drugs turn you crazy. The more you do the more crazy you get. You do enough of them and really crazy ideas start to sound OK. Even things like destroying private property, things like that, free love, women's rights, lesbianism – even jealousy, getting rid of jealousy, things like that all begin to seem possible. That's why folks like chemicals so much. They take you away from reality. They make you forget who you are, what you're doing. They make you feel like there are things possible which aren't possible. And then you get in trouble. Specially you get in trouble if you're a kid, or a woman, or a black. Stands to reason.

Everybody understands that, everybody knows that, 'cept for the ones who are already hooked. They don't know, they can never know because as soon as they start to suspect the truth they go out on a hunt for more chemicals to fuck them over.

The Scar was actually smiling. He'd turned round during Norman's cogitation and was leaning up against the rear of the Ford with a big smile on his face. 'It's good stuff,' he said. 'How much you looking for?'

'Ten big ones,' Norman said. He felt a small tic start up under his left eye.

'They're not that good,' the Scar said. His companion did a small nervous laugh. 'Maybe we can stretch to somewhere around five?'

'Jesus,' said Norman. 'Five? How'm I supposed to make a profit out of five? Listen, they cost me more than that. If I take five and go back to my supplier with five thousand, what do you think I'm gonna get? I'm gonna get about half as many weapons as I got now.' He scratched his head and looked off into the distance. 'I have to ask myself: "Is this any way to run a business." And you know what the answer says when it comes back? No, Norman, that's what it is. This is no way at all to run a business. Unless, that is, you

187

want to run the business into the ground. But what I hear coming from you guys is that you don't want me to run this particular business into the ground, because you've got a war on your hands. And having that war on your hands, you need more weapons than you can even think about to make sure you win your war against whoever it was shot up the big guy – Toby? – who we all buried yesterday.

'That's all on the one hand. On the other hand, you do want me to run this business into the ground, because you only want to pay half the value of the goods that this business is in the business of supplying. And any business on the face of this earth is gonna get run into the ground if it sells its products for half the face value.

'And that's on the other hand. And this hand and that hand add up to more than five grand whichever way you look at it. So I'll tell you again what I want to hear from you. It's ten big ones. Or no deal.' He looked at his watch, then he looked at it again. 'Time is money,' he said. 'I've got a whole lot of other things I should be doing. Places I should be. You keep me here yapping much longer, by the time I get home tonight it'll be fuckin' morning.'

'Six,' said the Scar.

'OK,' said Norman. 'We got a deal.' He did a quick smile. The kind you'd have to practise in a mirror.

The Scar got a brown envelope from the glove compartment of his V8 automatic and handed it to Norman. Norman passed the keys of the Ford over in exchange. The Scar got into the BMW and his mate slid behind the wheel of the Ford. They both waved as they pulled out of the car park, leaving Norman behind holding that fat brown envelope about the same size as Clint Eastwood's wallet.

'Yeah, Howard? Simon here. Listen.' The guy on the train was in full swing. He had one of those mobiles with the flip-down mouthpiece. He was sitting on an outside seat, next to the aisle, and his briefcase was open on the seat next to him. The table between the seats was covered with the guy's stuff, papers, a diary, some kind of electronic calculator or organizer. Norman didn't know what it was. He took the seat opposite the guy and watched him talk into the mobile.

'Listen, Howard, there's a truck on the wharf with thirty-five tons. I've had Dozy on to me, and there's no way they can take it in. I'm looking for a favour, Howard, I need a space for it. When? Well now, Howard, as we speak the truck is sitting on the wharf. The guy, the driver's threatening Dozy that he'll tip the lot on the doorstep.'

There was a sheen on his brow, a kind of patina to his face. This was the only indication that the man was driven. He was oblivious of Norman, of his surroundings, apart from the papers and gadgets. He was around thirty, wearing a pin-striped suit, and he had curly hair, thin, wiry stuff that he had to keep short or he'd have turned into a violinist.

'That would save my life, Howard,' he said into the mouthpiece. 'That would earn you a lot of points in Heaven. OK, I'll tell Dozy to contact you direct. No, don't do anything. I'll ask Dozy to ring you. In a few minutes. And Howard? I owe you a big one for this.'

He closed up the phone to cut the connection and opened it up again without looking at Norman. He pressed a one-touch button and looked into the phone as though it might have a screen attached. 'Dozy?' he said. 'Howard Screeton will take it in. Two days, maximum. I hated having to ask him, and he's going to charge us a fortune for it. But it solves your immediate problem. Look, what I suggest – are you by yourself? – OK, then get in the cab with the driver and take him round to Howard. Ring Howard first. Ring him now, as soon as I've finished. Tell him what's happening, then get in the cab with the driver and go with him to Howard's.

'What? Why the hell would I tell you how to do your job? I'm not telling you how to do your job. You come on to me saying you're at the end of your tether, the guy, the driver, he's going to dump a load on your doorstep. OK, Dozy, so what do I do? Do I tell you hard things, like you're on your own? No, Dozy, I don't do any of those things. I sort the thing out for you. So don't tell me I'm telling you how to do your job. Yeah? I should think so. You should be sorry. Goodbye to you, too.'

He closed up the phone again and put it on the table in front of him. He didn't look at Norman, but he sighed deeply, closed his eyes briefly, then opened them again. He took a foolscap sheet of paper from his briefcase and placed it in front of him. He pulled the electronic calculator towards him and began tapping the keys, making reference to the sheet of figures.

The trolley came into the carriage and the guy with the phone bought a sandwich and a coffee. Norman got a coffee. When the guy was paying for his sandwich and coffee his phone rang. He abandoned payment and went for the phone. 'Sal? Yeah,' he said. 'I've sorted it out. Dozy? No, he wasn't particularly. But that's life. That's the thanks you get. I'm the kind of man, I don't mind putting myself out for a friend. Somebody's in trouble, I'll give them a helping hand. Yeah, Sal, I know you do. I know you are. I'm the same. I think somebody doesn't ask for help unless they really need it. I wouldn't do that – involve somebody else – well, of course, everyone's busy. Busy as hell. I wouldn't do that unless I *really* needed it. Know what I mean? *Really?*'

The steward held out his hand for the curly-haired guy's money. The curly-haired guy looked annoyed but he reached inside his jacket and came out with a wallet. He handed the wallet to the steward, who extracted a ten-pound note and returned the wallet. The curly-headed guy threw the wallet into his open briefcase. 'I'm getting into a tangle, here, Sal,' he said. 'Being hassled for money.' The steward counted out change on to the table, and the curly-headed guy lurched forward to collect it. He caught the coffee cup and sent it over on to his foolscap sheet of paper. Some of it splashed Norman's hand.

'Oh, my goodness,' the curly-headed guy said into the phone. 'Going to have to leave this for a minute, Sal. Accident just happened. I need both hands. Be back to you immediately. Yes, I'll be back in two ticks. Don't go anywhere.' He closed up the phone and looked over at Norman with a smile. 'I'm really sorry,' he said. 'The steward was hassling me.' He raised himself slightly in the seat and shouted after the trolley, which was now several seats away.

'Hey, waiter, do you have some tissues? We've had an accident here.'

The steward ignored him.

'That's quite a thing,' said Norman. 'That telephone. I've never seen one of those.'

'Oh,' said the curly-headed guy, 'it's a life saver. I'd be lost without it.' He picked it up and gave it a smile.

'Can I see?' said Norman.

The guy handed it over.

Norman took it and snapped the mouthpiece off.

'Oh, no.' The curly-headed guy got to his feet. 'What're you doing?'

'Shutting you up,' Norman told him. 'Now, sit down and be quiet. If I get one more squeak out of you I'll shove both these pieces of telephone so far up your ass they'll come down your nose.'

The man sat down. Several minutes later he put all of his belongings into his briefcase and closed it. But he didn't speak. He didn't say a thing for the rest of the journey.

chapter 29

Janet had looked everywhere for Tabitha. But Tabitha was nowhere to be found. She had disappeared about the same time Norman had left for Manchester. Janet remembered seeing her curled up on the chair in the living room when Norman came back from the barber's. Then Norman had chosen which tapes he would take with him and driven away. Would he come back? Had he left her for good? Gone to find himself a woman with real breasts?

After that Janet had gone into the living room and fallen into the chair Tabitha had been curled up in. She noticed Tabitha wasn't there. She noticed immediately, because Janet had sat and cried in the chair for twenty minutes after Norman left. Venus was there. In the other chair. And

Orchid came in when Janet began crying, and stayed for the duration. Orchid had a heart. But Tabitha had a heart as well, and she didn't show up. Janet had thought it strange at the time, but Tabitha hadn't shown since, and that wasn't like her.

Janet thought that Norman didn't really like any of her cats, so she couldn't imagine, if he had gone away for good, that he would have actually absconded with Tabitha. And if he hadn't gone away for good, but had gone to Manchester on business, as he was supposed to do, he certainly wouldn't have taken Tabitha along for company. Not without saying. Though there was the possibility that Tabitha had got locked inside Norman's car by mistake.

A distant possibility. Not very likely. When Tabitha didn't turn up for breakfast the following morning, that unlikely explanation became the one that Janet fixed upon. She told Orchid and Venus, 'You know what Tabitha's gone and done? Got herself a trip to Manchester, that's what. The silly girl got herself locked in the boot of Norman's car, or maybe not in the boot, in the back seat, maybe. Anyway, wherever it is, she's gone on a long trip to Manchester, and with nothing to eat, probably. Norman wouldn't know what to feed her. She'll be starving when they get back. Serves her right.'

Janet had some money that Norman had left her. A twenty-pound note. She left a message for Norman on the kitchen table, in case he returned early, and went out into the town with the money. She walked along the city wall from Monkgate to Bootham Bar, looking at the beautiful gardens of the houses around the Minster. Imagining her and Norman living in one of those houses, those vast expanses of lawn, and the ancient trees. It would be paradise for the cats.

She went to the Arts Centre and bought lunch for herself. A cheese salad, only cost two pounds twenty pence, and there was nearly more than you could eat. Janet didn't like it inside the Arts Centre, because it was dark, and outside was bright sunshine. Also the people who ate there were odd. They dressed as if they hadn't any money, clothes from charity shops, hand-me-downs, but they spoke as if they had lots of money. They spoke posh. She couldn't understand that. It put her off her meal. But they served vegetarian food, and they didn't charge the earth for it, so she went as often as she could afford to. She never stayed for very long. Just ate the food and escaped as quickly as possible. She would have preferred to buy the food at the Arts Centre and take it over to the Museum Gardens and eat it outside on the grass. But she didn't suppose the people in the Arts Centre café would want her to take their plates so far away.

After all, how were they to know that she would bring it back? For all they knew she was a thief. But Janet knew she would bring it back. She wouldn't steal a plate.

It was in the Museum Gardens, while she was watching a peacock tantalize a group of tourists with its tail, that Janet first noticed the boy. He was trying to look as though he was part of the group, but he was watching her. He wasn't a man. He wasn't like Norman at all. He wore a soft leather jacket over a T-shirt, and he had a baseball cap which he was wearing sideways, the peak over his right ear. He was very thin, long legs, and a soft, effeminate face. He was not a real man, not what Janet called a man, anyway. She wouldn't be surprised to find that someone like him preferred other boys. So why was he looking at her? Probably because she had nothing up top. Maybe he thought she was a boy?

She lost sight of him for nearly an hour after that, though she still suspected he was hanging around. Once they got sex into their minds men tended to hang around sniffing for ever, or until they got it. After that it'd be you looking for them. But she didn't see him again until she was nearly home. She had taken the new path along the beck, way off the tourist track, and the locals didn't use it much either, only a few kids with bikes. So there was nowhere he could hide. He kept well back, but there was no doubt in Janet's mind that this strange young man was following her.

Perhaps he was the one, the murderer, the one who had done these killings in the town? Though she didn't really believe that. He was all skin and bone. There was no fight in him. Still, better to be safe than sorry. Janet slipped through a passage between two houses and got to her flat the back way. The boy, if he was a murderer or a nutter, someone who fancied a woman with no breasts, whatever he was, he had lost her – just as she had lost her beloved Tabitha.

'What I'm gonna do,' Norman said, 'tomorrow, is, I'm gonna get one of those phones. You know, without a plug?'

'A mobile,' said Janet. She watched him struggle out of his jacket. He had paid off the taxi outside and walked up the path into the house. He hadn't said hello. He'd come in and made this announcement about a mobile phone.

'Yes,' she said. 'I had a fantastic day. Went out for lunch. What about you?'

Norman looked at her. He had hoped she would be better by the time he got back, but there was still something eating her. 'It was OK,' he said. 'Did what I was supposed to.'

'Did you take Tabitha with you?'

Norman had to look at her again. Did she know? He didn't think so. 'Tabitha?' he said. 'The cat?'

'Yes,' said Janet. 'She's been missing since yesterday. I thought she might have got trapped in the car.'

'No,' he said, absently. 'I haven't seen her.' He walked through to the kitchen, crouched in front of the fridge with the door open, and gazed in there to see if anything tickled his fancy.

Janet felt sad. If Tabitha wasn't with Norman then she must be dead. She wouldn't just wander off, or run away from home. She must have been killed. Janet knew she would never see her again. She felt her face collapse, and several hot tears spouted from her eyes and ran down her cheeks. But she found control somewhere and immediately dried her eyes. Norman would get angry if she cried now. It would only make matters worse.

'It must have been that boy,' she said, when Norman came back from the kitchen. He had some cold rice and carrots in a Pyrex bowl, and was eating it with a spoon. It was the wrong spoon. Janet kept that spoon for the cats. 'Must've been one of them sadists. They take people's pets and torture them to death.'

With the spoon, Norman pointed to his bulging cheeks,

and he widened his eyes. He meant that his mouth was full and he couldn't talk without spitting rice all over the floor. Janet nodded to let him know she understood. She'd seen a programme on the television about kids who tortured cats. It had been on a council estate on Merseyside. They were nearly all boys. There were a couple of girls, but they were mainly boys. She thought they were younger than the boy who had followed her from the town, but maybe he was one of them, grown up taller now, and moved over from Merseyside to torture her cats. She looked around the room for Venus and Orchid. Both of them were there. She'd have to keep a sharp eye on them during the next few days. Make sure they came to no harm.

Norman had gone back to the kitchen. She heard him put his bowl and spoon in the sink and run water into the bowl. He wouldn't wash it. He would leave it in soak for her. He left everything for her. She wondered if he knew that she did the washing up, or if he thought it was done by magic. Same with the bathroom, the mess he left in there. Norman'd never dream that Janet cleaned up after him, he probably thought the fairies came in at night and cleaned the piss from around the toilet bowl.

He returned to the sitting room and took her by the hand to pull her out of the chair. 'Come on,' he said. 'Let's go to bed.'

'I can't,' she said. 'It's my time of the month.'

He had to work it out. You could see him doing it. He looked at you and he repeated the last four words, didn't actually say them but mouthed them to himself. *Time of the month* . . . Then a kind of dawning took place. Oh, *that* time of the month.

He pulled her to her feet. 'I don't mind,' he said.

Janet dug her feet in. 'But *I* mind,' she said. 'I don't like it when I'm . . . this way.'

'I thought you didn't have that,' he said. 'Time of the month, all that business.'

'I don't,' she said. 'I don't actually have it. But I have the *time* I should be having it. Which is the same.'

Norman smiled and continued pulling her towards the

bedroom. 'It'll be all right,' he said. 'C'mon.' He pulled her to the door.

'I don't want to do it like this,' she said. 'Don't make me, Norman.'

'OK,' he said. He put his arm round her shoulder and coaxed her over the threshold. He was gentle, but he was lying. He was going to do it anyway. She knew it.

'You're going to do it, aren't you?' she said. 'Even though I don't want you to?'

Norman showed his teeth. Must've felt like a smile to him, but it didn't make Janet feel any happier.

She'd been in the penicillin factory and had a bath. Norman had gone to sleep after ravaging her body. Her left nipple was bleeding again. She wished he'd give it time to heal. She didn't know why he had to use his teeth anyway. The sucking was OK, even though it was painful. She didn't mind the sucking. But when he bit her she fought with all her strength. It didn't make any difference, of course. He pinned her down and did it. Seemed to like it more. Thought it was a game.

After the bath she dressed in pyjamas and a thick towelling robe. She put on a pair of thick woollen socks, made herself a milky drink and sat on the sofa between Venus and Orchid. She played *Double Fantasy* quietly, so as not to wake her man.

She stretched her toes inside the woollen socks, and thought this is what heaven must be like. Except in heaven Tabitha would be there as well. And it wouldn't be a recording of John Lennon. It would be the real thing.

She smiled at the thought. He came on in bed like an army of occupation. It wasn't funny at the time, but later she could smile about it.

She must have dozed for a while after she'd finished her drink. Either she'd slept or been in that semi-conscious state between sleep and waking. She suddenly snapped out of it and was wide awake, and she didn't know where she'd been, what she'd been thinking about. The tape was still playing in the background. But Janet's eyes were fixed on Norman's jacket slung over the back of a chair.

There was something on it, the front of it, thrown into focus.

Janet got off the sofa and went over to the chair. She picked up the jacket and examined it carefully. She took one short ginger hair from the front, low down, by the right pocket. She looked at the jacket again. After a moment she took another short ginger hair from the lower part of the left lapel.

Norman didn't have ginger hair.

No human had ginger hairs like these. These were cat's hairs. These were Tabitha's hairs. Janet took the hairs back to the sofa and showed them to Venus and Orchid.

'Why?' she said to both cats. 'Why would Tabitha's hairs be on Norman's jacket?'

And neither Venus nor Orchid said a word. They knew what they knew.

Janet thought of her mother. She rarely thought of her mother, preferred not to think of her. Usually when Janet thought of her mother she became panicky. But this time she did not become panicky, because the thought she thought about her mother was not really a thought at all. It was more like a picture, a moving picture.

It was a memory.

Usually the memories that Janet had of her mother were negative. Painful. Disturbing. But this memory was not like that. It was positive.

Her mother was standing beside a stove. It was winter. It was Advent. A few days before Christmas. Janet's mother was happy. She had that soft smile on her face that came only once or twice a year. That smile that made everything seem all right.

Janet was twelve. Maybe only eleven. She had returned home from school and her mother had asked her to stay in the kitchen. They talked together for a time. Janet's mother wanted to know what kind of day her daughter had had. She also wanted to tell her daughter what she had been doing, and what she had been thinking.

Then she said the thing that Janet remembered now. The memory.

It wasn't like a pronouncement, or even a piece of advice really. It was a throwaway line. Something that slipped out. She said: 'Men were born to lie, and women to believe them.'

And Janet had forgotten all about it. She hadn't thought about it from that day until this. But she remembered it now.

chapter 30

Sam didn't have an appointment with the solicitor, George Forester, so he had to wait. Forester was talking to another client, who had thought to make an appointment. This information was given to Sam by Forester's secretary, a loaf-haired lady of indeterminate age and magnificent and terrifying demeanour. Her style was old-school. When she told Sam to sit there was never any question about it. He sat. But he didn't only sit, he sat exactly where the lady ordered. On his first visit to this office he had found himself squirming on that bench, shuffling slightly to the right, slightly to the left, until he was sure that the secretary was satisfied with his position.

He hadn't felt that threatened since his first day at school.

The last couple of times he had been to Forester's office he had been bolder, even tried to make her smile. But his attempts were still feeble, and unsuccessful.

Once having got him seated on the bench she would return to her enormous typewriter. She had the thing angled so she could keep a whole eye on the bench while she typed up her contracts and briefs. Her blouse, if that's what it was called, was gigantic and starched as stiff as a table top. It was cleaner'n a nun's imagination. Sam's mind tended to seize up at this point. The only thing he knew for sure was he would never invite her to his birthday party.

Forester eventually came to rescue him, though he came

out of his office in the guise of the absent-minded solicitor. He always looked as though he was suppressing a fart. He had a confused look about him, which was probably genetic. But Sam had a sneaking suspicion that he adopted these ways to impress his staff and clients. In reality, and in all his dealings with the man Sam was impressed that he actually did know exactly what he was doing.

He had been in the air force for several years – flying a desk – and he had many stories about it which he didn't mind repeating ad infinitum.

Sam followed Forester into his office and sat in a deep leather armchair. Forester also sat down and looked over at Sam. 'I can remember when this was a nice place to live,' he said. 'Now we have four murders in the last few days. That first couple, the gun dealer and his wife, they lived three streets away from me. My wife hasn't been out of the house since it happened.' He looked away from Sam, at an imaginary point up near the ceiling. 'And then Gus,' he continued. 'Have you got any leads?'

'We're not working entirely in the dark,' Sam told him. 'But you might be able to help. I need to contact a woman used to be known as Selina White, but married a local solicitor called Crumble, maybe seven years back.'

'Crumble,' Forester said. 'That'd be Freddie Crumble. He's dead. Cancer, I think, of the brain. About three years ago. And I met her, his wife, Selina. Pretty woman.'

'Is she still around?' Sam asked. 'In the area? Do you know where she lives?'

'No, I don't know,' said Forester. 'But I know a man who does. His ex-partner is still practising. I could give him a ring.' Forester took up the phone and asked his secretary to connect him to Freddie Crumble's ex-partner. Sam left his chair and went to the window while Forester talked on the phone. There was an ocean-going cruiser on the river, travelling very slowly to avoid collision with a host of smaller craft. It had a tanned god at the helm and a teenage bathing beauty on the foredeck. The hold, Sam mused, would be filled with gold.

This just goes to prove that it's people who screw things

up, Sam thought. Without the bronzed god and the beauty queen it was a real nice boat. Sam made a note to get one just like it, soon as he'd won the lottery.

'She lives alone,' Forester told Sam when he'd replaced the telephone into its cradle. He scribbled an address on to a compliment slip and handed it to Sam. 'Lives in Malton with her son. Three years old, born a fortnight after his father died.'

Sam thanked the solicitor and prepared to run the gauntlet of his secretary in the outer office. It was not painless. As he stepped his way gingerly towards the door she gave him a look that went clean through him and damaged the wall beyond.

He wondered if he should offer her an arm-wrestling contest. Sort out this conflict once and for all.

Sam pointed the Volvo in the direction of the A64 and followed it north to Malton. There was a police road block on the way out of town. The car ahead of Sam was waved to the side of the road, but Sam was allowed past. The police manning the block were obviously only doing random checks. Didn't really know what they were looking for. They looked bored. Earning lots of overtime, but not even inspired by the thoughts of what they'd spend it on.

Malton was a sleepy hollow of a town which Sam didn't know very well, and didn't want to. The kind of place you retired to and waited to die. God's waiting room.

He called in at a service station and bought himself a cling-film sandwich, then he drove past the semi-detached house of Selina Crumble, Norman Bunce's Snow White, turned the car and parked on the opposite side of the street in a position that gave him a good view of her front door and garden. Sam peeled his sandwich and settled down to wait.

Then the thought came, just like it always did, out of the blue. Wouldn't it be nice to have a bottle of beer. A cold beer to wash the sandwich down. Sam knew he couldn't allow himself to think it for more than a split second. He put the sandwich down and cast about for the clichés and aphorisms that he had used in the past to save himself from this situation. *It's the first drink that gets you drunk. There are a million excuses to drink, but not one good reason.* The first one, *It's the first drink that gets you drunk.* That had been a revelation to him when he'd first heard it. It had evaded him for years. It was so simple, so true, so glaringly obvious that he hadn't been able to see it. He would always remember hearing it for the first time at an AA meeting in Islington. A woman called Dorothy had said it, just dropped it into the conversation over coffee break, then made some kind of excuse, said she had to go.

Sam had wanted to hug her. He couldn't speak. He watched her put down her coffee cup and pick up her coat and bag. Then she went to the door and was gone. *It's the first drink that gets you drunk.* Hell, it was like being touched by God. 'That's amazing,' Sam said to another man who had been involved in the conversation. 'What Dorothy said. That's profound.'

The man smiled.

Sam couldn't remember the last time he'd been to AA. It was too long. Maybe three weeks. If he left it longer than that he would start to falter. Start to remember he was alone. It was only at AA meetings that he knew he was not alone. He would go tonight. Whatever else happened he would go tonight.

Snow White came out of the front door with her son in her arms. She put him down on the step and brought out a folded push-chair, unfolded it, and lifted the small boy on to the seat. Sam would not have recognized her from the photograph he had from her sister. But she did look like Princess Leia. Her movements were quick and nervous, and she glanced behind her occasionally, as though she couldn't quite believe there wasn't something or someone creeping up on her.

As soon as he saw her Sam knew that he would never tell Norman Bunce where she was.

He might have to use her as bait to draw Norman out of his lair. He might very well have no other option but to use her in that way. But he would never give her to him. She was free and beautiful. She had escaped. It would be unforgivable to give her back.

She pushed the little boy out of the garden and crossed the road. She walked tall, her shoulder-length hair swaying from side to side. When she drew level with the Volvo she glanced at Sam, gave him a look that made him wish he was younger and handsomer and worth a million, and assured him that he wasn't.

chapter 31

Sam drove home and got himself some coffee, took it out into the small garden. He left the door open so he could hear the tape, 'It's all over now, baby blue . . .' The sky was blue, the garden was mainly an expanse of grass with some stacked timber, a shed with a broken window and a felt-covered roof with green mouldy vegetation. All of this was surrounded by green hedges and trees. The sun was high in the sky, and a slight breeze played with one or two tulips down at the far end, couple of red ones and a yellow one. Roses. Incredibly peaceful, as if it was very early in the morning, no sound or movement apart from those tulips, and birds flying backwards and forwards. A robin dropped from the roof to the grass, hopping about. It was joined by a finch, and they were wary of each other. Both looking for the same snack.

I'm afraid to fall in love with Jennie, he realized. I'm afraid to fall in love with anyone since Donna. He carefully rolled a cigarette and put it to his lips. He lit it up and took a deep drag. There was a feeling of satisfaction which was soothing, but short lived. He coughed violently and shook his head; angry at his lungs for not managing better. But he dropped the cigarette on to the grass and ground it away with his heel.

He walked to the meeting. Left the car behind and legged it through the town. A woman in a doorway looked at him hard and long. He almost stopped and apologized to her for not being Gene Hackman. He recalled the thought about being afraid to fall in love with Jennie, and looked at it from the outside. When it had first occurred to him in the garden he had immediately banished it. But now he brought it back. Fear was something Sam understood. One of the few things he understood. He was an alcoholic. FEAR was an acronym. It meant: Fuck Everything And Run.

It was not Sam's home meeting, but not one he was totally unfamiliar with. There were twelve people there, six men and six women. They all knew each other, and Sam knew all of them but two. The average age would be somewhere between thirty and forty, and they had all, each of them in his or her own way, made some effort to present themselves positively. Polished shoes, an ironed blouse, creased trousers, immaculately applied make-up. They were all thoroughly decent people.

A man of about fifty detached himself from a small group and came over to Sam. 'How you doing?' Sam asked him.

The man smiled. 'Had the poor-me's for the last couple of days. But I'm coming through. What about you?'

'I'm sober,' Sam said. 'Haven't had a drink all day.'

'You know what's the difference between a normal drinker and an alcoholic?'

'Is this another of your famous jokes, Jed?'

'The normal drinker says, "I'm going to the pub and I'm gonna get drunk," but the alcoholic says, "I'm going to the pub but I'm *not* gonna get drunk."'

Sam laughed. He'd heard it before, but what the hell? If somebody tries to make you laugh, you might as well go for it. There're plenty of times when it's impossible to laugh. You might as well do it whenever you can. 'I don't have one for you,' he told Jed. 'People seem to have stopped telling me jokes.'

'It's because you don't go in pubs,' Jed said. 'That's where all the jokes get passed on. People pretending they're happy so they don't have to look at themselves.'

'Maybe,' Sam said, not committing himself.

The convener was trying to get the meeting started and Sam and Jed walked towards the chairs. Jed touched Sam's arm and whispered, 'I'll tell you something, though.'

'What's that?'

'This is no place to be if you want a decent drink.'

The convener asked a woman called Janice, who was seated next to Sam, to read the preamble. After that one of the men who Sam didn't know told how alcohol had affected his life. Sam listened subconsciously while he read the 12 Steps. He returned time and time again to Step 4 which was about making a 'searching and fearless moral inventory' of oneself. *Afraid to fall in love with anyone since Donna . . .* But why? In case you lose someone else? In case you have to face the fact of loneliness again?

During the interval another woman arrived and excused herself loudly. 'Sorry, folks,' she said. 'Couldn't find my sock this morning. I was looking for it for two hours.' She laughed, and someone put an arm round her. Her mouth was slack.

Sam remembered mornings he couldn't find his car. He remembered looking for a sock once. He remembered mornings when he couldn't find his legs.

After coffee some of the others shared their thoughts. Jed tried, but he was a shy sharer, and could only really communicate jokes. He said he was dry but not sober. 'Dry as a bone.'

They finished, as always, with the serenity prayer:

> God grant me the serenity to accept
> the things I cannot change,
> courage to change the things I can,
> and wisdom to know the difference.

There was a garden behind the building and Sam wandered through to it when the meeting broke up.

'Anything new?' Jed asked from behind him.

Sam turned and smiled. 'Yeah,' he said. 'Something every day. I've stopped smoking. I light up every day once or twice, but all that happens is, I remember I've stopped, so I throw it away before I smoke it.'

'I've got a woman,' Jed said. 'Met her at a dance. But I haven't told her yet.'

'That you're an alcoholic?'

'Yeah.' Jed walked off the path and trailed his fingers along a hedge.

They were both silent for some time. Then Sam said: 'Been arm-wrestling, too. I haven't won yet, but I get better every day.'

chapter 32

Geordie picked her up again on the same stretch of the beck. She'd clocked him before, when he followed her out of the town, and he hadn't seen which house she lived in. But now he had her on the return journey. If he could remain with her and stay out of sight he would find where she lived. Sam had said if they found where she lived, they would find where he lived, the guy called Norman. The guy who blew Gus away.

Geordie had been fishing. Well, what Geordie had been doing, Geordie had been pretending to fish. But that was first thing in the morning. While he was pretending to fish, but in reality waiting for the girl to show herself, he'd caught a fish. Didn't know what to call it, cod or haddock or salmon, or what it was you caught in muddy little becks like this. All he knew for sure was it wasn't a shark or a whale, or one of those fuckers with the teeth, piranhas they were called. Like in that film where the fisherman's wife has got the fire going waiting for him to catch one for their supper, but what she catches eventually is, she catches on that she's the supper.

So the upshot of that was that Geordie had this thing wriggling about on the end of his line and he didn't know what to do about it. So he had to enlist the help of a kid about half his age on his way to school. And the kid unhooked the fish and told Geordie it was his anyway. 'This is a beck, isn't it?' he said. 'There's no fish in it.' The kid had put this fish in there the previous night. This exchange gave rise to lots of questions in Geordie's mind, but he felt he didn't have time to pursue them. The whole thing ended with the kid offering to take the fish off Geordie's hands, and Geordie agreeing reluctantly, and the kid then going back the way he came with the fish and probably never getting to school for the rest of the day.

Some of the schools were closed down anyway. Talk about panic. With the murders, people were closing up their businesses, a good percentage of the town was closed, because the staff refused to come to work. The hotels had lots of cancellations earlier in the week, when tourists had decided to visit other towns. But their rooms had all gone to journalists and the TV crews who were being shipped in by the busload to cover the manhunt. There was a different chief inspector or superintendent or police spokesman every time you turned on the telly. But none of them knew what they were looking for. They didn't even have one of those identikit pictures that always look like nobody you ever saw. Nobody had seen nothing.

Geordie was intrigued by the girl. He remembered the first time he saw her, when the guy called Norman caught her shoplifting in Woolworths. He remembered how Norman had taken a grip of her arm, and the way she had looked up at the man and something in her face had fallen away. Geordie had wandered off then, somehow he'd given in, surrendered, just like the girl to the inevitability of the Norman guy's dominance. Celia said Hitler had been like that, all those dictator guys, they'd had this charisma thing which made people think they were superhuman. And Geordie remembered telling Gus what Celia had said, and then Gus said that they weren't superhuman at all, they were just fuck-ups. And that made Geordie smile, the memory of Gus and how he used to talk. And the smile made him feel guilty for smiling when Gus was dead, so he stopped smiling and carried on thinking about the girl instead.

She was skinny but she had a really nice face. He hadn't noticed the first time, when Norman caught hold of her arm, but the second time when she'd been in the Museum Gardens watching the tourists watching the peacock, she'd been smiling. Then he noticed her face, because of the smile. A rounded kind of face it was, which you didn't expect on somebody skinny. With skinny people you expected more a long face. But this girl had a rounded one, and it suited her just fine.

Geordie had thought about her five times since then, and he couldn't make out why a girl with such a nice rounded face would get involved with somebody who was going about killing people. He didn't know *how* to think about it. He didn't know where to start. Not rationally, anyway; what he could do very easily was fantasize about it, which didn't help because it always ended up with Geordie and the girl getting tangled up together in a clinch. In the fantasy, body parts got accidentally touched, and the lighting changed so they were in that kind of soft focus they use on the TV ads. And at the end of the fantasy you didn't feel any better about it. You just wanted to scream.

Peacocks don't scream. Peacocks shriek from the ancient walls at dusk. Before Sam got him the flat Geordie used to sleep in the Museum Gardens from time to time. But he would avoid the place at dusk, when the peacock was calling to his mate. If the harrowing sound of the peacock got lodged in his brain then, he would sit up half the night with Barney, not daring to close his eyes. The peacock's call was disembodied, alienating, seemingly having nothing at all to do with the peacock, but more connected to the lost souls who inhabited the ruins of the ancient fort. It was a trumpet after a battle, a trumpet played by a dead soldier with no lips.

Gus was a dead soldier. When Geordie tried to think about where Gus was now that he was dead, it was hard to imagine. Like was he in a box under the ground, which is what Gus himself thought happened to people when they died. Or was he in heaven, which is what Celia thought happened to people when they died.

Sam was useless with questions like that because he couldn't make his mind up what he believed. He seemed to have his own private religion, which he didn't want to talk about, and whatever you suggested to him about it, he'd say it was up to everyone to make up their own minds.

As far as Geordie could work out, he – Geordie, that is – was a humanist. If you was a Christian you believed in God and heaven and hell, and a whole lot of other things like creeds and hymns and women priests. And if you were an atheist you just believed in yourself and being worm food when you were dead, and probably being worm food when you were alive as well. Buddhists and Muslims and agnostics were other things that you could be, if you could ever find anybody to explain them to you so that you were left with the tiniest idea of what they might mean. Geordie hadn't found anyone at all who could explain them, and he seriously doubted that he ever would meet anybody who could do that.

But what Geordie, as a humanist, believed was that all the love that people had for God would be better employed if people gave it to each other instead of giving it to God. So all in all Geordie really believed that Gus was in a box under the ground. Except sometimes he didn't feel so sure about it. He never saw Gus as like an angel, with wings and white robes, stuff like that. But he sometimes felt him in the breeze; and it was difficult to explain that, even to yourself. Specially if there wasn't a breeze blowing at the time, which sometimes happened.

And the last problem with all this metaphysics – thank you, Celia, keep the words coming – was Barney. That was because Barney didn't know anything about God, but he loved all the people in the world, didn't care what they'd done or nothing. Which was like being a humanist. In fact it wasn't *like* being a humanist, it *was* being a humanist. But he wasn't a human. He was a dog. So how do you work that one out?

The girl wasn't going anywhere. She was taking a walk. Geordie had thought she was going into town, but when she got to the end of the path she turned around and started walking back again. Geordie had to do an about-turn and get off the path before she clocked him again. She might've given him the slip once, but she certainly wasn't going to do it again.

She got to the house and went inside. That's where she lived. There was every reason to believe he lived there as well, the Norman guy. Might be he was in there right now.

Geordie couldn't make up his mind what to do about it straight away. Needed time to think. He walked around the block. It would be crazy to go into the house, even to knock at the door. If the psycho was in there, to go knock on the door would be like volunteering to go through a mincer. And Geordie didn't want to do that.

He stopped at a pay-phone and tried ringing Sam at home and at the office. He got two answering machines. Sam was probably sniffing round Jennie, Celia's niece. Which is what Geordie had hoped he would do, but now he wished that Sam was on the job, instead of sniffing round skirts. There was a time for sniffing round skirts, Geordie thought, or if there wasn't a time for it, there ought to be a time for it. And that time wouldn't be right now, it'd be much later in the day.

What you did in a situation like this, you kept your head. You waited it out, watched what happened, took everything in your stride. You sat tight. Rang Sam every half hour, or every hour, whenever you could. And you hoped that this Norman guy, if he was in the house, didn't go out and get lost before the reinforcements arrived.

Except he did come out. His beard was a little thicker than it was the last time, but it was him all right. He came out of the front door of the house, and he was lugging something after him. Some kind of case or box. Geordie eventually thought it looked like a kind of cat box, or cat carrier, he couldn't think what it was called. But that's what it was.

He also had a camera slung round his neck. Expensive looking job, with a huge lens stuck on it. Like one of those the Japanese tourists carry round with them.

The guy was preoccupied. The Norman guy kept looking behind him like he expected someone might be coming after him. But he kept looking back at the house, as if he wasn't worried that someone like Geordie might be following him.

It was more like he was worried that the girl with the round face might be following him. And Geordie didn't understand that. Why would the guy be worried that the girl was following him? He lived in the same house with the girl.

Geordie took off after him, because he didn't want to lose him, and because he was really very curious to know what the guy had in a cat carrier.

Norman took the new path down by the beck, and when he came to a quiet stretch he went over to the bank of the beck and put the cat carrier into the water and pushed it off. It was like a boat. It sailed into the centre of the stream. Then it capsized slightly, must've shipped water, and soon it was beginning to sink. Norman didn't even look back. He was on his way into town now, and he was not loaded down by a cat carrier any more. He was walking with that sexy swagger some guys have. Geordie really hated the way the guy walked.

This whole area was supposed to be an Urban Nature Park, but it was actually neglected. The gravel footpath was overgrown with trees and shrubs. It was scrubland, very different to the tourist areas of the town, which were coddled by droves of gardeners. This was a paradise for dock leaves, nettles, dandelions and untrimmed hedges.

When Norman was out of sight, Geordie rushed down to the spot where the cat carrier was still visible, and got a couple of long branches to try and pull the thing in to the bank. He tried for several minutes, but the carrier had shipped a lot of water by now, and the force that was pulling it down to the bottom was much stronger than any force Geordie could exert to get it in to the bank.

Just one corner of the carrier was still visible, and disappearing fast, when Geordie felt himself violently pushed aside, and a figure flew away from him, off the bank of the beck, and landed with a splash in the water.

chapter 33

When Janet returned from her walk Norman had got out of bed and was already dressed. 'I've got to go out,' he said. 'Business.' He was sitting in the deep chair, and as Janet walked past he put his hand up her skirt and took hold of the inside of her thigh. He gripped her hard, nipping the flesh there with his fingers. But he was preoccupied with something, not really communicating. 'What's it like out there?' he asked.

Janet told him it was fine. 'Hot again.' At first she hadn't struggled, because Norman got angry if you struggled against him. If you frustrated whatever it was he wanted to do to you. She'd learned that these last few days. But he had hold of a particularly sensitive spot, and he was beginning to lay it on, really trying to hurt her. Digging his fingernails in. She pulled away, and his brow darkened for a moment. Several moments. Janet thought she should have stayed put, let him hurt her. When he went dark like this she thought he could easily kill her. But he wasn't really interested. He was preoccupied with something. He dug his camera out of a drawer and put it round his neck. She couldn't think what kind of 'business' he might be doing with a camera. Janet went out into the back garden to put distance between herself and the man, and to look for Orchid and Venus. To see if a miracle had happened and Tabitha had come back from the dead.

Something was wrong, because Venus was at the end of the garden, hanging around the shrubs there, and she didn't come when Janet called. Even moved away a little, as though she was frightened. And there was no sign of Orchid.

Janet would have felt better about it if Venus was missing and Orchid was there on her own, because Venus was that kind of cat, one that would wander off. When she was younger she sometimes wandered off for a day or two. But Orchid never did anything like that. She rarely went out of the flat during the day, let alone out of the garden.

While she was trying to coax Venus back into the flat, Janet heard the front door slam, and realized that Norman had left. Something wrong with him as well, going out like that without saying goodbye. He'd said he had to go out, but he hadn't said where. He hadn't said when he'd be back. This was a typical pattern with men, as far as Janet was concerned. A few more weeks and he'd have gone altogether. Probably already had another woman.

Which was fine with Janet. She'd be glad when he was gone. He thought he could hurt her any time he wanted. Didn't pretend any more. Just bit and scratched as much as he felt like doing. Punched as well. Didn't even try to be nice.

Janet walked down the garden to where Venus was waiting. When she got level with the garden shed, she noticed that the door was open and veered towards it. She kept the door shut. Some of the neighbourhood kids would steal anything that was visible. And she couldn't understand why the door was open. Norman must've been looking for something. Though there was nothing in the shed that could possibly interest him. She only glanced inside before shutting the door, but she noticed immediately that the cat carrier was not there. She closed the door, then opened it again to check she wasn't mistaken. It really had gone. And Orchid had gone.

And Norman had gone.

Janet didn't close the shed door again. She ran back to and through the flat, out of the front door and into the middle of the road. She realized that she had left the front door open, but she didn't go back to close it.

Instinct took her towards the new path.

Later Janet tried to remember the thoughts that went through her head as she ran along the path. But she couldn't remember what they were. She had this vision of Norman walking along the path with Orchid in the cat carrier. He was taking Orchid away. He was certainly going to kill her, as he had probably killed Tabitha. Janet knew that she had to catch him and take Orchid away from him. Orchid was Janet's responsibility. Orchid was dependent on her. Janet would not let her down.

She ran so fast that she didn't register at first that the cat carrier was in the centre of the beck, sinking, and that the boy from yesterday was poking at it with a long branch. She ran right past that scene. She saw it happening but carried on running along the path for several seconds more.

Then it hit her brain and she turned round and ran back again. She didn't stop for an instant at the bank, just pushed the boy aside and leapt into the beck. By the time she got to the cat carrier there was only one corner visible. She struck out for the bank, dragging the carrier behind her. The boy stretched out his hand for her as she approached, but the carrier was full of water now and she couldn't quite reach his outstretched fingers.

She watched his face. He looked at her, and when he realized that she couldn't make it he didn't hang around any longer. He stepped into the beck beside her and helped her lug the carrier on to the bank. Then he climbed out and pulled Janet up beside him.

The boy released the catch on the cat carrier and Orchid was out of there like a shooting star. She was along the path and out of sight before Janet could shout her name.

The boy looked at Janet and Janet looked at the boy, and they were both stunned by the speed of Orchid coming out of the carrier, and even more stunned because they'd both been in the beck with all their clothes on, and the whole operation seemed to have been a success, and they both looked like drowned rats. So Janet laughed. The boy laughed as well, and told her she looked funny, and Janet said he ought to look at himself before he started insulting other people. And then a couple of people on the path stopped to look at them, and then someone else came along, and Janet said there would be a crowd in a minute, and did he want to come back to her flat and get dried. And the boy said he'd thought she'd never ask.

So they got to their feet and walked back up the path to Janet's flat, and the boy walked as though he'd wet his pants.

And he wasn't very handsome or sexy, not what Janet called handsome and sexy anyway. But there was something vulnerable about him. And she liked that.

And he was funny as well. He made her laugh. He said they must look a sight walking along the street like that, the two of them wetter'n a frog's drawers. Janet had never heard that one before.

What did it mean, handsome and sexy, anyway? Norman was handsome and sexy, and he was also a rotten bastard. Janet wanted to check that Orchid was all right. She wanted to have a shower and put on some clean dry clothes. Then she wanted to get her Charter Arms Undercover .38 Special and find Norman and put a few holes in him. There might be a possibility for him then, if he had a few holes in him. Maybe something like compassion, whatever it was that couldn't get through his skin, perhaps it could get through the bullet holes.

chapter 34

'Was it Norman?' she asked.

'Yeah,' Geordie told her. When they got to the house he noticed that the front door was still open. The girl pushed her way in, and Geordie followed.

'What's your name?' he asked.

'Janet,' she said, and smiled at him. It was a quick smile. Her face was streaked with dirt from the beck. 'What's yours?'

'People call me Geordie,' he said. Then he had another thought, and added: 'There's a kind of disease you can get from rivers and becks. Caused by rat piss.'

There it was again. That quick way of smiling she had. By the time you got round to returning it she'd given up. 'I'm gonna have a quick shower,' she said. 'Get changed. You can get in after me.'

She went up the stairs and Geordie had a look at her record collection. Lot of stuff by John Lennon, most of it he didn't recognize. Sam would know it all; he liked John Lennon, all that old stuff. Geordie liked it as well, specially when Sam talked about it, told the stories around the songs. He could put on a song you'd never heard before, and you'd only be half listening to it, and then he'd say: 'I remember this. When this song was released I was in San Francisco . . .' Or something like that, then he'd go off into what he was doing in San Francisco, or wherever he was, and all the characters he knew, hippies and general madmen, geeks and perverts, and by the time he'd finished, you'd think you knew the song yourself, maybe even ask him to play it again.

Geordie left the record collection and looked at a few other bits and pieces in the sitting room. Mainly girl stuff, but one or two things from Norman as well. Something looked like a silencer for a gun, and, the biggest surprise in a very surprising day, Gus's dictaphone.

Which proved that the guy did kill Gus. There was no other way he could have got his hands on this. Geordie picked it up and hit the Play button. Nothing, so he rewound it to the beginning of the tape. When he hit the Play button again he heard a recording of Gus's voice: 'Norman Brown is sitting outside Celia's house at the moment. He knows it is Celia's house. He knows the house is connected with us. How? Why?' Then the tape went dead.

Geordie rewound and played it again.

When he switched it off the house seemed strangely silent in the aftermath of Gus's voice. Geordie looked at the dictaphone and tried to assimilate what he'd heard. Then there was the sound of a step in the hall, outside the door. Geordie felt the hairs on the back of his neck stand up. They did it completely unaided. He couldn't see them because they were behind him. But he could feel them sticking out like the quills on a hedgehog. There it was again. Another step.

Next the handle of the door turned with a slight squeak, and whoever had been outside was now inside the flat. Someone moving stealthily. Someone moving quietly. Geordie picked up the dictaphone. He would have liked something heavier. He would have liked a gun. A very big gun. But in the absence of anything sturdier, the dictaphone would have to do.

He moved swiftly and silently to a spot behind the door. He looked around for a more effective weapon, but there was nothing to hand. He lifted the dictaphone above his head, ready to bring it crashing down on the head of the psycho when he came through the door. Geordie held his breath as the door handle turned and the door was slowly and quietly pushed open. He waited, expecting to see the barrel of a gun come through the opening. But instead of that there came a sound something very close to the call of a peacock.

'Yoohoo.' It was a high-pitched female voice, and it was very close, and very loud, and totally unexpected. And it very nearly caused Geordie to have an accident in his trousers.

'Yoohoo, Janet,' the voice came again. And it was followed by a small, dumpy woman with bleached hair and dark roots. 'Ooh,' she said, and giggled shrilly, when she saw Geordie. 'Who are you?'

'Geordie,' said Geordie, bringing his hand with the dictaphone down, in case the woman thought he might be using it as a weapon. 'Janet's having a shower.' He was so relieved that it was whoever it was, and not Norman, that he forgot to ask her name.

'I'm Trudie,' she said. 'From upstairs.' Then she giggled shrilly again and looked at Geordie's crotch. 'You're all wet,' she said.

'Yeah,' Geordie agreed. 'We had an accident with the cat. Down at the beck.'

Trudie backed away. 'I'll come back later,' she said. 'Tell Janet I called.'

When Janet came down she looked extra clean. She had white jeans and a white blouse. She wore white trainers, and was swinging a white leather shoulder bag. 'I've found these,' she said, handing Geordie a pair of shorts and a T-shirt. 'They're Norman's, but they're about the only things that'll fit you.'

Geordie took the T-shirt and shorts upstairs and figured out how to use the shower. The bathroom was filthy, and when he switched the shower on it gave off two completely separate jets of water. The main jet went upwards rather than down towards the bath, but if you kept moving around you could eventually get enough water to make you wet enough to begin to feel clean. There was only one towel, which Geordie assumed was the one that Janet had used before him. Smelt a little like her. A good smell, though, one that he felt he could inhale deeply, and under different circumstances might have lingered over.

The only thing that stopped him lingering altogether was the thought that Norman the psycho might be over at Celia's house. If anything happened to Celia, Geordie would never forgive himself.

Janet laughed at him when he went back down the stairs. Then she said she was sorry, it was just that the shorts were a bit too short. 'I wish there was something else,' she said. 'But there isn't.'

'I don't mind,' he told her. 'But I don't want you laughing. It's bad enough having to wear this stuff, belongs to a madman.'

They left the house, and this time Janet locked the door behind her. 'Did you actually see him put Orchid in the beck?' she asked.

'Yeah,' Geordie said. 'I saw him.'

She was quiet for a moment. 'I knew it,' she said, eventually. 'When Tabitha went missing I suspected him. I suppose I didn't want to believe it.'

Geordie walked quickly along the path, Janet having to run every few steps to keep up with him. 'Where are we going?' she said. 'Norman could be anywhere. It would be better to wait at the flat for him.'

"S'up to you,' Geordie told her. 'I think I know where he is, and if I'm right, there's somebody there'll need some help.'

Janet ran a few more steps to catch him up. 'I'm sticking with you,' she said.

chapter 35

Barney was in his basket in the office. One eye on Sam. Occasionally he'd cock an ear. When the telephone rang he cocked an ear and stood in one movement.

Sam was at his desk. When he answered the phone and heard Jennie's voice, Sam asked her where she was, what she was doing. 'I'm sitting at Celia's dining table, pressing keys on my portable PC,' she said. He imagined her being very animated. Her voice rose and fell every time she turned up another scrap of information about Norman Bunce. Sam imagined the way her hair swung over her eye, momentarily obliterating part of her face. He kept seeing her the way she had been the previous evening, her white breasts, her long legs, her shyness which she confronted and braved, her determination.

'What?' he said. 'Four balls. You've gotta be joking.'

He heard Celia's voice then, unexpectedly, fought the confusion and quickly realized she was on the extension in the hall. 'Sounds like a serious disability,' she said.

Sam laughed. 'Hell,' he said, 'I could see the guy was a freak. But four balls. That's gotta be some kind of record.'

'It's not the only way he's handicapped,' Jennie said. 'He's got all kinds of troubles. He'd never have been released from prison. He's almost completely psychopathic. Has no remorse for any of the crimes he's committed. According to the medical staff I talked to he showed no progress whatso-ever during the time he was in prison. There was even a suggestion that he might be getting worse. Becoming more paranoid, more violent.'

'Did you actually meet this man?' Celia's voice asked.

'Yes,' Jennie said. 'He was part of a control group we were studying. I remember him particularly because of the way he looked at me. Most male prisoners, well, high security prisoners, they look at women, they watch you out of the corner of their eye. But they manage to do it surreptitiously. Quietly, with a degree of subtlety. But not Norman Bunce. He'd just look at you full on. He'd drool right in front of you. He'd fix his eyes on your breasts and lick his lips, then follow a line down your body until your flesh was creeping. Ugh.' Sam imagined her shaking her head. 'Less than a minute with him in the room and you felt as if you'd been raped.'

'You really don't want to come across him again, do you?' said Sam.

Jennie was quiet. He felt her shake her head slowly from side to side. 'I don't want you to either,' she said. 'Or Geordie, or any of you. He's one of the most dangerous people I've ever met.' Sam heard the keys on her PC clack away. 'Here's something else,' she said. 'We were measuring motivation for change. Violent prisoners give all kinds of answers when you ask them why they think crime is the answer to their problems. They like showing off, or they think the girls look at them. They could get off on the excitement, or crime makes them feel good in different ways. But you know what Norman Bunce said, when we asked him that question? He said he was into crime, violent crime, for the *laughs*. And when I say violent crime, in his case that means torturing and killing people and animals in the same way. He killed a couple with their dog because the dog barked at him. He thought that was funny. "You shouldda seen the look on their faces," he said.'

Sam couldn't get that flap of hair which covered her eye out of his mind. He saw it again for a moment and sighed inwardly. He was listening to what she said, but a large part of him wished they were still in bed. He wanted to inhale her again. Or just sit and look at her nakedness. The reality of last night was being ground out of his mind by the reality of the violence of Norman Bunce. Sam was fighting it, but he could tell last night was going to have to lose out. Norman Bunce represented a kind of reality you ignored only at your peril.

'There's something else, as well,' said Jennie. 'His concept of his own personal space is way off beam.'

'Personal space?' That was Celia's voice again. 'How do you mean?'

'Most people you can get fairly close to,' Jennie said. 'Most normal people will let you get as close as twelve inches, eight inches. If you get closer than that they start to feel uncomfortable, like you might touch them.'

'I hate that,' said Celia. 'When people stand next to you and you can almost feel them.'

'Well, Norman Bunce starts getting uncomfortable if you're within about four feet of him,' Jennie said. 'And that's from the front or the sides. If you come up behind him, you'd better be more than six feet away or he's liable to attack you.'

'Your Mr Norman Bunce,' Celia said. 'He sounds about as much use to a woman as a copy of *Good Housekeeping*.'

Sam and Jennie both laughed. With Celia you had no idea what was living inside her brain. 'Good one, Celia,' Sam said. 'He's one of those people who would be enormously improved by death.'

'You didn't say anything about his intelligence,' Celia said to Jennie. 'Sometimes these people are very bright, aren't they?'

'Not this one,' Jennie said. 'Norman Bunce could count to twenty-one if he took his boots and his pants off.'

Sam laughed again and Celia's voice did a continuous chuckle, which slowly faded and then ended abruptly when she replaced the phone.

Marie walked into the office as Sam replaced the telephone in its cradle. 'Police everywhere,' she said. 'You can't move for them.'

'They're investigating a murder,' Sam said. He bit his tongue, but the words had already got out.

Marie smiled wryly. She took a breath. 'Any news?' she asked.

Sam told her about Norman Bunce. 'Sounds really mean,' he said.

'Was that Jennie?' she asked.

'Yeah. At Celia's house.'

'I just talked to Celia a few minutes ago,' Marie said. 'I was on my way round there. Invited for coffee.'

'He's got four balls,' Sam said.

Marie looked out of the window, down at the square. 'The telephone's going to ring,' she said.

The words had barely left her mouth when the telephone rang. She turned to face it, and Sam looked at her, his head cocked to one side. He raised his eyebrows and collected the instrument from his desk. 'Yeah,' he said. 'Geordie. Where are you?'

'On the trail of this psychopath,' Geordie said. 'Listen, Sam, I think I know where he's going. I found Gus's dictaphone.'

'Slow down,' Sam said. 'Just tell me where he's going, and where you are.'

'He's going to Celia's,' Geordie said. 'We're trying to get there as well. But he's gonna be there before us.'

'Quick as you can,' Sam said. He replaced the receiver.

'Come on,' he said to Marie. 'The killer's on his way to Celia's.'

Barney was out of his basket and at Sam's heel before Marie had fully assimilated the message that they were going out. 'Sorry, Barney,' Sam said. 'You're not coming.'

Barney didn't even bother putting on an appealing face. He knew nothing would change Sam's mind when that tone was in his voice. He walked back to his basket and sat on the floor. 'I'll make it up to you,' Sam said.

Marie followed him out of the office. 'Is this it, Sam?' she said. 'Is this the showdown?'

A journalist tried to stop Sam for a comment but he brushed on past the man, with Marie following closely behind.

She caught him up and matched his strides for a few seconds. 'Did you say he had four balls?' she asked.

chapter 36

There is a stretch of the old city wall that takes up one side of Lord Mayor's Walk. Immediately after the city wall, in the area that used to be a moat, there is now carefully cropped grass, and early in the year the local council plants daffodils to delight the tourists. The shape of the moat is still visible, and Norman stationed himself on the stretch of grass that would have been on the wall side of the water. He was directly opposite the house, and had hoped that he would see Squishsquash go in, alone.

But he had seen nothing. He expected that the old woman would be with her in there, and that was a drag, because he'd forgotten the silencer for his gun. When he discovered this, he'd immediately bought himself a washing line to truss the old biddy up. The washing line was in a plastic carrier bag, by his side on the grass. It was one of the new kind, the nylon twine encased in transparent plastic. The Nikon was slung around his neck. He thought he might as well record this one. Show Squishsquash with that first surprised look on her face, then a couple of shots with her undressing. Maybe get her to do some posing, like in the skin mags. Pouting and touching herself up. He hadn't been able to work out how much film was left in the camera. But he'd take as many shots as he could, just hope there was enough to get her when she was really scared.

He was finished with Janet now. She'd know it was him who took Orchid out of the house, and even if he denied it, she'd still know. This was a great pity, because it meant that he would not be able to get his hands on the last cat, Venus the penis. Not easily anyhow, he'd have to wait around at the bottom of the garden, prowl around at night with a sack.

Janet was no good anyway. No tits. She wasn't a real woman, not like Tina. Norman had done her a favour, really, giving her a chance with a real man. Probably the only chance she'd ever have. She was a real crap cook as well, couldn't leave things alone and let them stew like they were supposed to. Always stirring the pot. Weighing everything. Real cooks didn't carry on like that. They knew better. Cooking was instinctive, like Norman himself. If Norman took up cooking – and some men did do that kind of thing – he'd probably end up famous, like being a chef in the poshest hotel in the world. Next thing you'd see him on the TV, one of those big white hats on his head, tasting sauces off the end of his fingers. Doing a bit of slobbering for the masses.

But Janet, Jesus, he wouldn't even employ her to do the washing up. He could see her turning up at this big hotel where he would be the chef. 'Hey, Janet,' he'd say. 'Take a walk. I'd like to help, babe, but you'd be a fucking liability. I've got a reputation to think about.'

The thing about Norman, one of the most important things about him, and one that most people didn't realize, was that he was multi-talented. He was a workaholic, that was true, which meant he didn't hang about too long thinking about what to do next. He got on with whatever it was needed doing that moment. But almost whatever it was that had to be done, if he thought about it, he could do it. Whatever it was. It might be armed robbery, say, which is a job a lot of people would flinch at. Some people just wouldn't be able to do it. When you're doing an armed robbery, you often come across problems, you have to think on the hoof, deal with whatever comes up. You might have to pop somebody. An old guy, say, or some biddy sticks her nose in. Well, they do. And you have to finish them. It's no good leaving them half dead, so they can recognize you. Next thing you know you see your own mug shot every time you turn on the telly. Policemen start looking your way.

That's one thing you might have to do. Another thing you might have to do, teach young people how to face up to life. Norman could do that as well; he'd done a lot of it in prison. All his life he'd really fancied himself as a teacher. Not that he'd had any training. He hadn't actually, formally, trained for anything. But that didn't mean he couldn't do it. It only meant he didn't have a piece of paper saying he could do it.

When you were a student of human nature you had to be flexible.

Money, writing, driving cars, he could manage all that with no problem. Well, writing wasn't easy. But he could talk better than most, which made up for the writing. Reading? Someone had called him illiterate once, because he didn't read books. But that guy, the one who'd called him illiterate – means showing a lack of familiarity with language, because Norman had looked it up in the prison dictionary – the guy who'd called him illiterate had an accident in the kitchen three days later. Sonofabitch got a kitchen knife stuck through his hand. He was careless. Anybody could see that.

So. Squishsquash. Prison psychologist.

Norman was finished with Janet, but that also meant he was finished with York. He'd go to Manchester. Much bigger town. Lots of opportunities. And Tina was there. Maybe he could buy her off the Jamokes. If he offered enough money, they'd sell her. Why not? Norman the liberator. There was a lot of mileage left in that girl yet. Whatever he had to pay for her, she'd earn it back.

There was still the question of Snow White. But Norman couldn't remember when he'd last thought about her. He really regretted giving the private detective that money. Snow White was in the past. As long as she stayed lost Norman could forgive and forget. Revenge had seemed as though it would be sweet when he was banged up in prison. But now it didn't seem so sweet at all. Of course, if he ever did come across her he'd give her a hard time. Who wouldn't? After what she did to him. But as long as she wasn't available he wasn't gonna lose no sleep over her.

Only one thing left to do in this place. In York. One thing. Squishsquash.

And now was the time to do it. He picked up his carrier with the washing line. Checked the shoulder holster to see if his gun was waiting. Then he strode across Lord Mayor's Walk. He tried the door, found it open and walked inside.

A voice, must be the old lady's because it wasn't Squish-squash's, called through to him.

'Hello. Marie? Is that you?'

Norman didn't say a thing. Fingered the washing line and stood there really quiet. Wait for the old biddy to come to him.

chapter 37

Geordie took Janet up on the city wall at Monkgate and they walked along the battlements. Geordie saw Norman while they were still a hundred yards away, but Janet didn't see him until they'd drawn almost level. When they got to the spot just above him, Norman got to his feet and walked across the road away from them.

'Where's he going?' Janet asked.

'That's Celia's house,' Geordie said. 'Celia's our secretary. She's also a friend of mine, and a teacher. She teaches me English.'

'What's he going there for?'

'I don't know,' Geordie said. He began running back along the wall. 'Come on,' he said. 'I don't wanna think what he's doing to Celia.'

Janet followed. Geordie ran down the narrow stone steps and along Lord Mayor's Walk to Celia's house. When he got there, he saw Marie and Sam coming towards them from the opposite direction.

'Any sign of him?' Sam asked, looking strangely at Geordie's shorts. Then he looked over at Janet.

Marie smiled at Geordie. 'Who's this?' she asked. 'I don't think we've been introduced.'

'I'm Janet,' said Janet. She accepted the small fat hand that Marie presented.

'Marie,' said Marie, still smiling. She was fat, Janet thought, but it was fat that fitted her like a tailored suit. Out of a hundred overweight people, men or women, there were only one or two could say that. Fat that fits.

'The guy's just gone in there,' Geordie said. 'Norman, the guy who . . .' He had intended to say, 'The guy who killed Gus,' but couldn't finish the sentence with Marie being there. He looked at the house. It looked like it had always looked before. It was not possible to tell what was happening inside. Was Norman in the process of killing Celia and Jennie? You looked at the house and you couldn't tell anything. It looked as though there was no one at home.

'What shall we do?' he asked.

'They're expecting me,' said Marie. 'Celia just asked me round for some coffee. I could knock on the door, then when they answer you could rush in.'

Sam shook his head. 'I'll come in with you,' he said. 'We'll play it by ear.'

'I'll go round the back,' Geordie said. 'Over the wall. You go in the front way. If everything's OK, come back out and tell us. If you don't come out in a minute I'll go over the back wall.'

'No,' said Sam. 'Get on to Delany at the police station. Tell him what's happening. I've got a feeling we'll need all the help we can get.' Marie nodded. She started for the door, then hesitated for a moment. Geordie thought she was going to crumble. Turn round and say she couldn't do it. Something like that. But Sam drew level with her and touched her arm and she cast a backward glance and went to Celia's door. She knocked and walked in, Sam following.

Geordie looked at his watch and counted off the seconds until sixty of them had gone by. Marie did not come back out of the house.

'OK,' Geordie said to himself. Then to Janet: 'Look, I'm gonna ring the police then I'm going round the back and see what's happening. You stay here.'

'You must be joking,' she said. 'I'm coming with you.'

'It might be dangerous,' Geordie told her.

Janet laughed. 'Might? It might be dangerous? What you talking about? It is dangerous. It's Norman. You should tell me it's dangerous. I've been living with the guy. He tried to kill my cats.'

chapter 38

Norman came into the room holding Celia by the scruff of her neck. He had the barrel of his gun close up against her temple. Jennie leapt to her feet. She could see only Celia's eyes. Larger than she'd ever seen them before, almost coming out of her head. They were fixed, unblinking, and there was no sense of recognition.

'Sit down,' said Norman. He pushed Celia on to her knees on the carpet and waved the gun at Jennie. His camera, swinging wildly around his neck, caught Celia on the side of the head. He knocked her over on to her side and leered at Jennie.

'That just leaves you and me, babe,' he said to her. He walked over to her and backed her up against the wall. He pushed the barrel of his gun against her chin, eased her head back with the pressure of it, then let the barrel slip down her neck and come to rest between her breasts. Jennie flinched at the touch of the metal, and Norman did a chuckle that anyone else in the world would have had to practise. 'How far would I go?' he asked, fully conscious that he was imitating questions she had asked of him. 'Would I squeeze your tits, or would I shoot your fucking nipples off?' Then he backed up and aimed the camera at her. 'Say cheese,' he said, and he hit the shutter button.

There was no flash, and Norman looked at the camera for a second or two, slight confusion in his eyes. But he shrugged and looked back at Jennie. 'I want you to walk across the room,' he told her. 'Just walk natural, from here to there and back again.'

Jennie tried to walk normally across the room. She was shaking, but Norman didn't seem to notice. With every other step she took he said: 'Squish.' Then with the next step: 'Squash.' Norman took another couple of photographs. She had known that they called her that in the prison. Squish-squash. She'd heard the prisoners, some of them, repeating it under their breath when she walked past them. But she had thought it was a general comment, aimed at all women. She realized only now, for the first time, that it was something they'd invented specifically for her. She didn't know exactly what it meant, but she realized it was erotic. It was turning Norman on.

When she got to the other side of the room, Norman said: 'Now take your skirt off.' He squinted through the viewfinder on his camera. Every time he lifted the camera to his face he exposed his tie, which showed two women, one black and the other white, caressing each other. They were cartoon-like, with luscious lips and swelling breasts and thighs.

Jennie shook her head. 'No,' she said.

'I'm not asking,' he said, and he started to cross the room towards her. 'I'm fucking telling you.' She remembered him from the prison. The pointed determination of his features. The overwhelming will power. Someone had called it magnetism. For an instant she let herself think that she wouldn't be able to resist him, and for that instant she was lost. There was a resilience in her that would not go down without a fight, and that resilience did not abandon her. But he was powerful. My God, he was powerful. He was demonic. She didn't doubt for a moment that he intended to cause as much pain as possible, and then he would kill both her and Celia. He'd tear them apart with his bare hands if necessary.

But before he could reach her there was a knock on the front door, followed by the sound of the door opening.

Marie's voice came through to the sitting room: 'Hello? Celia, it's me.'

Celia lifted her head from the carpet. 'It's Marie,' she said. 'I'll put the kettle on.' But she didn't move.

Norman changed direction quickly and headed out into the hall to intercept Marie. As soon as he was through the door Jennie picked up a cake knife from the table and pushed it down inside the waistband of her skirt. Even while she was doing it she saw the inadequacy of it. A cake knife. But in the face of someone like Norman anything was better than nothing.

Norman returned with Marie and Sam on the end of his gun. Marie had turned bright red. 'Got a fat one and a detective,' Norman said to the room in general. 'Down on the floor,' he said to Marie, pushing the gun into the back of her neck, but keeping his eyes glued on Sam.

Marie went down on all fours, and Norman pushed the gun harder into the back of her neck. 'Flat,' he said, and Marie fell forward. 'On your hands,' he said, and Marie lifted her head to look at him for a second, but she put her arms under her.

Then he looked over at Sam. 'It's Mr Detective,' he said. 'Hey, you owe me money.'

Jennie watched Sam carefully. She wanted to go to him. Be close to him. She wanted to tell him about the knife in the waistband of her skirt. To hear his plans about turning the tables on Norman Bunce. But she knew she daren't move. Knew she had to stay where she was and wait.

'Don't tell me,' Norman said, looking from Jennie to Sam. 'Let me guess. Squishsquash and Mr Detective are an item. Am I right?'

Neither Sam nor Jennie had anything to say about that.

Sam wanted Jennie to talk to the guy. Distract his attention long enough for Sam to make a grab for the gun. If Norman made one mistake they could overpower him. Four to one should be enough. Then he looked at Celia again and reassessed. Three to one.

'I can see you thinking it, Mr Detective. But you know I'm capable of using this little baby.' Norman indicated his gun. 'You try anything at all and I'll blow a hole in you. And in this one,' he said, cuffing the top of Celia's head with his free hand. 'Your Grandmother, whatever she is.'

Sam wanted to throttle him with that lurid tie he had round his neck. He wanted to even up the odds, take Norman's gun out of the equation, and then stride over there and take the guy by the neck. He wanted to lift him off his feet and squeeze the life out of him. Throttle him with the camera strap. But he didn't move. He knew if he tried anything that wasn't immediately successful Norman would shoot him, and then he would shoot Celia as well, if only because he'd said he would.

You had to make a decision and whatever the decision was, you had to stick to it.

That's what the situation demanded. And that's what Sam did. He decided to wait his chance. Whenever it came he would be ready. Any perceptible chink in Norman's armour would do. When it became apparent Sam would spring.

'I want you on your knees,' Norman told him. 'Hands behind your back.'

Sam did as he was bid.

'Now, Squishsquash,' Norman said to Jennie. 'I want you to tie this rope around Mr Detective.' He threw her the washing line. 'I want you to tie it as hard as you can,' Norman continued. 'So the rope bites into his skin.'

Jennie proceeded to tie Sam's hands behind his back, and then, following Norman's repeated commands, she wrapped it around his arms and legs, and pulled it at every twist and turn until the sweat stood out on her brow. Norman took another couple of photographs while she was doing it. When she'd run out of rope she helped Sam to stand and then helped him to jump and hobble to a deep armchair. Norman pushed him into it, and then he dragged Celia to her feet and threw her into the chair on top of Sam.

Sam tested the ropes and confirmed what he already knew. There would be very little chance of escaping from them. Had he been otherwise unencumbered it would still have been difficult, but with Celia on top of him it was certainly impossible.

Celia groaned and Jennie leaned forward and stroked her hair.

'Keep away from them,' Norman said. He kicked Marie in the leg for no apparent reason.

'I'm going to make her comfortable,' Jennie said. 'She's an old lady.' She lifted Celia's head and rearranged her arms. Using her own body as a partial shield she slipped the cake

230

knife out of her waistband and let it fall down the back of Sam's chair, towards his hands. He squirmed and spread his fingers, and felt the blade of the knife fall into his hand. His face registered nothing, but Jennie knew he had received the knife. Sam thought that Norman had seen the knife pass between them. But the man said nothing, registered nothing on his face, so maybe he hadn't? Was it ever possible to be sure about anything with Norman?

'I thought you wanted Snow White?' Sam said to him.

Norman stopped at the sound of the name. 'You found her?' he said.

'Yes,' Sam said. 'I found her yesterday. She agreed to see you.'

'Where?' said Norman, going over to Sam's chair, pushing Jennie aside. 'What's her address?'

'Not so fast,' Sam said. 'We should be able to come to some kind of deal over this.'

Norman laughed. 'You've got nothing to deal,' he said to Sam. 'I've got all these women belong to you. When I've used them all up, which won't be long, I think you'll give me much better terms than you're thinking of at the moment.'

'Now,' he said, returning to Jennie and taking her by the hand. 'You can take that skirt off yourself. Or Norman'll do it for you.'

Jennie was wearing a calf-length blue cotton skirt that buttoned down the front. The buttons finished just above her knees, and from there on down the skirt was open. She wore it with a plaited leather belt. She and Norman stared at each other for the best part of a minute. Then Jennie loosened her skirt and let it fall to the floor. She stepped out of it and picked it up. Folded it neatly and placed it over the back of a chair.

Her legs were bare. Her white cotton top, which had a cable design down the front, was not long enough to hide a pair of white stretch lace briefs. Her breathing was loud in the room. She glared at Norman with open hostility. He leered. He brought his camera up to his face and took a picture.

'Got any questions?' he asked. 'Like about social skills?

231

For example, what do you imagine will be your principal problem when I've got you stripped down to nothing?' He laughed and moved over to her.

'I know you,' Jennie said to him, putting on a brave face though it was obvious that she was very frightened. 'Your principal problem is people, Norman. It always has been and it always will be. Because you're basically frightened of almost everyone.'

Norman laughed. He turned to the others in the room and laughed loudly. 'She's trying to do her psychology on me,' he said. 'Even now.'

'I'm telling you how it is,' Jennie said. 'You don't want to hear it, but that doesn't stop it being true.'

Norman had a fixed grin on his face. He walked over to the chair which contained Sam and Celia, and he took Sam by the hair and pulled him forward. He reached down behind Sam and came out with the cake knife that Jennie had given him. 'Oh, look at that,' Norman said. 'I found the knife before he could cut through the rope.' He let go of Sam's hair and waved the knife at Jennie. 'Clever Norman,' he said. 'And silly Squishsquash, thinking she could work that one over on me.

'Walk,' he said. 'Walk over the room and back, all squishy and squashy. And I'll tell you what. You do it nicely and I'll shoot your boyfriend before I fuck you. You give me any more psychology and I'll fuck him as well.'

Jennie began to walk.

'Squish,' said Norman. And he clicked with the camera.

'Hey,' he said. 'Here's one for you. How about if you get down on the floor and undress the fat girl?' He indicated Marie. He looked back at Jennie. 'How'd you like that?'

'You're disgusting,' Jennie told him.

Norman smiled, like he'd received a compliment. 'Lift her skirt,' he said. 'And pull her knickers down. I might give you a demonstration. Show you just what I'm gonna do to you.'

'Go to hell,' said Jennie. 'Do what you like. I'm not taking any more orders.'

Norman poked the barrel of his gun into Celia's ear, holding eye contact with Jennie all the time. He said nothing.

Jennie sobbed, she slowly inched her way over to Marie, sat down on the carpet behind her and lifted her skirt. Norman walked away from Celia to get a better view of the action.

Sam saw Janet through the window before she smashed the glass with a handgun. She hit out at the window and the glass shattered. There was a flash of red as the falling glass bit into her arm. Norman turned away from Jennie and began lifting his gun in the direction of the window. But he was always a breath behind Janet. She took aim and fired, and the bullet from her gun grazed Norman's forehead. He was caught off balance and fell forward, his gun dropping from his grasp and spinning away from him across the carpet. His face connected with the camera on the floor.

Marie was up on all fours and she scrambled forward and straddled Norman. She grabbed a handful of his hair and banged his face forward on to the carpet. She repeated that movement several times. She picked up the camera and hit him over the head with it once. But she didn't seem to like that for some reason, and threw the camera into the corner of the room.

In the meantime Jennie had picked up Norman's gun. She went over to where he was pinned to the floor by Marie and stuck the barrel of the gun into the back of his head. Sam could see she was crying. 'You bastard,' she shouted. 'I ought to blow your fucking head off.'

Sam was pulling frantically at the rope around his hands, trying to get himself free.

'Help me,' he said to Celia. He wanted to sort this scene out before either Jennie shot Norman in the head, or Marie smashed his face to pulp. Or the other one, the one he'd glimpsed with Geordie outside, the one with the gun, who'd smashed the window, came in the house and did the job for them. He glanced up at the window, and saw Geordie taking the gun away from the girl out there. He couldn't figure out where Geordie had got the shorts from.

'Fucking shoot me,' Norman shouted at Jennie. 'But get this fat cow off my back.'

Marie continued banging his head on the carpet. It had a

233

thick pile and didn't do much damage, but it was obvious that he didn't like it.

Celia came back to life and got out of the chair. She pushed Sam forward and loosened the rope around his hands. He got to his feet and pushed the rest of the rope away from him. He took the gun away from Jennie and led her across the room to a free chair. At the same time Celia pulled Marie away from Norman. Geordie came in the back door with Janet's gun and he and Janet began tying Norman up with the rope that had originally bound Sam.

'Who the fuck are you?' Norman asked Geordie. But he didn't get an answer.

Norman moved fast. He'd shaken the rope away from his hands and taken the gun away from Geordie before Sam or any of the others realized what was happening. Norman pushed Geordie in the chest, and Geordie went over a chair and landed on his back. Norman reached out for Janet and held her round the neck with his free arm. He backed up against the wall and waved his gun at Sam. 'Now put your gun down,' he said. 'First wrong move you make and this one gets killed. After that I'll kill the others one at a time.'

'Fuck,' said Marie.

Janet struggled against Norman. 'Just shoot,' she shouted at Sam. 'Kill the bastard.'

Norman raised the hand which held his gun, as if to bring it down on Janet's head. Sam didn't think. He could see that Norman's gun wasn't actually pointing at anyone. Most of Norman's body was shielded by Janet, and if Sam had had time to think about it he wouldn't have attempted a shot. But he didn't have time to think. He just brought his gun up, pointed it as accurately as he could at Norman's head, and pulled the trigger.

Norman's body went into a kind of spasm. As soon as the bullet hit him, he dropped Janet. He dropped his own gun. Then he dropped to one knee momentarily. Everyone in the room thought he was gone at that point. But they didn't understand Norman. There was still breath in his body, and as long as that remained he was a danger. He retrieved his gun and stood again, looked over at Sam and moved forward. There were sounds coming from him. Not speech, no recognizable language. Something between a string of curses and the howl of an animal. He fired his gun, twice. One bullet lodged itself in the wall above Sam's head, and the second one went through the door and ricochetted around the kitchen. Jennie screamed, and everyone except Sam threw themselves to the floor.

Sam aimed and fired his gun and Norman's left shoulder seemed to drag him to a stop. Then he came forward once more. Sam fired again, and again, and eventually Norman was halted. He staggered backward and his good eye, the one that didn't have a bullet in it, closed slowly, and his whole body twisted against the wall before he fell to the floor.

Janet ran over to Geordie and helped him to his feet. Sam walked over to Jennie and put his arm around her. Marie took hold of Celia's hand. And they all looked at the body of Norman Bunce. Sam wondered how such a small, and now totally inactive, bundle of flesh and bones could have caused so much trouble.

Geordie looked over at Sam. He smiled. 'Is that it, then?' he asked.

Sam nodded. He looked around the room at the others. 'I think so,' he said. 'Everybody's still shaking. But it'll look a whole lot better tomorrow.'

Also available in Vista paperback

Poet in the Gutter

JOHN BAKER

Introducing Sam Turner, who bluffs his way into a
job as a private eye – and then discovers he's good
at it . . .

'Set in York, Baker's debut novel is engagingly
credible, off the wall, romantic without being sen-
timental, with a sharp sense of humour . . . A great
cast of characters I look forward to encountering
again' Val McDermid, *Manchester Evening News*

'Neatly plotted and engagingly and wittily written:
Sam's next case is something to look forward to'
Tim Binyon, *Daily Mail*

'Exceedingly cunning, laid back plot . . . Genial,
fast and funny' Philip Oakes, *Literary Review*

ISBN 0 575 60045 4

VISTA

Making the Cut

JIM LUSBY

Exactly what was Billy Power – machinist at the plastics factory, keeper of greyhounds, and Jack-the-lad about Waterford – involved in?

Unshaven, unorthodox and unpopular with his superiors, DI Carl McCadden finds straight answers about Power, or anything else, hard to come by. And as McCadden searches for the truth through the bleak and dilapidated housing estates, the bars and the dog tracks of Waterford, byzantine business machinations and self-righteous politicking serve only to muddy the waters . . .

'A distinctive and original debut, with more feeling for atmosphere and more sense of character than most crime stories' *Evening Standard*

'An exciting read, a fine first effort from a welcome newcomer' *Irish Times*

ISBN 0 575 60013 6

VISTA

Flashback

JIM LUSBY

The Belview Guesthouse overlooks the City of
Waterford, Ireland. Popular in theatrical circles, it
takes the discovery of a woman's naked body,
bludgeoned and flayed and tangled in blood-
soaked sheets in one of the bedrooms, to bring
Inspector Carl McCadden to the residence. But
before he's had time to dig out his copy of *Hamlet*
another body is found in similar circumstances
across town in Gracedieu, and McCadden finds
himself plunged into the murky world of amateur
Players, 'home-movie' makers and the local alternative comedy circuit . . .

'The Irish setting makes for a pleasant change and
Inspector Carl McCadden has just the right degree
of laid-back charm' *Guardian*

'McCadden's a lively old type, full of maverick
offbeatery . . . Lusby's prose is similarly lively'
Oxford Times

ISBN 0 575 60066 7

VISTA

A Gollancz Paperback Original

King of the Streets

JOHN BAKER

Whenever he talked about it later, Sam Turner would say the whole thing started with Jeanie Scott, who looked like the woman from Scottish Widows. She was scared – her ex-husband Cal had been murdered the day before and her house broken into. Thinking the two events must be connected, she wanted Sam to investigate.

Sam and his unlikely sidekicks start asking around, and it's not long before their office is trashed. Never one to back down, especially when he's being so obviously warned off, Sam digs deeper. He uncovers unexpected links between both break-ins, Cal's murder and the case of a missing boy who had turned up dead a couple of days earlier in Brownie Dyke in York, minus his genitalia.

All the threads are drawing Sam back to an old enemy he's been watching for a long time, but who has always seemed to be above the law. He's not sure how it all fits together, but you can bet there'll be trouble for someone when he works it out.

Sam just hopes it won't be for him . . .

ISBN 0 575 06548 6

VISTA

Other Vista crime titles include

VISTA books are available from all good bookshops or from:
Cassell C.S.
Book Service By Post
PO Box 29, Douglas I-O-M
IM99 1BQ
telephone: 01624 675137, fax: 01624 670923

VISTA